UNDER THE STILL STANDING SUN

UNDER THE STILL STANDING SUN

BY DORA DUECK

Kindred Press

Winnipeg, MB Canada   Hillsboro, KS USA

Canadian Cataloguing in Publication Data

Dueck, Dora, 1950-
    Under the still standing sun
    ISBN: 0-919797-93-8
    1. Mennonites - Paraguay - Fiction. I.Title.
PS8557.U435U6 1989 C813'.54 C89-098073-X
PR9199.3D843U6 1989

UNDER THE STILL STANDING SUN

Published simultaneously by Kindred Press, Winnipeg, Manitoba
R2L 2E5 and Kindred Press, Hillsboro, Kansas 67063

Publication of this book has been made possible, in part, by a grant
from the Manitoba Arts Council.

Cover Design by Sleeping Tiger Art Works, Winnipeg, Manitoba
Printed by Christian Press, Winnipeg, Manitoba

International Standard Book Number 0-919797-93-8

Note

All the characters in this novel, and their experiences, are fictitious. I have, however, tried to reflect accurately the geographical, social and historical setting of the story: namely the 1930 settlement of over fourteen hundred Mennonite refugees from Russia in the Chaco region of Paraguay, South America.

for H.

PART ONE

Chapter 1

When the *Apipe* docked at Puerto Casado I strode off with my head high. My eyes were wide and unblinking, and my lips were parted, ready to smile. I was sixteen, and though a refugee, I was full of hopes and ideals. I had set myself to welcome my new home.

I nearly stumbled on the solid, unyielding pier because my legs had taken on the rhythm of the gentle, rocking boat. But my unsteadiness was brief. Eagerly I crossed the wide wooden platform. My feet touched the grey shore.

"I'm here," I murmured reverently. "I'm finally here in the Chaco."

Just beyond the dock I stopped, slipped my sack of possessions onto the ground, and began my inspection of my surroundings. I had waited over eight months for the Chaco, that region of Paraguay where we Mennonites from Russia would settle. I wanted to embrace it with all my heart.

The sun hung low in the west, red as embers, as intense as if it had gathered all day, not given, and was now full for departure. Tones of fiery red and orange radiated across the sky in waves, beginning with the most brilliant and then fading gradually into the muted blue of the eastern horizon.

To my right, I saw a tall smoke funnel. It belonged, I guessed to the tannin factory. I heard cheerful voices and clanking and swishing of machines. I noticed the dwellings of the port. They were pale pink or green or blue, or simply whitewashed, but all of them were overlaid now with the rosy veneer of the setting sun.

And the trees! Palms with dark, towering trunks and long graceful fronds; scattered fern-like plants, imitating the trees in miniature; stately eucalyptus trees with slender leaves; and many others I didn't recognize but would learn about soon.

Shielding my eyes against the sun, I looked at the swift, wide river. The water glistened as it moved; it seemed to dance. Then I remembered what it hid: hordes of treacherous piranhas. So the sailors had said, grinning at us.

But it didn't matter what moved beneath the surface, I thought. The river was important because it brought us here. Lapping against the high, sandy banks it whispered: you're home, home, home.

I narrowed my eyes, and the water was compressed and gleamed even more as it ran away behind the steamer. The shining golden line broke into the stream of my people straggling off the boat, noisy and uneven like brown water over rocks, filling the dock as if it were a pool. The *Apipe* cast its shadow over them.

I saw our leader, Mr. Schroeder, greeting the port officials and gesturing grandly with his gaunt, vein-lined hands. He was probably trying his few words of Spanish. His trim, pointed beard rose and fell with the movements of his chin as he spoke.

Several dark-skinned Paraguayan women in bright dresses and kerchiefs, balancing cloth-draped baskets on their heads, slipped into the crowd. I watched one of them stop suddenly in front of Hans Wiebe, swing her basket down, and flick aside a napkin to reveal a mound of cream-yellow baked goods. Strange words poured from her mouth. Wiebe scowled and shook his head.

The woman persisted, blocking his way. He blushed. Finally he darted around her, looking both ashamed and pleased at his escape. The vendor laughed cheerfully as if she had sold him everything, covered the rolls with one smooth motion, and whisked the container onto her head again. I laughed too.

Other women leaned in doorways, following the *Apipe's* arrival with casual curiosity. I thought they were lovely. Although their skin was dark and their hair black as night, they had an aura of color; they were like flowers and their teeth flashed white when they smiled.

The workers on the boat shouted to each other, and waved at the women. They looked at us too, in our greys and navys and browns.

One of the sailors caught my eye and called to me. Gibberish, this Guarani or Spanish, whatever tongue it was he used. But I smiled back. I felt happy. Why not show it? He grinned, and on the strength of an exuberant whoop heaved a wooden crate onto his shoulder.

Paraguay was wonderful, I decided. The air was moist and sweet like a ripe tropical fruit. Strangest of all, the season was winter. Never had winter been so pleasant.

We left Russia in winter. The night we turned the corner on the road out of our village in the Orenburg settlement for the last time it was bitterly cold, and the sharp wind threatened to bring us a storm.

We fled in secret, in great haste and agitation, scarcely able to grasp what we were doing. I looked back at the turn, but our farmyard was lost behind swirling snow.

"Good-bye, dear home, good-bye," I had breathed, my eyes blurring with tears.

During the hour's icy ride to the station not one word was spoken by any of us huddled under robes and blankets. I had stared at the immense grey sky and tried to swallow the fact that I would never come back. I knew that.

In the months that followed I felt my life as something I carried. It seemed like a piece of luggage I was waiting to set down and unpack.

Now I touched the Chaco. My existence could be fastened here, secured, moored, even as the steamer had been bound to the dock.

This was a moment of great significance for me and I felt I must celebrate it. I closed my eyes. Mentally I repeated the names Russia and Paraguay. I followed the distance between them again. My mind, like a finger tracing the lines of a map, travelled the road in the village to the turn that hid my childhood home from sight, then the kilometers of train tracks to Moscow and beyond, over Germany, with our stay at the refugee center in Moelln, and the long journey across the Atlantic. I pronounced Buenos Aires, Asuncion, scanned the bends of the river beyond small hamlets and reached Puerto Casado, the Chaco at last . . .

"Anna!"

I jumped.

"Oh Mama, you scared me!"

Recovering, I cried: "Isn't it pretty?"

Mama, a stout woman, puffed from exertion. "Pretty? What?"

"The Chaco is pretty!"

"The Chaco! My dear child, what are you talking about?" Her eyes moved rapidly through the milling crowd of people.

"I'm trying to find your father," she said. "Have you seen

him? And I've lost Klaus and Maria too . . . Oh that man! He forgets I can't keep up when he walks so fast!"

"And you," she continued, "every time I need your help, you're gone. What are you doing? Standing and dreaming again, I see!"

"I'm looking," I said. To her first question, I added, "Papa will be missing you in a minute, you know. Stay here. He'll come."

Mama sighed. "I don't want to see water again!"

Dear Mama; she'd been sick much of the ocean passage. Then, when we left the large liner in Buenos Aires and boarded the small river steamer, the service fell far short of her expectations.

"Untidy! Crowded! And the Spanish food! It's very trying for us Germans," she had complained. "We've left European civility far behind, I see."

"No more voyages, Mama," I comforted. "We're here."

"To be sixty and heavy, and travelling like a gypsy instead of ruling a kitchen is no delight, I tell you Anna."

Suddenly Papa appeared.

"See?" I nudged Mama.

"There you are!" he declared triumphantly, as if we had tried to hide from him.

"I'm finished with boats and water forever, I hope!" Mama announced.

"You've come to the right place then, my treasure," he said, not smiling. "The Mennonites who already live in the Chaco say the water situation is desperate."

"Oh, I don't mean *that*!" Mama clucked in exasperation. "Now, where are we supposed to be sleeping Abram? Come Anna, bring your things. What's happening Abram?"

"We take the train inland tomorrow."

"And then we're there?"

7

"No, no! From there, several days by wagon. Ox-drawn wagon! The *Kanadier* will transport us. Come."

"I think I'll like it here!" I said. "It's wonderful."

Without responding, my parents lifted their hand baggage and began to walk away from the dock area. I followed.

Papa stopped suddenly, but I wasn't watching, and stumbled against him.

"Oh!" I giggled, skipping to gain my balance. We met in a half-circle and, thinking they hadn't understood me earlier, I said:

"You know, Paraguay's actually nicer than I expected. It's a lovely home, don't you think?" My joy wouldn't settle; I was stirred by the significance of our arrival.

Papa glared at me.

"You keep your tongue, Anna," he said. "You're barely off the boat, and you're babbling and making pronouncements!" He brought his face close to mine. "Paraguay is actually worse than I expected, if you want to know what I think. It's like erasing fifty, maybe a hundred years for us."

He whispered, but I felt the hiss of his rebuke and scorn. I flinched from him as if struck by a spark.

"You're blind if you think it's a place to leap about," he concluded, turning abruptly and wiping his mouth.

"Where's Klaus and Maria?" Mama interjected, glancing anxiously from him to me.

"Stay here."

Papa strode away. I heard him mutter "Oxen." as he left.

"Look for Klaus and Maria, will you?" Mama called.

He didn't turn.

I waited until Papa was out of sight. "Well," I pouted, "this *is* the Chaco we're standing on, isn't it?"

"Papa doesn't want to be here. He's still thinking that we might have gone to Canada." Mama adjusted the black shawl on her head.

"Yes, but — "

She lifted her arm to my shoulder. "Each day brings us closer," she said, sighing. Just as suddenly her arm dropped. "We're weary, that's what. Waiting is harder than working. Yes, it's the waiting that makes me so weary."

Why wasn't she listening to me? I looked at her. She gazed at something in the distance. Perhaps the birds hovering over the *Apipe*, or the wide river? Did she see what I saw at the port?

People sometimes told me I resembled my mother. We were the same height; my eyes were greenish-blue like hers; I had her mouth, too wide, and the full lips. Her expressive, sometimes dramatic manner of speaking also; we shared a lively spirit.

But I couldn't see myself in the woman before me. I was sixteen, I was slim, and she was heavy and old, with once-blond hair that had greyed unevenly, giving it an unappealing yellowish hue. Her face looked tired, as if it could no longer be held taut.

She was meticulous about herself and her clothing however, insisting on cleanliness and neatness of dress. Sometimes she hinted at earlier beauty. (If it was true, my sister Maria was her heir, not I.) In public she tried to carry herself erectly and proudly in spite of her build. It amused me. I thought she should be past vanity.

"Waiting and travelling," Mama broke her reverie, "it's no way to live. I thought I might enjoy some serenity in my latter years, and I'm seeing the world. Just to start again? From the beginning?"

"But, Mama — "

"That's why you shouldn't go on the way you do, Anna. Angering him. We haven't done any work here yet. When we've got a house standing, done something with our hands, you may praise it. Papa's not one to be pleased with fancy emotions you know."

"It's not that!" I protested in a rush. Why would Mama scold me too? "You have to look about. It's our new home!"

"Look about!" She repeated the words disdainfully as if I knew nothing.

If you looked about, I wished to reply, the waiting wouldn't be so hard. All you and Papa think of is how it used to be.

Yes, I knew my parents hadn't abandoned our beloved home in vast, magnificent Russia willingly. I knew we had, in effect, been driven away.

I also knew we had nearly been too late. And very nearly too early too; the clearing of the Moscow suburbs had already begun when we arrived. Even on the way, as another train passed us, we glimpsed Hein Martens from the village next to ours. Hein Martens! What was he doing? He had gone to Moscow for papers earlier, and now he travelled east? We all saw him, for the light focussed his face as the other train slid past ours. There was no doubt, window next to window, it was the Hein Martens we knew. He looked ahead, and he seemed pathetic and shabby, shadowed, even in the sun.

We learned later that he volunteered to return to his farm. "Volunteered" had an ominous overtone.

And we, coming neither too early nor too late, were allowed to leave. We were among the few who escaped! Yet my parents still wound their lives around deceptive Russia as tightly as thread on a spool, with not even a short frayed piece left for any place else.

But it wasn't that way for me. My life lay ahead of me. I collected this arrival into the scrapbook of my mind, not because it ended something, but because of what it began.

Couldn't they see that? Couldn't they understand that I had few memories as important as this, that everything I experienced here would be of monumental consequence?

In spite of my father's rebuke and Mama's condescension, I brimmed with feeling, for I walked on new — to me, holy — ground. The Russia I left was a land without promise, godless and frightening. I didn't care for it any longer. I wouldn't miss it, I decided. They could think about it if they wanted. I wouldn't.

I wasn't happy though to be alone in my fervor and out of sorts with Mama. If only I could tell her what I meant! And had she already forgotten what she said as the train stopped, just before crossing the border? We were instructed, before leaving Moscow, to take no Russian money out of the country. So when a tattered beggar passed along outside the train cars, holding his hat to the windows, it seemed a good opportunity for the immigrants to rid themselves of their last currency. His hat was nearly full, his eyes incredulous, wild with joy, when he reached our wagon.

"It's the greatest fortune of his life," someone remarked.

"Perhaps he thinks we're a visitation of angels," another commented.

It gave us a moment of pleasure amid the tension we felt (the tension which wouldn't subside until the Red Star crossing was clearly behind us).

"He's full and we're empty," Mama observed quietly. "But he doesn't know that we're better off than he is. We're leaving, and he must stay."

It was a good insight, a statement to admire.

"Remember what you said about the beggar, Mama?" I asked her now. "That we're better off?"

"It's still true," she said mildly.

I was glad. I had to push, sometimes, for these concessions. I gratefully squeezed her hand as we waited together in the darkening port.

Chapter 2

We spent the night in several large shelters with open doors and dirt floors. I slept fitfully. It was warm, uncomfortable, and crowded, and I felt insects crawling over me all night, though they were more imagined then real, perhaps, for I brushed at them and they didn't move.

I awoke, instantly alert, before the sun rose. I groped in my sack for my clothes, and dressed quickly, awkwardly under my blanket. Then I tiptoed past my sleeping mother and sister and stepped outside.

The air was fresh and invigorating. I stretched. Had anything changed? No. Yesterday's excitement was still with me, my feet stood in the Chaco, and today we would proceed inland. Very soon, we would live in a house, till the soil, be settled again.

Papa was already up, seated on a rough backless bench. He was a long man; all the parts of him — head, arms, body, legs — were long and narrow, and their length was emphasized by habitually-stooped shoulders and a full head of dark, rather unruly hair. He was staring at the ground, and seemed sad, brooding.

I wasn't surprised to see him, for though I usually woke early, I rarely preceded him. But his presence dismayed me, reminding me of last evening's reprimand. We hadn't exchanged words since then.

Unable to retreat, however, and not daring to walk past, I approached him.

"Good morning, Papa," I said.

"Anna. Yes, good morning." He looked up. "Sit down." I obeyed. Together we watched the sun come over the earth's rim. It moved as resolutely, as joyfully, I thought, as a diligent man or woman to work.

"Have you noticed how quickly the sun rises and sets?" Papa asked suddenly. "Have you noticed that the moon fills and empties the opposite way? Did you know we'll have Christmas in summer?"

I didn't answer, knowing he didn't expect it. His questions were statements.

Then he bent over and tried to mark something in the dirt with his finger. The ground was too hard; it allowed no impression. Papa walked to a spiny bush with small leaves and broke off a short branch. With this he scratched a triangular shape on the earth in front of me.

With the stick, he indicated a spot on the upper right side of the shape. "This is where we are now," he said.

He swept his hand over the crude drawing. "This is the Chaco. The part of it that lies in Paraguay. It goes into Bolivia here, Argentina here. Here is Brazil." He waved to the three sides of his map as he named Paraguay's neighbors.

"We came up the river. We'll enter the Chaco along the railway." He scraped a line running west from the point he had first marked as the port.

14

"Here is where the *Kanadier* live — you know, those other Mennonites, from Canada, already there — west of the railway's end. North and west of them, that will be us."

Papa dropped the branch and straightened.

"Compared to the Chaco, this port is like a seed," he said. "Like a seed beside a full-grown tree. That small. And bearing that little resemblance. I haven't been any farther than you. I haven't seen it either. But I know that much."

He hadn't looked at me while speaking. When he did so I quickly nodded. I didn't understand him, but I realized that this instruction concluded yesterday's scolding, and that it was conciliatory. Papa was a strict, quick-tempered man, but he was fond of me. I was the youngest, his favorite, his *Liebling*.

But there was no concession to my view.

"It won't be pretty, Anna," he continued, sounding nearly angry again. "Pretty is a word for children."

"Yes, Papa."

"So, I've warned you."

I was intent on the strange sketch, trying to remember what it meant, still puzzled by Papa's words, when Johann Walde joined us.

He and Papa greeted each other, and immediately Johann seated himself between us and began to talk. I politely said Hello to him but he appeared not to hear me; it made no indentation in their exchange.

Walde, as he was known, was a small but solidly-built man in his mid or late twenties. He had an attractive face with a charming smile of even, good teeth. Sitting beside him, I was aware of the faint odor of perspiration he exuded. It made me feel too close to him, but I didn't move.

Johann Walde and his wife Leni came from the Orenburg settlement in Russia, as we had, but we didn't know them there. During the organizational meetings in the refugee center in Germany, he and Papa discovered they would settle the same village in Paraguay. In spite of the disparity in their ages, they became good friends, often sitting together on the deck of the ship. Walde talked much more then Papa did. Sometimes, I thought, he lectured Papa, though he did it respectfully enough, and even stated matters in question form, as if suggesting Papa could correct him if need be.

Once Mama complained to Maria and me, "Walde helps himself to every conversation, whether invited or not. Then people repeat what he says, as if he knows everything."

I countered, "But he knows a lot." What Walde said might be contested, even spawn an argument, but his opinions held, I noticed. At least they held with Papa.

Johann's wife Leni was young, but her features were drawn and pinched. I had watched her on the ocean journey, as I watched all my fellow passengers, and had felt contemptuous of her. She seemed weary and worried and unhappy. She didn't enjoy her children as I believed a mother should. She had three daughters, all of them barely ten months apart, so she was busy enough, it was true. Johann didn't help her. He sat and visited with the men.

The baby seemed never to be out of Leni's arms; always she was nestled against her mother's neck, like a gourd on a plant, I imagined, hiding beneath the leaves. Leni might have stroked the smooth fat cheeks, for the child was as round as a piglet, but she complained, as if she wanted to shake the child away.

"Leni's pregnant again," Mama had informed me, sighing, as if that explained everything.

Then yesterday, for the very first time, Leni had spoken to me. She happened to pass me and she said, cheerfully, "Isn't it a relief that we're finally here? And safely too, without one of my little ones pitching into the Atlantic? Or plopping into this awful river?"

It so surprised and delighted me that I wondered if I had been wrong in my assessment of Leni.

I remembered her words now; and I heard Johann speaking. He was intelligent and determined. He had the makings of a leader. It made me proud to sit with him and Papa, to be associated with a fine couple like Johann and Leni.

"The first group arrived the very last day of the year right here in Puerto Casado," Johann was explaining. "1926. Last day. At the hottest time of the year. By the time they'd all come, there were over 1770 of them. Over 1770 who left the Canadian plains for this lovely jewel of the South. Can you imagine?"

They were talking about the *Kanadier*, as we called them, the Mennonites from Canada who had entered the Chaco several years earlier. They had originated in Russia too, but had left it for Canada in the 1870's. They were more conservative than we were; they wanted to keep to themselves. And when their freedoms to do so were threatened in Canada, a group of them sought another country.

"One of the main issues was language," Johann said, "and the right to decide on education. They were supposed to give up German in the schools."

"It'll be a help having them here, I guess," Papa said halfheartedly. With his shoe he absentmindedly erased the map he had made.

"If they hadn't come, man, who would have thought of it?"

"Who would have indeed?"

"There are two sides to the story though," Johann said with an air of wisdom.

Papa murmured assent. For a few minutes, the two men sat without speaking. The sun had warmed the dawn air. There was increasing activity in the sheds. People were getting up;

17

near us several women were lighting fires and beginning breakfast preparations; small wisps of smoke rose into the morning
air and disappeared, leaving a faint pleasant aroma. The leaves
of the palms waved gently in the morning breeze, as if they were
giant fans.

"Well, we can be thankful for one thing," Johann said suddenly. "They got us the *Privilegium*. Our own schools,
language, religion. Freedom from military service. Forever. Not
many countries like that left, willing to make those guarantees."

"Countries break promises," Papa said glumly.

"Right, right. But listen, Abram, Paraguay will keep her
promises for a long time. They need us here. We've already
seen how poor they are. They need us!"

"We're poor too."

"Yes, but we know how to work! They'll give us no help
starting, but we'll be helping them in time, just you see!"

"I suppose. I suppose. But I'm sixty-three. That's too old
to begin again. And without my sons too."

"You have Klaus," Johann returned.

Papa sputtered, "Klaus!" and they both laughed.

My five brothers had been the pride of Papa's life. The
way he spoke of them, Maria's husband Klaus was nothing. He
wasn't a farmer. His father left the farming life to stand behind
a counter in an Orenburg store, and Klaus worked as an office
clerk. But did it mean he wouldn't learn?

"I'm too old to start without sons," I heard Papa repeat
despondently, as if seeking encouragement.

"I'll be there, Papa!" I declared eagerly, breaking into their
conversation for the first time. "I'll work hard!"

"You've got Anna," Walde agreed, pointing to me as if he
had just now seen me beside him. "The lovely Miss Sawatzky is
worth as much as a son or two." He smiled at me.

"And it's still better to be here than in Russia," I said

18

earnestly, directing the comment to Walde.

"You're right, girl, absolutely right," Johann responded. He rose. "Indeed, we've been delivered from hell."

It was a fact. Our release had been a miracle.

Then Johann laughed, not merrily, but in a grating, cynical way.

It added something to his statement. He mocked me.

Chapter 3

We left Puerto Casado on the tannin company railway —
a small, narrow-gauge train, slow and primitive compared to
what we knew from Russia — which linked the port with the
rich reserves of red quebracho, from which tannin is extracted,
in the Chaco interior.

This journey was a strange one for me. We crossed mar-
shes, filled with reeds and water grasses, and dotted with palms.
The track cut through this warm, green world, moist, brimming,
fecund; we were surrounded by it, yet I had the sensation of
looking at the scene from the top of a hill or at a great distance.
It was something apart from me, contained, complete in itself,
and it didn't notice me. At the same time it provoked my
curiosity, and my longing.

The palms varied in maturity from young trees poking
above the grasses to tall, magnificent giants. Their tops were
graceful mounds of green with old brown fronds drooping
beneath or hanging limply along the trunk. In my opinion, they
sadly detracted from the trees' appearance. But it was a small

thing, I reasoned and supposed it had to be that way. The tree apparently grew taller by casting off its lower branches, and the trunk, straight and mottled, could only reach its full height by this sacrifice. Couldn't they drop off sooner? I wondered. And were those hanging branches dead or still partially alive?

Strange, beautiful water birds rose out of the swamps, their motion smooth, effortless. In the moment it took me to catch a breath, they were airborne. What startled them into flight? What did their calls mean?

Oh to be a pure white heron! To spring up and see the Chaco from above — what a thrilling view it must be — instead of traversing it slowly on this odd, noisy train. To see it all!

"Farewell!" I wanted to cry, "I'll meet you there. I'll wait for you."

Perhaps the others would want to join me. If only we could all be granted flight. I imagined the men on the open, roofless luggage cars, spontaneously ascending from the train, their legs no wider than sticks dangling behind, floating majestically to the new settlement. The women and children seeing this, rising immediately to follow. Klaus and Maria, Mama . . .

I giggled. A preposterous idea, indeed.

I remembered what Johann Walde had told us about the explorer Fred Engen. He worked for General McRoberts, the New York lawyer who negotiated the *Kanadier* Mennonites' emigration to Paraguay.

"Engen was determined to get to the heart of the Chaco to see if it could be settled. He was enthused about a 'state of pacifists' here. He managed to push beyond the marshy region that floods every year when the river overflows. And he found campo. Grasslands that could be used for crops.

"When he returned to Asuncion, he telegraphed his employer, 'I found the promised land'."

So that Engen-man knew his Bible, I thought. He knew

about Jordan rivers and special lands and special people. I sounded his phrase within myself. "I found the promised land."

Oh. Perhaps he simply meant he had done what he promised he would. He had fulfilled his obligations.

What had he meant?

Johann hadn't explained but continued the history, telling how that incident led to another and another. It led to this. To this slow voyage through a muggy green sea. How long it took! The train scarcely moved faster than a man could walk.

Jokes about it circulated. Someone said, "I'd rather walk; at least I'd be doing something while I get there."

"But this way you don't miss anything that goes by," his neighbor replied.

Later another man grumbled, "We don't even move fast enough to make wind."

But his friend held his nose, saying, "Even when we stand still, you make wind."

The day wore on, it grew hot, and humor and conversation lagged. My hands were damp; I was perspiring. I wiped my forehead, and swatted at insects, I was tired. It was an effort to keep my eyes open to the Chaco vista. Indeed, I found myself irritable with the dense, green view. Its sameness was flat and unending. I had seen enough; already it seemed as if I had grown up with it. I was impatient for a corner and the possibility of something less familiar.

Then, my first doubt about this adventure: a small, unsettling thought, which troubled me as if it were a temptation. Just yesterday I celebrated our arrival in Puerto Casado. The place was chosen arbitrarily, yes — I might have selected Buenos Aires as the point where we touched South America, or Asuncion, the capital of Paraguay. Or I might have waited a few days until I sighted the campo on which our village would be established.

But I had chosen Puerto Casado because we left the water, there. There began the solid, continuous mass called the Chaco; weren't we like Jonah, spit up on the beach and given another chance?

I knew it would take four or five days for the trip inland, although I couldn't visualize this in terms of either the distance or the hours, with the speed of transportation here unlike my previous experience. But this did not cause my uncertainty.

Rather, I experienced a hesitant but nagging suspicion that after yesterday's significant juncture, nothing was different. My happiness changed nothing. My people sat, as before, in their various groupings, with the same faces, the same voices, the same jokes and complaints and weariness from the older ones, the same innocence in the eyes of the younger. And I too, Anna, a day older, but unchanged, observing and waiting, carried along. The landscape was new, but already it seemed old. What did home mean?

I closed my eyes. How very tired I was, and soon, just around a bend, I would come to a station. We would reach it soon, nearly hidden by fog and the steam of warm breath in the sub-zero air, and underneath, the vibrations of a train and the stamping of boots on a wooden platform and voices, calling in Russian . . .

I jerked, tense with fear, and opened my eyes. The warm, green bush on both sides, the pale blue sky, the flies buzzing about me were a relief.

My heavy eyelids closed again. But I must not sleep! No, I must not sleep, but pray; I must pray. Oma's last words to me were, "Annchen, I'll be praying here, and you must pray as you go."

So I must call to God fervently through every terminal, past every fur-robed, mustached officer, asking without ceasing, God be merciful, help us please! Be gracious, Father, hear

24

our prayer! I must never stop praying.

Again I jerked awake, terrified, and realized where I was and that I was dreaming. There was no fear, no hurry, no necessity to pray on this slow, easy train. No fear! We were welcome here, weren't we? I could close my eyes and relax. I could lean against Mama or Maria and shut my eyes.

When I opened them again, having napped, though I don't know how long, it was to my first view of a Chaco campo. *Campo*. It was the Spanish word for this plain stretching before us, trees here and there, as if it was a park, planned for us. It seemed friendly, accessible, inviting us to walk in it.

Oh, I thought, it's pretty!

I remembered: "Pretty is a word for children."

I won't say it, I thought defiantly, but Papa doesn't know what I'm thinking.

And what was that swift activity over the long dry green grass? Strange creatures were running, fleetly, between the scattered trees. They were long-legged, long-necked.

Ostriches. I heard that new word and learned it too, agape at the comical shape and stride, but thrilled because of their speed and their gracefulness in spite of their awkward-looking bodies. The wind seemed to stir over the plain because of them. I closed my eyes again to hold the stunning sight, to keep back my tears.

Chapter 4

When we reached Endstation, the farthest point we could travel by train, *Kanadier* men, straw-hatted and barefooted, waited with their wagons to transport us to our settlement. It was several days' journey away; we had to enter the Chaco still deeper, westward.

Every hour, every day, we spent on the narrow trail, two grooves the width of the wagon wheels apart cut through the bush, moved us closer to our land. Yet our pace was so halting, so laborious, it seemed to me we made no progress.

The landscape, however, had changed. Dense grey-green, thorny, compacted woods surrounded us here; they didn't deserve the name forest, with its suggestion of height, coolness, shade and mystery. With memories of forests we had seen in Europe, we knew instinctively that this must be called by the simpler, slighter, inferior name "bush". It was very dry.

At a distance the bush appeared a tangled, complex, crowded mass of spiked bushes and scrubby trees. Cactus dotted the area. A closer look revealed astounding variety, millions of tiny, intricate leaves. These plants were adapted to heavy clay soil, sub-tropical heat, the vicissitudes of the rainfall. Vines wove in and around the other plants like threads.

I heard Johann Walde explain these things as we moved slowly, torturously slowly, through the bush. (Of the oxen, he said, "It's remarkable how much dust their hooves can raise even at this pace, enough to make you cough." He was right. When they raised the dust, it hung in the air, waiting for us to pass through it.)

I heard questions asked of our *Kanadier* driver, a Martin Toews, about the rain and the weather, and what plants were suited for the region. Mama wanted to know about raising chickens and pigs, about gardens and fruit trees. Taciturn Toews answered every inquiry patiently, but otherwise revealed nothing.

These conversations seemed secondary to what I saw and thought. Perhaps I didn't get the details or follow the connections, or I trusted my parents to learn what was needed. I was trying to define for myself what had altered in the Chaco since we left Puerto Casado and the river. The changes had occurred too subtly, too gradually, for me to remember the variations. The scenes couldn't be collected like pictures, to be spread out and compared later. I was already forgetting how the port had looked.

We travelled endlessly, it seemed, yet were always stopping: to water and graze the oxen, to eat and sleep, to eat and sleep again. When the sun was setting I felt as if it had just risen and we hadn't moved. The place where we camped for the night, I felt sure, was the same place we had left in the morning.

Occasionally we traversed campo, seemingly empty, but we didn't unpack there. We might farm *here*, I thought each time, but the wagons rolled on. Why would they put us so far away?

28

Neither the sun nor the sluggish pace of the oxen would help me believe we going to reach our destination. Everything looked the same; there were no landmarks. Nothing was familiar, nothing had a name. Dusty crippled bush blocked any sense of horizon, trees that looked starved or stunted mocked me. Birds shrieked raucously at us; I didn't hear them sing.

Chapter 5

When Wilhelm Froese began to speak, his story didn't interest me, for words about Molotschna, war, the revolution, famine and bandits were the notes of a too-familiar melody. I had heard plenty of accounts of suffering already. For my elders, the experiences of Russia were like the village well, which they shared and from which they could draw at day's end or when subjected to lengthy periods of inactivity during travel. They had time to carefully document every person who was mentioned — who his father or his grandfather or his neighbor had been, where he had lived — as if to find every mutual connection and ensure that the story, however distantly, belonged to them all.

I was more intrigued with Froese's large, protruding ears. When he spoke or gestured, they did not move but stood stiff, as if guarding his head. His daughter Susi, a year older than I, had inherited those ears. But being a girl, she had long hair, which she pulled tightly over her ears and wound into a neat bun at the nape of her neck. There was only a small bulge on each side of

Susi's head. I hadn't made any particular effort to befriend Susi; she was too quiet and her personality too bland to suit me.

But I had, that very day, noticed her older brother Hans. My feelings for boys at that time were much like the flight of a bird from tree to tree. They had alighted on him for the small reason of observing how lithely, how smoothly, he sprang to the ground from one of the large wooden wagons in which we travelled. He wasn't bad looking and I wondered what he was thinking.

I didn't anticipate talking with him, however, for he was as shy as the rest of the family. All the Froeses — Wilhelm and his wife, Hans, Kornelius, Susi, Greta and the three younger children — were reserved.

Thus, it was unexpected that Mr. Froese would tell a story. But I listened because of Hans.

"There was nothing to eat," Froese said, "nothing but a few slices of bread. My dear wife, she said to me, 'Wilhelm, we need something more, for the little ones especially. What shall we do?' I walked out of the house without answering. I didn't want to see their pleading faces again. The children's eyes looked so hollow. They hid behind their mother's skirts every time she came to me with news like that. The older ones understood, but not the little ones. We'd already lost our baby . . . "

Mr. Froese talked in a soft voice, too quickly; several times he stuttered. When his voice caught on a word he breathed deeply, closing his eyes to concentrate, and flung his arm forward and down in a punching motion and then the flow of words came again.

"God had always provided something. Every time. But this day, I felt we were truly at the end. He won't let His own suffer hunger, I told myself. But I knew some of His own had died. I didn't understand; He let some of them die. So I ran out of the house to the fields to pray, like I had before, for something, some little help, from somewhere. I couldn't give Him ideas, for who had anything to share? Yes, some still had small stores, but I couldn't beg. I threw myself on the ground. It was hard. It was frozen. But there was no snow.

"I tried to pray and always the question in the children's eyes faced me. They seemed to think it was my fault, I was their father and . . . "

Froese's voice stopped. The muscles of his face twitched

"And then lying there in despair, I saw a mouse run by," he continued. "Only a few inches from my outstretched hand. It let itself be caught! It wasn't so skinny either. It was too cold for it to be out, so my dear wife couldn't say anything when I brought it. It's from God, I told her, so it'll be all right. We had soup. Two days later the relief supplies from America arrived in our village."

As if his tongue had been loosed, Wilhelm Froese told us a second story.

One night a band of anarchists came to their house, he said, demanding a meal. While Mrs. Froese cooked the potatoes, which was all they had then, the men searched the house. There was little of value left, but they took some woolen stockings, a watch, some candles, a shirt.

"Then they looked at the women," he said. "At my wife. And the officer in charge spotted our Susi. He was a big man and he had the pistol. That's why he talked so boldly. He said, 'I'll take her later'."

A sudden fear seized me. How would the story end? Where was Susi? I was relieved that she wasn't sitting with us. I ducked a little, hoping the deepening dusk would help conceal me, so I wouldn't be noticed at the edge of the circle.

"They ate all the potatoes, while we sat in the other room. They didn't leave over even one potato. And then the leader came in. He stank of the wine which they had brought. He belched and then he said, 'I'll have the young lady now.' He came straight to her and touched her. He touched Susi . . . "

Again Froese's voice stopped though his lips still moved as if speaking. His face contorted as he struggled to control himself.

My premonition exploded into fact. I didn't understand the villainy of the man's touch. But during Froese's pause, my heart pounding like thunder inside me, I grasped that something unspeakably terrible had been done. All thoughts of Hans were replaced by the reticent, sweet-faced girl.

Stunned, I tried to fit her into the scene, as her father went on. "He touched her with a sneer. I cried, 'No, no!' I offered him something, another shirt, maybe; anything instead. With his other hand he pointed the pistol at me. My dear wife hurried the children into the small room, and Susi was crying. He tore at her dress."

If anyone attempted to stop Froese, I didn't notice. Only partially comprehending, though hearing clearly, I listened as he described the rape which he had been forced to watch. Froese seemed determined to give the details of the assailant's conquest, though many of his words seemed to choke in his throat. Mrs. Froese had sung loudly behind the closed door in the next room, he said.

"I didn't know what to do," Froese stated. "I saw that he intended to do it, really do it and not just tease us with it so he could enjoy our terror. He almost forgot me because he was looking at her and feeling her. I couldn't stand by, so I sprang up. I wanted to kill him, I think, yes, I guess I would have . . .

"He heard me and turned in a flash. Then he tossed the pistol to a comrade and said, 'You keep the man out of this, I can't concentrate on two things at once.' The other fellow was almost crazy with desire himself, I could see, but he held the pistol at me. Then I calmed myself. Susi said in Low German, 'It's okay,

34

Papa. Let it be.'

"I looked at the man who had to guard me, hoping for help, but he wouldn't look at me. I didn't know what to do. I could see that he wouldn't help me, because his mind was on what his leader was doing. He wasn't thinking about me. I might have knocked the gun out of his hand, but then I thought about the others, outside. Some of them had knives. Their sabers would end us all.

"So I fixed my eye on the edge of the door and listened to my wife. Susi didn't struggle, and then it was over and they were outside . . .

"That brute was so satisfied! He puffed his chest, walking out of the house. I went to the other room and stayed with the children while my wife went to Susi. She prepared the water to wash."

Froese removed a large handkerchief from his pocket and blew his nose noisily. For a moment he gaped, startled, at the spot where his family had set up camp, as if fearing he had revealed too much. He dabbed at his eyes with the handkerchief. I could hear him sniffle; once he sobbed. Then all was still.

Unnoticed, the sun had set while Froese ended his account. I was suddenly conscious of the darkness and the rustling, hushing noices of the bush. It seemed to know I listened. I thought I heard an eerie distant scream. I shivered. The night and the story were one, surrounding me, alive, mysterious, almost a menace.

I was also keenly aware of something else, something quite wonderful, new to me, as I stood on the border of the adult world: a nearly tangible compassion extended to Froese from the circle of people about him. The men near him stared at the ground; they may have been as unprepared for Froese's agony as I was, but they absorbed the experience and guarded it as carefully as one would protect a fragile heirloom. They seemed

35

to fill the silence for him in case he wished to add something; they didn't intrude with comments until he regained his composure. Heinrich Pauls. Papa, and my brother-in-law Klaus. The young *Prediger* Rahn. Johann Walde. Jakob Bergen, his son Jakob. They could have been adolescent schoolboys reciting their verses at the village Christmas program, so clear was their mutual commiseration and support.

Also included were Mama, Leni Walde nursing her baby at a distance, Sarah Rahn, me. All of us were bound together, in the storytelling and in Susi's tragedy. It changed my attitude toward her. She had become a different person in my eyes. Now she excited my admiration. How had she borne it, I wondered? What had it been like? She was my superior, and I hadn't known. I wanted to have her as my friend.

Now Froese asked quietly, "Did I do enough? What is non-resistance, when I did nothing but hate the man? When I cried, God deliver us, let us out of Russia, He did. But I wasn't pure in everything. I know I wasn't."

He waited, as if this admission would shock us.

"I didn't deserve to be released," he continued. "If I could say I suffered and remained pure, maybe. But at the moment, what could I do? I don't know. I just don't know . . . "

There was no reply. The silence spelled uncertainty, rather than discomfort; it still pulsed with understanding. Who would answer him?

Finally *Prediger* Rahn spoke. "You did all you could, Wilhelm. Not one of us would have done better."

Immediate murmurs of assent, throats cleared, several "yes's" confirmed that the words had been right. The tension ebbed; someone started another subject of conversation.

That evening I saw the strength of community. Surely, I thought, our chief asset was that we were together. And I belonged to these people. How I loved Susi. How I loved

36

everyone! If there were no one but us in the wide Chaco, it was enough.

Chapter 6

It almost seemed as if Papa had had no childhood, for when he talked about his life, he began in Orenburg, the settlement to which he had come as a young husband and begun to farm. He told the farm's history as if it were his own. When his turn came to tell a story, he shared the events and particulars important to a practical man — the dates and years of this crop or that purchase of machinery, the colors and kinds of horses (even information about their personalities), the size of the barn and the plans for the new, larger house whose construction had been annoyingly interrupted by the Great War, which in Papa's opinion set Russia on its head, never to be righted and it took his sons away when he needed them most and when they were at the peak of their youthful strength. He spoke of good years in *puds*, the Russian measure of weight, and losses by the amounts of the quotas the local Soviet demanded. Through such details both his prosperity and pain were gauged.

As his daughter I knew a little more about him. To me there was another narrative, and the main twist of it was the way it turned out with my brothers.

By the time my parents were married eight years, they had already been blessed five times over with a son. Papa was happy for Maria and me, but I knew that nothing matched his joy in the births of those boys.

"All five of them, blond and fair-skinned like their mother, but built tall and solid, with clear blue eyes looking to the future!" he would say. "Imagine! Five of them, like olive plants circling my table, as the Psalmist says."

It hadn't turned out well at all, for at sixty-three he was a disappointed, disillusioned man, coming to Paraguay with a remnant; he was without his sons.

Two of them were dead.

Gerhard, the second youngest, was a fun-loving boy, though of all the sons, he was the most likely to arouse Papa's temper because of his pranks and his apparent sloth. He joined the medical corps during the war and was killed in 1917 when his train car collided with another and exploded.

Reuben was the middle son, the one whose pet name for me was "the little cat".

"That man understood the land; he had a shrewd sense of business," Papa said of Reuben. Seemingly wrapped with Papa's mantle, he was destined to take over the family farm. He died three days after collapsing with a severe headache during threshing. That was in 1927.

One day I came upon my father sobbing in the barn, his head pressed against a post. The horses were munching their feed, flicking their tails, paying no heed. I hurried away, noiselessly, not wanting him to know I had seen him.

Reuben and his pretty wife Christa had lived in the large room of our house for awhile, also in the summerhouse. They had no children, so she returned, after his death, to her parents. Eight months later she married again. Papa was displeased.

"Why shouldn't she be happy?" Mama defended her.

"I just don't understand how she can forget him so soon," Papa said.

My oldest brother Abram, Papa's namesake, seemed already a man when I was a child, and I didn't know him well. I knew of his reputation though: by fourteen he kept pace with the adult men of the village in farm work. In whatever he did, driving the horses, flailing the wheat, pitching hay, he wouldn't slacken or stop until the others had.

But he and my father quarreled. My brother married young and moved to his father-in-law's farm instead of joining Papa to buy neighbor Boldt's farm as Papa wanted. Later Abram and Susanne moved east into Siberia to the new Mennonite settlement near Omsk.

When he served in the medical corps during the war he stopped for a few days on his way to the Front. He didn't say much; he visited us as a stranger might, speaking of his wife and children as if they were our former acquaintances.

In Moscow we met an Omsk family who knew Abram and Susanne. Mama pressed them for news. "Something's wrong, I'm sure of it," she worried. "They won't say much. But Susanne is disheveled and careless, I've learned that much. She wasn't like that earlier." Abram had formed a collective with some other Mennonites, and was, as far as we knew, in no danger. He didn't want to join us in Moscow in our attempts to leave.

Peter, the second son, served during the war in a hospital for disabled soldiers on the shores of the Black Sea. He returned to the farm after his term. Then a delegation visited the Orenburg settlement to organize those interested in emigrating to Canada. Peter signed up.

"I'm going with or without your blessing," he told Papa. "It won't get better. I've prayed about it and I'm going."

Of course Papa tried to persuade him otherwise. He

41

believed those running to Canada were weak, terrified. He thought then that the upsets of the Revolution would be temporary, a national fit, probably of short duration.

"I was wrong," Papa said later, an enormous admission for him. "Now Peter, the quiet one, is safe," Peter worked in a factory in Winnipeg. At age thirty-two, he had recently married a widow, also an immigrant, with two daughters. The infrequent letters we received were cheerful and devout.

And David! David, the youngest of the row of five boys, and my favorite. He was handsome, gregarious, charming.

"Every girl in the village is in love with our David," Mama said.

David put me on his knee when I was small and sang to me with his fine tenor voice, usually something in Russian which I didn't understand.

He was also rebellious. He joined the army. He had no use, he claimed, for Mennonite non-resistance. The war seemed an adventure for him; he came home occasionally on leave, and told us fascinating stories, including his brushes with death. He carried good luck, he claimed, like a song always ready to be sung.

Our last letter from David was in 1920, posted from Moscow. He had stayed with the army after the war ended, but wrote now that he wished to leave. He regretted he had joined for he knew now that war kills. More than the enemy, he said. He was seeking forgiveness; was there anything he could do, he wondered, to ease our hurt?

"How I wish I had heeded your words," he wrote. "I should have served, like Gerhard and Peter. Death would be better than this. Can you forgive me?"

My parents read and re-read the letter. "Of course we forgive him," Papa said. "So why doesn't he come home?"

Mama worried, however. "I'm sure he's ill. It doesn't

sound like David at all." After months without news or a response to their inquiries, Mama begged my father to travel to Moscow to look for him.

Papa couldn't find David. He seemed to have been neither dead nor alive. After searching for two weeks he was angry. Had his son been a phantom? He came home, and publicly gave him up for dead.

But since there was no absolute proof of David's death Mama retained hope he was alive. She had a recurring dream: it began with her stirring a pudding, thick and creamy, made with fresh eggs and milk. On the table stood the wild cherry sauce to spoon over it later. As the pudding started to boil and thicken she saw, through the kitchen door, David walk out of the trees at the yard's edge. He wore a uniform and walked with a stiff soldier's stride. But now the pudding was boiling so violently that she couldn't leave it to meet him; she had to stir it vigorously a few moments at least or it wouldn't be right. Before she could see him clearly, he disappeared from view, but he must have entered the house through the barn, for she heard his boots clicking and his greeting, "Mother!" She turned, her heart leaping with gladness, but he had vanished, and she would waken.

"If only I could have seen his face!" Mama moaned at the end of her recitation of the dream.

It annoyed Papa. "The boy is dead, Gretel, and you make yourself miserable with your wishing. I don't let myself fancy such things and I don't dream dreams about them either."

"I guess so . . . I know he's dead, but . . . Perhaps it's a rebuke that I set too much pride on him and I'm not allowed to see his face."

"Don't think of it like that!" he roared.

Several years passed, and one day near winter's end, when the wind was mild and the sun bright and shining, teasing us with thoughts of spring, David actually walked onto our yard.

He was thin and colorless. I didn't recognize him. But the voice was strong, the same. "Mother!" he called first. Then, "Father!" and "My little Anna, how you've grown, and so beautiful you are too!"

Papa remembered Mama's dream then, and with tears trickling down his cheeks, called it a prophecy. All of us were afraid to take our eyes off David, lest he would be gone. But it was true; he was home.

He wouldn't talk much about the years since the letter. He recalled it well enough, but had been ill, he said, and it erased huge chunks of months. He had been converted, he said, and then worked in the forests in the north, where the snow didn't melt.

"They don't want believers in Russia. Not one!" he said mysteriously. "They want to rid the country of Christ, scrape it clean." He gestured with his hand on his cheek as if pulling a razor. I stood in awe of him and these expressions. Although I knew the government didn't like religion, our village worship hadn't been hindered yet.

The returned David was eager to be baptized. He spent hours reading a Bible, hunched over it and occasionally muttering. When Papa and Reuben made plans for the farm and rented more land or bought an implement he tried to discourage them with apocalyptic predictions. "You don't know what's happening!" he warned. David's presence brought tension into our household because of his gloomy outlook about the future of Russia.

Then he announced he wanted to go east, to the new settlement near Blagovensk. Hans Isaak was going, and would welcome his company.

"Isn't that nearly in China?" Mama cried.

"Nearly," David said.

"You'll need a wife then," I burst out.

"I know." David laughed and gave me a hug in the former charming manner. "God will provide."

The resurrected brother had gone again. Would he settle, farm, have a family? David was very altered. Where was he now?

We heard rumors that individuals were escaping Russia over the Amur River into China. Would he try it?

David was the one I wished most to see again. Perhaps, I thought, he would join us in Paraguay someday. He was especially blessed, wasn't he?

By 1928 Papa finally realized that matters in Russia would never return to what they had once been. By 1928 it was clear the Five Year Plan with its relaxation of government interference had been temporary, almost a lapse, and what followed would be an even more determined effort to equalize society and obtain the goals of the revolution. The Soviets re-ordered village life; the church building was requisitioned as the district office.

By passed in the first skimming off of the rich, my father and other middle-level farmers in the settlement rose, as cream rises in milk, to take their places. The local soviet, saying they acted only on orders, became more demanding. Papa had tried to cooperate, but he couldn't meet their quotas. They insisted he was lying. Of course he had more to give. *Kulak*! The tight-fisted one! He would have to bring it, or else . . .

Then came the evening of decision. This was a story I knew from memory.

Papa was in bed that Thursday night in October, 1929, when a faint knock shook the bedroom window. He was instantly alert, he claimed, and with his heart thundering in his chest went to the door. Icy air blew into the house.

"Who is it?"

"Bernhard," a voice responded, and his nephew, Bernhard

45

Sawatzky, a teacher who sometimes worked in the village soviet office, stepped out of the shadows.

"What do you want?" Papa shook, terrified, freezing.

"I just want to warn you, Uncle," Sawatzky replied, glancing nervously about him. "You're not in the soviet's favor. Perhaps you'll be questioned, or . . . " He didn't need to finish. Papa knew what he meant. *Taken.*

"Are you sure? How do you know?"

"Of course I'm sure." The younger man was impatient. "And don't ask how I know. Can't you see there's no mercy for the likes of you? The revolution must run its course, and you, with your thinking, well, it's not appreciated, not now." He paused, obviously unsure how much he should reveal.

"Listen, Uncle Abram," he said, "would I risk my life to tell you this if it wasn't true?"

"Is . . . is there nothing you can do . . . do for me?"

"Nothing. Nothing more. I've spoken for you before. But I have my life and family too."

"I see."

Bernhard turned and had taken several steps when Papa remembered he had not thanked him.

"Bernhard!"

His nephew stopped immediately, jerked about fearfully.

"I appreciate it, Bernhard. That you came."

"It's only because you're a relative," came the reply.

"And what about you?"

"I'll survive." Bernhard turned and hurried into the darkness.

That night, Papa didn't sleep.

In the morning he said, his voice calm, controlled, "We're going to Moscow too, Gretel. We'll try to get papers to leave."

"And to Canada?" Mama nearly squealed. She would have left with Peter, had she had her way.

"Hush. We leave in secret."

"God be thanked," she said. "When?"

"Tonight."

"Tonight? How shall I get ready?"

"You'll be ready."

"But who?"

"We and Anna, of course. We'll send a message to Maria."

"I have no sons to take, you know," he added bitterly.

Chapter 7

On the third morning of our trek into the Chaco our driver, Martin Toews, announced that the oxen had wandered while feeding; they were nowhere in sight. The men of our group offered to join the search.

We women and children waited beside the muddy waterhole where we had camped. We cleaned up the eating utensils and packed our clothes and placed them in the wagon. In the thick water through which the oxen had trampled I washed several diapers for Maria, and hung them on branches to dry. We all worked with dispatch, expecting to be leaving shortly.

As the sun rose higher and the men didn't return, we removed some blankets from the wagons and spread them in the shade. We didn't talk much, except to call to the children: Come away from the bush, come out of the sun, come get your hats on, come and sit.

I wished I could have accompanied the men to seek the oxen. Then at least I would know what was happening. What was keeping them?

The children were restless. Maria rocked the crying baby

Margarethe. My sister swept her hand repeatedly over her forehead as if to push away stray strands of hair, but there were none there. Leni Walde too tried to hold her daughters close to her.

"I'll watch your Agnes," Susi offered, following the three-year-old as she scampered away across the clearing.

"I'll help," I said. I called my nephew Nikolaus, and we persuaded the children to join us on a blanket and play a game with some twigs and leaves. We took turns moving them into different positions to form shapes.

Then Leni Walde tucked her younger two daughters firmly on either side of her body and lay down with them. They wiggled to get free, but her arms, as if metal, held them tightly. Both girls gradually ceased their efforts and their whimpering and fell asleep. Leni's eyes closed also. She was on her back, her pregnant belly strangely small in that position, her arms relaxing but still rounded about the children. Soon she too slept, her mouth opening slightly.

"I don't know how she can sleep like that," Mama remarked. "On this hard ground. In the daylight."

"It's nice she gets some rest," Susi said to me. Susi's eyes were too large, but they were full of compassion. My secret knowledge of her ordeal in Russia plumped the narrow, bony face. There was beauty in her gentle demeanor, I thought.

"Where are the men?" Mrs. Froese, Susi's mother, complained. She jerked at every unusual sound.

"Try to rest too," Susi soothed. "Just don't worry."

"I do believe they've left us," Mama declared, yawning noisily. "I wouldn't be surprised if they've decided to walk back to the river and leave us to fend for ourselves in this wilderness."

A frightened look crossed Mrs. Froese's face, and she thrust her body into an upright position as if it might truly be so.

"Of course not, Mama," Susi calmed her mother. "Don't worry."

"My mother doesn't mean it," I whispered to Susi.

She nodded. She seemed grateful for my interest.

Then we heard voices and glimpsed one of the white oxen sauntering nonchalantly into the clearing.

"At last!" I greeted the men joyfully. "At last we can move on again."

Mr. Toews looked stern. "We'll eat and drink, and then we'll have a siesta, and then, when it's cooler, we'll travel on."

We've lost nearly a day already, I thought miserably.

As if reading my mind, though not directing it to anyone in particular, Toews said, "The word to learn here in South America is *mañana.* Tomorrow, there's always the tomorrow."

On the last day of the wagon trip, we passed through several of the Menno Colony villages. We watched for clues how the other Mennonites were doing.

"They had more to start with than we do, looks like," Papa remarked to Walde in a near-whisper, not wanting our driver to hear him.

"They had capital," Johann returned. "They had good farms in Canada to sell."

"I still can't understand why they would have left."

"They can go back. They have Canadian papers."

"We should have left Russia sooner," Papa said. "We'd be in Canada now. They were taking immigrants by the thousands just a few years ago."

"Our fathers or grandfathers should have left." Walde proposed.

"But then," Mama interrupted, "you might have ended up here anyway! Like the *Kanadier!*"

Papa scowled at her. But Mama was amused with her unexpected wit. I was pleased too. It made me think: yes, If my father's father, or my great-grandparents, had left Russia . . . well, where would I be now? Who would I be? Why, my parents might not have met then, so I wouldn't be myself at all. That was impossible. But, what kind of other lives might I have lived? *If.*

As a child whenever we travelled anywhere, I always longed to take the roads from which we turned, the tracks we passed. I wished to be on trains that went both directions, all directions, to see where each of them led.

If, supposing, my foreparents had left Russia earlier, or if we hadn't been among the fortunate ones to leave last winter, or if we had been permitted to enter Canada now, or not had trachoma . . . Then we wouldn't be here. I would have missed this!

God was leading us here. I had heard this often, and I believed it. This was my road; I was following it because I must. And I didn't mind either, in spite of my desire to lead all of the many possible lives which intrigued me. We were separated from the rest of the world now, with only the stars over us as evidence that other places existed, but we were with God. He had reasons for everything that happened.

Suddenly driver Toews announced, "We're here!" We had reached the central campo of the fledgling Russian Mennonite colony. Papa and Johann Walde sighed, in unison.

Several days later, ten days after reaching Puerto Casado, we unpacked our belongings on the piece of land assigned us by lot in our yet-to-be-built village.

"But where is home?" four-year-old Nikolaus asked. There was nothing here but softly waving bittergrass, nothing but scattered trees, nothing but a band of bush around us at the far edges of the campo, and the immense sky above.

"This is our home. This is our village," I assured him. I bent down and repeated the statements, enjoying his innocent confusion. "This is *our* place."

Pegs marked it. There would be one wide street down the middle of the village, the school and teacher's *Hof* in the center, and farms ranging along both sides of the street with the fields stretched behind.

Papa immediately dug away a tiny patch of grass. At every stop into the Chaco he had poked into the ground. The soil here was sandy and pale brown like the earth of all his samples, yet I knew his practiced eye could detect slight differences from one campo to the next.

"We have a good farm!" he said, standing upright again.

"We have a good farm!" I repeated for Mama.

"Fine." She was pacing about, wondering where the house should stand, where she would put her temporary kitchen.

"Good news," I called to Klaus and Maria. "We have a good farm."

"Well, " Papa said, "let's get to work."

Chapter 8

We grubbed out the wild campo grass to erect our first dwellings, tents. The white canvas tarps were gifts of the German government, the supporting poles the first offering of the virgin bush. We used two thin posts to stake the ends and a pole as a bridge over which the tarpaulin was hung. Under this shelter we piled dried grass for mattresses, spread our blankets, and arranged our few items of clothing and household effects which we had received as part of our refugee outfit.

Mama and I dug a hole about three-quarters meter deep with a slanting entrance for an oven. Mama bustled about with remarkable energy. She planned to construct a proper oven out of clay soon, but for now she had a place to cook. She made bread. The kafir flour, coarsely ground, didn't hold together — the dough ran over the edge of the pan — and it crumbled in our hands as we ate it. But it tasted delicious. When Papa said so, Mama glowed like a young wife with her first culinary accomplishment. We quickly learned the secret of baking with kafir flour: a little wheat flour would hold it together.

Papa began to make some simple furniture and learned

about the various trees of the area. Most of the wood was extremely hard. He fashioned some benches, stools, and a makeshift table out of the paloblanco wood which grew in slightly lower spots in the bush. The tough paratodo we used for oxen yokes and collars.

It was slow work, for both Papa and Klaus had dysentery. In spite of his reluctance to settle in Paraguay, his age, and the absence of sons, Papa refused to remain idle to the challenge before him. There was work, so much word, to do. His stomach tortured him, he said, and he was clearly frustrated with this weakness, but he worked, long after he should have stopped to rest.

"There are two things to do," he said. "We have to get the land ready for planting and we have to build a decent house."

Some of the settlers from the groups which arrived before ours already had houses, many of them little more than huts of mud pasted over wire or stick frames.

"I'm not doing that," Papa grumbled. "We'll make a sturdier house — we'll make it of bricks, even if it takes us longer."

I helped him excavate a trough, about a meter and a half square and half a meter deep, for making mud bricks. We gathered piles of grasses from the campo, and mixed it with clay and water in the trough. Then Maria or I trampled it with our feet, making a mixture of even consistency.

I enjoyed the mud on my bare feet, the prickling of grass stalks on my soles, the stems pushing through between my toes. It was cool, and delightfully oozy. Sometimes I permitted Nikolaus into the mud with me — for him it was play — and we held hands and danced and sang as we stomped. Then we scooped the prepared mud into a box frame about thirty centimeters long and twelve wide, pressed the dark mixture firmly into every corner of the container, and carefully dumped it out to dry in the sun.

We needed hundreds of bricks to begin a house, but we were fortunate: not once did it rain before a day's bricks were dry. We didn't know then, of course, that there was no danger of rain dissolving our efforts: we didn't know that we had entered the Chaco in a year of drought.

Very quickly we found out how difficult our life in the Chaco would be. Dissatisfaction spread rapidly, as if it were a living, growing organism.

This was the list of our complaints.

The corporation which handled the arrangements for our arrival hadn't finished surveying or preparing the land. It also seemed that the company was mismanaging finances — getting rich at our expense, we were convinced — adding needlessly to the huge debt for land, outfit, and food we would need to repay over the coming years.

The supply of food staples was erratic. The white flour assigned to the first group, for example, hadn't accompanied them in proportions adequate to their numbers. The nine sacks they had with them were soon gone, and there was no white flour to add to the dark kafir-corn flour. And how could the women make *Zwieback*, the double buns for Sunday *Fespa*, without white flour?

When the flour arrived, the supply of cooking oil ran out. For over three weeks the fledgling colony was without oil. The food itself, what there was of it, was of poor quality: the flour and beans wormy, the oil rancid.

Another problem was the water supply. One well after another was dug, producing only salty water. Well-digging was both tedious and dangerous. First the sandy clay layer must be removed, and then a layer of greyish yellow sand, so loose it could be taken out with a bucket. At that point the digging became easier but also unpredictable because of the threat of a sudden cave-in.

At about eight meters the ground was moist and after another meter or so of digging it was wet enough to squeeze out a first sample of water.

Time after time the ritual was repeated. "I'm going to try it," came the call from below. Those above waited anxiously.

"Salty!"

Silently the bucket was lifted up and passed from mouth to mouth until enough had confirmed the disheartening news.

Sometimes, though, there was wonderful, sweet water. But that too fell short of expectations. Well water was lukewarm. What kind of place was this that even deep in the ground it wasn't cool?

"Hell's in the middle of the earth, " said Johann Walde irreverently, "and we're that close to it."

(We learned to chill the water somewhat in earthen containers, in a tree at night, and in a corner of the coolest room in the house by day.)

Another difficulty was the bush. It seemed sinister, and we hesitated to enter too deeply, fearing we would lose our way. (Incidents of this had already occurred; only the Indians, at home here and blessed with a keen sense of the wild, could help then.) But it must be penetrated in search of wood: wood for fires, wood to build houses and furniture, wood for yokes and collars, posts for gates and fences.

In the bush there was hardly a tree without thorns; these tore mercilessly at our clothing. There was no wind in the bush, the heat nearly unbearable, and it was full of mosquitoes, flies, and tiny hovering insects we called by the Russian term *moschki.*

And we discovered that what had seemed a still and silent landscape teemed with living creatures of all descriptions. There were ants: tiny ants who bit fiercely; small red "sugar ants" whose sense of smell was extraordinary — they invaded the supplies of sugar, syrup, and bread wherever they were stored; larger ants who marched in columns up and down walls, across rooms, over tables, especially at night, seeking the kafir pile; poisonous black ants with red heads whose bite could cause dizziness and mild illness; large "Schlepper" ants, leaf cutters, who cut young plants off at the base, delighting especially in the fresh corn, kafir, vegetables, even blooming peanut plants.

It was fascinating to watch the "Schleppers," in spite of the frustration and anger they aroused, because of the way they worked together, led to their booty in long lines by large-headed shiny leaders, cutting the plants with their scissor mouths, and carrying the spoil back to their nests in neat lines exactly the way they had come. No obstacle seemed too difficult for them to surmount. In the nest the leaves were cut fine by other diligent workers, mixed with a spittle and worked into a field that produced a fungus off which they fed. There was not one kind of leaf cutter, but three. The "minera" was the most difficult to eradicate.

There were also flies and mosquitoes, termites, "Sandfloh" who burrowed into human feet, scorpions and spiders. Little spiders, medium-sized spiders, and huge spiders up to eight centimeters long filled the world with their webs, working alone or in groups of hundreds. Grasshoppers hopped about, as did crusty-backed black beetles of various sizes and crickets. There were bugs that stank terribly when killed, and bugs that, when brushed aside, released a liquid that burned on skin like fire. And there were worms.

Perhaps the severest trial was the climate, whose vagaries we soon experienced. We arrived in winter, usually characterized by little rain, extremes in temperature, and beginning in about July, the *Nordsturm*, a hot wind blowing out of the north. Usually it was too warm, but sometimes the temperatures dropped sharply. July, we discovered, was unusually cold that year, and there were frosts. We huddled around fires. Papa wore his heavy fur coat from Russia, and without snow, looked as absurd as a polar bear would in a desert. When he wasn't wearing it, the coat closed the openings of our tent to the frigid air.

Then in August the terrible heat began, and the *Nordsturm* unleashed its steady blast. From morning to night, sometimes even through the night, it blew as from a funnel, carrying heat and fine sand which it lifted from every bared bit of earth. We weighted the lid of the cooking pot with a brick so it wouldn't blow away and let the wind spice the beans with sand.

Over the noon hours the wind roared into a fever pitch. It was a horrible, depressing wind: a wind not for winnowing, but for destruction, not for refining, but for carrying refuse before it.

One afternoon Papa emerged from the tent where he had taken a noon siesta and said, "I heard the wind and dreamt I was in Russia."

"I thought I was napping by the fire," he continued, unusually communicative, strangely willing to be caught the fool, "and that the winter winds were howling. This didn't disturb my rest, for the animals were safe, the house cozy, Mother had preserves enough and there was grain for bread. Hadn't I worked like a madman all summer? Shouldn't I now enjoy the lazy winter rest of the Russian farmer, safe, and warm?

"Then I turned on my blanket and felt the sand against my chest. Bah! That woke me quickly enough. Only the sound of the wind is the same. Only the sound! . . .

"When it's cold you can warm up, as I used to, coming in with my bones stiff, and then thawing, at the stove. But how do you stop the sun or this wind? Where can you hide from it?"

He muttered, "And if it was hot, we hung the mutton over the ice-cold water of the well in the barn. It would be fresh for days!"

Mama didn't respond to this monologue. She rose from the bench where she sat mending his pants and carried the blankets out of the tent, one by one, to shake off the fine sand which had accumulated. It flew along with the wind over the campo.

"Why do you bother?" I asked, irritated. "You just have to do it again in the evening before we sleep."

"You don't let it pile up, Anna," she said sternly.

I felt dirty and sticky much of the time now. But baths and frequent washing weren't possible until there was more water. The villagers lined up at the village well and ladled the precious liquid as it oozed up. We watched each other carefully to see that each took only a little for cooking and drinking.

We needed more wells, better wells! The men were digging, but there was so little strength for it. There was so much to do at the same time; everything was needful at once. Yet many of the settlers, like Papa, were ill; they felt weak, had headaches, rashes, and diarrhea.

And then they wasted their time bickering. I saw this clearly, more clearly than ever before, for I was allowed around adult conversations as freely as if I had been invisible. As a child I was sent out to play or to bed, but now, apparently, it didn't matter what I heard. Whether my parents decided this consciously because I no longer attended school and worked all day in the kitchen and on the yard or fields like an adult, or whether it resulted from the loose structures and loss of privacy in pioneering, I didn't know. I spent Sunday afternoons and some evenings with Susi and other girls from the village, attending choir and occasional youth meetings. Nevertheless, I overheard many adult conversations — our *Hof* was a gathering place for our neighbors — and I discovered to my disappointment that, though I hadn't regarded my elders as faultless, they were more flawed in wisdom, love, and endurance than I had realized.

I had my people set in peaceful, happy circles — I walked the wide village street and felt a surge of emotion as I considered the specific people belonging to this tent or that lean-to or the next *Hof* or that: the Rahns and Bergens and Waldes and Froeses, us, the Derksens and all the others. We were a community. Together, we had lifted, as it were, a cheesecloth into which Onkel Froese's story could drop like an egg and not break. On Sundays we met for worship on the campo, under the open sky, and sang in harmony of God's love and our love, of how we would follow and He would guide through all the sorrows of this life.

Now that vision of our unity seemed distant, like a cloud with a wonderful, billowing shape, but out of reach. Immediately at hand were the disagreements, the gossip, the failures of our leaders, our neighbors, our friends. Papa was loyal to Walde — he didn't speak behind his back — but I wondered, did Johann keep the same trust? What was said about us in our absence?

There was continuous tension in political matters of the colony. (Women weren't directly involved, but we found out easily enough what was discussed at the meetings). Though bonded by a common heritage, we were strangers thrust together from a dozen or more localities in Russia, each with its unique way of doing things. Those from Omsk thought they were so smart! Others from the Krim, as if that were something special! We from the Orenburg colony understood each other best; didn't we have a knowledge of the world that the others lacked? That's how it was, each feeling separate from the others, though some hung on to the distinction of their place of origin more than others.

During this period I was more alert, as well, to the teachings of the Bible, particularly the life of the disciple as presented in the Sermon on the Mount — blessings resulting from meek, merciful hearts, shining with good works, pure in thought and deed; the gospel penetrating the very motives and imagination; loving the enemies and gladly giving whatever might be required; contentment with food and raiment; entering at the narrow gate; praying "lead us not into temptation but deliver us from evil . . . all power is yours, O Lord."

The simplicity and purity of it was compelling, and I embraced it wholeheartedly, only to be frustrated by the gap between the life I hoped to see and that which my people, particularly my parents, lived.

I judged Mama less harshly than Papa. I could oppose her in a single, even petulant, remark when I felt her too unkind and complaining. She often let it go, unanswered, so I felt it was received. But with Papa, I could say nothing. I harbored my criticism of his failures like a pain. I was silent, listening, and unhappy.

He and Johann might spend an entire hour speculating, for example, what had happened to our horses.

"I sent the horses back with a young fellow, Igor who sometimes worked for us — "

"He came to the station?"

"I took him along. He happened to be in the village."

"He couldn't have known?"

"How? Nobody knew. He appraised those horses. I saw him; his eyes were like hands over them. I said, 'We're visiting our relatives and the neighbors will tend to them until we return. You stable them as usual!"

"He probably knew."

"He was appraising them. Sure, he was thinking, 'You won't be back,'and 'How much are they worth?'"

"He guessed what you were up to."

"I said, 'Take them home, stable them as usual. I've asked the neighbor to look after things,' and he said, 'Yes, Mr.

Sawatzky'."

"Lying."

"Sure."

They carried on like that, wondering: had he taken them back, waiting until morning, or did he drive them to his village that night, directly from the station? What did he do with the money? The one might have fetched this much, and the other that much. They considered every possibility, until it seemed as if the night was black because of the earth's one wretch, Igor. Because of him, everything else was wrong, and especially the awfulness of not knowing what he had done that night after we pulled out of the station. When I heard Johann say, in Russian, "But by now you wouldn't recognize them, you know," I felt I could bear it no more. I rose quickly and fled to the street.

Anything to be away from those voices with their needless petty worries and hatred, I thought. We had abandoned the horses, so what did Igor's honesty or dishonesty have to do with us? But let them talk, I thought miserably, as long as I didn't hear them and feel this anger and shame.

Another evening, a Friday evening, when several of our neighbors gathered informally around a fire on our *Hof*, Papa remarked, some time into the conversation, "I don't understand why they didn't let us into Canada. We have a son there."

"Our second. Peter," Mama inserted.

"How many times did I say to the officials, 'We've got a son there'? A son!" He spewed the word at us, as if we were the foreigners who doubted and hindered him.

"Those stubborn Canadian doctors," he said, "they claimed we're not healthy. They made up sicknesses to keep us out! I'm not so young, but I'm not sick! It's just because I'm old . . . "

Papa, I wished to interrupt, your eyes were the worst of ours all, the doctors said. Only Maria's children and I were en-

64

tirely free of trachoma. Besides, I continued to argue mentally, we were supposed to come here. The doctors didn't deliberately turn us away. And if they did? Wasn't it all for a purpose? Wasn't it God?

No one challenged Papa. Instead, as if troubled with his exact doubts, our visitors chimed in with similar stories of recalcitrant immigration officers.

Then I softened slightly, sensing in their confirming stories a certain kindness, as much a support of Papa perhaps, as of his grim view of our rejection.

"I'm old, and they think I'm useless, no sons to help," Papa reiterated.

"God will work even this out for your good," *Prediger* Rahn said. "God's grace still surrounds us. He brought us out, and he ... "

His comment was strangely thin and mechanical, but he spoke the truth.

Papa spat. The spittle landed at the edge of the fire and sizzled.

Rahn drew back in surprise. Walde laughed nervously but stopped abruptly as he realized my father timed the gesture for contempt.

The walls of support shifted; I was sure I could see them move.

Papa spat again. My heart beat rapidly. No! Don't! I cried inside. I felt humiliated, unable to look at anyone but Papa. We held our deliverance high, and he minimized it. It had been momentous, awesome, and he made a sacrilege of it. Why did he oppose Rahn and the others that way? Papa wiped his mouth with the back of his large hand and turned to Walde. It was the signal for Johann to talk; he began to explain the propensities of the peanut plant. Again I stood up and walked deliberately away from them to the street.

Chapter 9

"So, what do you think of the place, Anna?" my brother-in-law Klaus asked jovially as we carried firewood from the bush.

At that precise moment I was looking with great concentration at the grass before me, watching for snakes. Although I had not yet seen a snake, I had heard about many dangerous varieties, and I was duly afraid and careful. The rough grass stalks scratched against my legs. It was hot. Insects flitted around my face but with my hands full of wood I couldn't defend myself against them. His question made me uneasy. In it I heard a challenge to which I felt unequal.

Klaus had insisted that he and Maria live with us as one family. "I'm sick," he said.

"He's scared because he doesn't know how to farm," Papa grumbled to Mama.

"He really isn't well," Mama countered. Indeed, Klaus seemed to thrust Maria back to us with urgency. "Let them stay with us," she pleaded.

Klaus and Maria had their separate tent for sleeping with the two children, four-year-old Nikolaus and baby Margarethe, but we shared meals and all the work. Klaus helped, as he could, without complaining, taking orders each morning from Papa, and making no suggestions as to how the work should be done. He was drawn and tired, very different from the animated, though soft-spoken, young man who married Maria.

During the courtship Maria had gushed, "Oh Klaus is so easy to talk to!" and "He has such wonderful ideas," and "He knows everything." My sister's revelations, though little more than exclamations, made him, in my mind, a person of remarkable substance. I was her ally, hoping that Papa would consent to the marriage. He shook his head and said, "Sweet conversation won't put bread on the table." But Maria pleaded until Papa submitted. Maria was a beautiful woman, less spirited than I, but very intense and charming then. My parents realized she wouldn't be satisfied until she married Klaus.

Papa never warmed to his son-in-law. And Maria's ardor waned. Her main concern was her children — most of her words and actions involved them. I couldn't dislike Klaus, for he was a thoughtful and kind man, but none of us paid much attention to him. He was Maria's husband, that was all, or perhaps someone to pity because of his ill health. He became withdrawn, slept much, spoke little, and played no important part in the blend of personalities on our *Hof*. Even his children ran to *Opa* rather than their father.

Once I saw Klaus reading a Bible, which startled me, for he wasn't religious. He had been baptized as a youth, but rarely attended church. I wondered what he was thinking and what he was reading, and felt a twinge of guilt because I didn't know him better.

But it wasn't right, I often thought, that Klaus made no effort to mollify Papa. He didn't seem to care what the older man thought of him, and that showed disrespect, I felt. Did he consider himself superior because he had a few more years schooling?

Klaus hadn't wanted to leave Russia. "I'm no *kulak*," he said simply.

"Does the man count himself one of these communists then?" Papa roared to Mama and me later. "Is he as godless as that?"

When Papa's message that we would meet them in Moscow arrived, my sister and her husband packed and followed. Klaus gave no reasons for his change of mind.

And now he asked what I thought of the Chaco.

"Well," I answered slowly, repeating a statement I'd heard numerous times from Mama, "here we are, and that's to be made the best of, I suppose."

"That we must," Klaus agreed. "Just as Mama says." He began to whistle.

What did I think of it? The pests were terrible, that was sure. They were smaller then flies, smaller than mosquitoes, but as relentless as both together. The wood rubbed against my arms and I felt the perspiration rising over my body. The sun shone brightly in a cloudless, pale purple sky. I stared at the wide campo, pleasant and quiet. Here and there a small house, barn or corral rose out of the earth like a bit of turned sod or some sticks, the white tents like patches of shrinking snow on a field in spring. Snow! It wouldn't snow here. Never. Better to imagine them as flour sacks spread to bleach in the sun, soon to be folded, put away.

I noticed the campo, but it didn't heed me. Its sound was that of rustling, small noises, as if it whispered; but it sang to the sun as it always had, not to me. We might have been ants on its surface, so insignificant and unnecessary was our presence.

"You know, anything we'll know of civilization, or culture, or convenience will have to be made by us — by our own hands," Klaus said. "It'll take a lot of work."

He didn't need to tell me that. I had done plenty already: carried water (many women considered this work too heavy, but not I), dug a latrine with Papa's help (I who hadn't held a spade before), dug away the grass to gradually enlarge the yard, clearing it so it was brown, bare, and hard, made bricks, washed clothes.

"Actually it's kind of pretty," I said.

"It's not without its delights," Klaus agreed. "Might take some getting used to, though, wouldn't you say?"

"A little."

"It's been a disappointment for you, hasn't it?"

It was too personal. A blush covered my neck and cheeks, and I refused to look at him. It wasn't his business; disappointed or not, I did not require his comfort.

"Oh I don't know," I said lightly when I could trust my voice.

Klaus resumed his whistling.

I decided to initiate a conversation to show my composure. "How are you feeling?" I asked, interrupting his trilling. "Maria says — "

"Maria's right. I'm a sick man and I won't live to be old. Not old enough to see the Mennonite paradise that will be built here."

"Oh don't say that."

"A paradise for sure. As close as we've ever come before."

"No, I mean about not living so long — "

"I'm sick and dying, girl."

Wasn't he afraid? How could he speak about it so casually?

"If you talk like that, doesn't that hasten it along?" I asked shyly.

"Maybe it does. Maybe it doesn't." After a moment's

70

reflection, he added, "I suppose it's like a ball. All sorts of sides to it."

"About the paradise, though," he continued, "It *will* come, you know. Sure. As sure as there's nothing good about this place, it'll come. Our forefathers had their share of hardship too, no matter what region of Russia you want to consider. The Ukraine, the Krim, Turkestan, Siberia. Sure. Sod huts, poor crops, hunger, bandits, everything. It was always hard, starting out."

"Yes," I said, though I didn't know the details.

"Mennonites are devoted to land, to self-preservation," he explained. "And eventually it pays off. It works. Now look Anna, here we have the perfect situation again. We're alone, except for a few Indians. We have a government that's given us all kinds of rights. We don't have to enter the military. We can run our own schools. So we'll do it again, because we're just made to work and set things in order. And someday this wilderness will be full of us! A paradise!" Klaus laughed.

"It's hard to believe now," I said seriously.

"You're right. Sure. It's difficult now, everything so crude and primitive, and maybe it'll get worse before it gets better, who knows. After better, maybe worse again. But someday, for a while, it will be quite wonderful."

"But it's hard to believe, to see it that way," I persisted.

"You don't have to believe it," Klaus said. "You look at your people, you study a bit of their history. Then you know how things will turn out."

"Yes," I said slowly, not from reluctance, but thinking about his words, and feeling, suddenly, safe with him.

"It's good it will be like that, isn't it!" I said warmly.

"I'll tell you something else," Klaus said, as if this had given him the freedom to reveal a secret. "You'll suffer and your children will enjoy."

"What do you mean?"

"Just that. You'll build up the place, give your youth and health to do it, and the next generation will enjoy the fruits of it."

Klaus stopped abruptly and dropped his wood. "I read something strange in Isaiah," he said slowly. "Someday, whether it means in some new Jerusalem or heaven or the millennium, I don't know, but God promises that those who build houses will live in them, those who plant will eat. Each one will enjoy the work of his hands. I mean, every generation will be complete in itself! That's what I took from it. That will be a turnabout, won't it?" He chuckled. "That would be fairer, wouldn't you say, Anna?"

"I guess so. . ." I looked at the ground. "Now you'll have to pick up all your wood again."

He waved my concern aside. "Personally, I wish we'd start mingling with others. If we learned to live in cities we'd have something for our work sooner."

I knew his penchant for city life. Papa had spoken scornfully of it: in Orenburg Klaus had Russian friends, he sat in cafes with them.

"What would it do to our faith?"

"It wouldn't have to hurt it, Anna. Do you realize that?"

I shook my head doubtfully.

Klaus threw his arms open. Passionately, mockingly, as if addressing a crowd in the field, he cried, "Let those with more blood than will power in their veins stroll the streets of the cities! Let them enter shops and suck on sweets! Let them buy things! Let them sit with their friends and watch the passing of time!"

He struck his chest with exaggerated fortitude. "And us? Let's stay here alone! Let's do it with gladness! Let's eat beans and perhaps some rice for the rest of our lives! Let's eat and work over and over until we die!"

72

I couldn't help laughing.

"You're odd," I said, but I was teasing him, as a friend.

My load felt heavier, my arms were getting numb. I wanted to get to the *Hof*.

"Hey wait!" Klaus called. "My wood!"

"You dropped it, you pick it up," I called airily, marching on.

Chapter 10

As part of our outfit, supplied on credit by the Mennonite refugee organization, we received an ox and a cow with a calf. Milking "Brownie" was my job.

Brownie was thin and wild, had to be hobbled tightly before each milking, and refused to let down her milk unless started by her calf. After the calf began to suck, I pushed him away, jumped onto my three-legged stool and squeezed and pulled on the cow's ragged teats.

I had learned to milk in Russia, where we always had at least one cow. I rated myself a skillful milker, and enjoyed milking. But Brownie was nearly more than my patience could bear. All too often, when I was nearly finished, the unruly beast would kick loose, and overturn the tin bucket of milk.

Little Nikolaus often accompanied me, and then ran ahead announcing to his mother and grandmother how it had gone. "We have some milk today," he cried if the venture was a success. And, "May I have some please, please?" He seemed to crave it like a richer child might desire sweets.

When the cow's swift hooves robbed us of our small supply of the cherished white liquid, he called woefully, "There's no milk today. Brownie kicked the pail over!" I hated to come to the outdoor kitchen table then. Maria's eyes sought to meet mine and reproach me.

"Can't you tie her better, Anna?" she asked one morning.

"You try!" I responded shrilly. "Just see how easy it is!"

"I was just wondering," she said.

The next day I didn't move toward the cow. Let Maria find out how it is, I thought. Just once. I busied myself sweeping the *Hof* with short belligerent swishes of the straw broom.

"I'm sorry," Maria said at breakfast.

I couldn't forgive her that easily. "I'm not touching Brownie until you've milked her at least once," I declared. I began to cry. "Just so you know."

"What's the matter with her?" I heard Papa ask.

"She doesn't want to milk today."

He didn't command me but left the table. So I remained firm.

"You go, Maria," Mama said, sighing. Both of us looked at her in surprise. Then Maria shrugged, and went, giving Klaus a helpless look as she left. He grinned at her.

I could hear the tumult in the pen as Maria tried to calm and hobble the beast. Nikolaus' high childish voice shouted instructions. I refused to look in the direction of the small corral.

"You certainly are a stubborn one," Mama told me under her breath.

When Maria returned, Nikolaus didn't publicize for her as he did for me. There was a little milk in the pail, I noticed, but barely a quarter of what I got on the good days. I felt vindicated.

Milking seemed somewhat easier after that, although the animal never responded as I hoped she would. She seemed to hate me. Sometimes I would lean into the hairy leather hide and pull at the teats with more ferocity than necessary, and then the tears slid down my cheeks, though I wasn't sure why I cried. I had hoped so much to tame her, to win her over.

When Brownie was dry, the Wilhelm Froeses, our neighbors across the street, who had a tamer and better milker, said we could get a cup of milk from them each day. Nikolaus and I walked together to get it.

"May I have what spills into the saucer?" the winsome blond boy begged.

"Oh, you're just like a little cow yourself, with your big brown eyes," I teased him.

"Please. . ."

"I'll have to walk very carefully so that none spills over."

"I know, but if a little does spill, may I drink it?" His pleading touched me.

"Yes, you may have it then," I said.

At the edge of our *Hof*, I permitted a little milk to spill into the plate. He slurped it noisily. This, plus a quick visit with Susi, became a daily ritual.

"Don't you get a whole cup, Anna?" Maria asked.

"I never bring a full cup home," I said.

Brownie calved, but the calf was tiny and sank down weakly, bleating, after each attempt to stand. It died within three days.

"How will we get Brownie milking now?" I worried. "She won't let down her milk without a calf."

Mama suggested we try to fool her. We skinned the deceased calf, stuffed the hide with grasses and propped it against the milking post. Brownie looked suspiciously at the strange creature, nevertheless allowed herself to be drawn toward it. I nuzzled the lifeless hide against the mother's lips and then against the full udder. I began to milk. It worked!

Brownie yielded several liters. All the while she nosed the skin, alternately mooing and sniffing.

We couldn't trick her the next morning. She wouldn't allow me near her udder, and although she bawled for days because of her painful distention, she finally dried up.

We also received some chickens in the initial outfit. The hens roosted in the trees at night, and scavenged the yard by day. But they weren't safe; one day Mama drove a bold fox away with a stick.

"We need a dog!" she said.

"We need a chicken pen," Papa replied.

"A farm has to have a dog."

"There are no dogs."

"I've seen Indians with dogs."

"They won't part with them. They love those skinny hounds like children."

Then one of the chickens was stolen. Mama caught only a glimpse of the predator when the poultry's squawking alerted her. She couldn't be sure, but the creature bounding away seemed cat-like.

"We need a dog," Mama began again.

"Someday we'll have a dog too," Papa told her.

"We need a dog now, even if I have to sacrifice something to get one." Chickens were indispensable to her, first providing eggs and then a tasty chicken noodle soup.

The next morning Mama left the yard with her brown dress, her oldest one, tucked under her arm. When she returned several hours later, she cradled a skinny, shaking mongrel. The ribs showed through his matted hide. He looked at us with dull, doleful eyes.

Papa blinked. "What's that?"

"A dog."

"I can see that much. But where — ?"

"Traded it for my dress," she said.

"But — "

"They won't part with their dogs, no, but they want clothes too. They couldn't refuse, it being as big as it was!"

Papa shook his head. "She did it again," he commented to me.

Patiently Mama fed and trained the dog, Rolf, over the next weeks. Her tender efforts were rewarded with a faithful companion and watchdog. She loved to tell the story of how she traded her large size dress for the dog, while Rolf sat at her feet, wagging his tail occasionally as if he understood and entirely supported her version of the tale.

Chapter 11

As if our present difficulties weren't enough, we suffered a typhoid epidemic.

The months in which it raged in the westerly three villages, when nearly a hundred people died were the longest and strangest months of my years in Paraguay. The intimate presence of Death stretched them and vividly fixed certain scenes on my mind. It set my emotions in such sharp, yet distant relief that I sometimes felt I was watching myself experience them. The village graveyards were marked with one fresh mound of earth after another, the soil turned to the air the way our fields should have been, open to seed. Ironically, our pioneering energies were expended in caring for the sick, cutting trees for coffins, and digging graves. Yet rather than anger or bitterness, I felt a numb sort of awe. Fear altered us all for awhile.

We were eating pancakes the evening Johann Walde brought the news. The pancakes were a welcome, wonderful break from our monotonous diet of beans or rice and coarse bread and tea. The meal was festive. Even Mama's intention to make them, passing from one family member to another as good news, had cheered us.

Nikolaus darted immediately to Mama's side and watched intently as she mixed the dough: cracking the eggs and measuring in the flour, pouring the milk, stirring in a bit of precious sugar, and beating it smooth with a wooden spoon. He followed her to the fire, guarding her and the pale cream-thick dough. He also got the first pancake, which he carried to the table like a live chick in his hands. Then he said "It's good," after every mouthful.

Impulsively I hugged him, saying, "Oh Nikolaus, I love you!" He pushed me away; he had no interest in Auntie Anna then.

"It nearly fills me up, seeing him eat like that," Maria said, her eyes moist.

The pancakes were delicious, tasting of the outdoors and the smoke and smell of wood. The wind had calmed, the sun was low, and the air mellow. We all ate heartily, except for Klaus, who said he wasn't hungry.

Then Johann hurried along the worn path between our farms.

"It's been established," he called eagerly. "It's typhoid fever."

"So the cause of the deaths is the typhoid," Papa echoed.

"A plague!" Mama gasped.

Walde's message gave a name to several deaths which had already occurred and to the widespread diarrhea, cramps, vomiting, and weakness in our villages. So it was something more than simply adjusting to a new climate and food. Immediately I saw the implications of his statements. We had no medicines, no medical help. It would be dispatched from the capital, Johann said, but how many weeks would that take? I glanced at Klaus but he was looking at Johann with an expression of unconcern.

Before we could learn the details from Walde, we were interrupted by a flock of parrots alighting on several trees about eighty meters away, loading the branches with the color of exotic blossoms, and filling the air with their harsh squawking.

"Caw, caw, caw!" they screeched, utterly without melody or grace. They seemed to mock us.

Walde and Papa ran to the trees with pieces of firewood which they heaved into the din. "Away from here! Away! Away!" they shouted.

The birds finally moved on. The two men stayed in the field, talking; Klaus crept into the tent to sleep; we women proceeded to our duties with the dishes and the children.

Over the next weeks, the deaths continued. In one village, a quarter of the inhabitants died. The news of each incident passed from *Hof* to *Hof*, by word of mouth or by way of an invitation to the funeral. Initially, I felt excitement — albeit subdued excitement — in hearing who had died. The turns the invisible enemy took, fed my imagination "Ratzlaff sobbed so loudly the neighbors heard it" people said, and "Mrs. Siemens screamed, 'He's in hell! He's in hell!' She'd been begging, and he wouldn't give in."

Soon, however, I was weary of the reports. I didn't actually expect to die myself, and yet, I was afraid, for what was sure? Each morning I wondered, do I have pain anywhere? If there was nothing besides hunger, I was glad and jumped up energetically. One day I felt a slight pressing discomfort in my lower abdomen and dizziness. I prayed anxiously as I worked. When I realized they were menstrual cramps I was jubilant, as if God had answered and given me reprieve.

I watched my parents and Maria and the children. I watched Susi. I watched everyone I loved, asking them, "How

83

are you feeling?" If the answer was "All right" I was relieved; we had gained time. Help was on the way, but we didn't know when it would come, so every minute of health was hoarded, saved like insurance for a favorable outcome.

One day Mama said to me, "Some families need help. We're three women here, so one of us can be spared. You and I will help, as we can. You don't mind, do you?"

I didn't understand why she asked me so formally. Didn't I always obey her?

"I don't mind," I said.

"It's our Mennonite way," she sighed. "We stand by one another."

"It doesn't matter. We're all getting behind in our work because of this. We're all in the same situation."

"It's not that," Mama said. "It's just that . . . well, anyways, tomorrow you'll help at Penners."

The Penners' *Hof* was in chaos, but empty of any human activity when I arrived mid-morning. Several pieces of clothing hung over a cord, other garments soaked in a basin of dirty water, and still other pieces were strewn on the ground. The table was thick with crumbs and flies, half a loaf of bread, some lard, a cup of sour milk and in the middle, a bar of hard soap which was grey with dried foam and grime. The axe lay on the ground between the woodpile and the corral, and a little further, a hoe, the blade turned up. Chickens scuttled about. Apparently someone had slept outside, for a blanket and pillow were crumpled together under a tree. The entire scene offended me.

I was suddenly startled to see a boy of about eight, their youngest child, staring at me from under the table where he was playing with some pods and sticks.

"Where's your mother?"

He pointed to the tent.

There, Helene Penner lifted herself feebly. "I'm still in

bed," she apologized weakly.

"I'm here to help. Mama told you I'd come, remember?"

"I'll get up to show you."

"It's all right," I protested.

"Lying in bed, the sun risen?"

The thin woman struggled to her feet. Her stomach was loose from bearing many children and bulged through her shabby dress. Her face was pale, and streaked as if she hadn't washed, though the discoloration seemed to come from beneath her skin, and her hair was uncombed, oily, and had fallen onto her shoulders. She was ugly, and difficult to look at.

"I've brought a bit of meat," I offered. "Mama sent it. It came from the other villages." I set the bowl on the table.

"We'll make a soup," Helene puffed. She stumbled to the water pail, then cried reproachfully, "There's no water!"

I sprang to take the pail. "I'm sorry," I said. "I'll go. Please lie down."

Then I ran from the *Hof*, not looking back, afraid to see if she had fallen. The hot sand of the street burned my bare soles and I felt like crying. It would be another white, windy, hot day.

Maria was at the well, alone.

"What a mess at Penners!" I called, glad to see her. Then I saw her eyes, red and unhappy. "What's the matter?"

"Well Klaus is dying, you know."

"Are you sure?"

"Of course, Anna. You know it too! It's so hot in the tent, he can't bear it. I hate to be in there. He won't eat. I come in and the flies are crawling in his nose. He doesn't even notice!"

Her voice was shrill and each sentence ended sharply, as if to cut through my stupidity. But she looked at something in the distance, not me. When she finished, she swallowed, and her chin and lips trembled. Tears gathered in her eyes again.

My beautiful sister Maria! She seemed young and vulnerable, and I dropped my pail and put my arms around her. "I know, I know," I whispered, patting her back, moved by her need and what I hoped was, at that moment, a renewal of our once-open, loving relationship. I had always admired her, adored her. Now she would let me console her.

Then she moved, like an animal wary of another strange beast, and I had to release her.

Picking up her pail, she resumed a peevish tone. "You're lucky you have nobody to lose with this sickness. Just be thankful you're not responsible for anyone yet, no husband or children! I'll be alone with two children!"

"I know that Maria!"

"You should think of it more, how fortunate you are."

I remembered Mrs. Penner, swaying like a broken straw in her yard.

"I have to go," I said.

I found Mrs. Penner slumped on a bench with her head on the table. Her son hadn't ventured from his play spot beneath. She was conscious, so I half-lifted, half-guided her to her pallet in the hot tent. She resisted, however, grunting and muttering "ouch" while I moved her.

Helene continued to moan inside as I made a fire, cooked the broth, and cleared the table. I wished, the entire time, that I could get away, home, away from her and the disheveled surroundings.

I reported everything to Mama when she came to check near noon.

"You shouldn't have let her get up."

"She doesn't listen to me."

"She's a mother, and her conscience won't let her rest when there's work to be done. But you shouldn't have let her get up."

"What can I — "

"You simply take charge if they don't know any better."

Mama taught me an important lesson that day. She went to Mrs. Penner's side, spoke in soft tones at first, and then rigidly. "Helene, don't get up again. If you need something, ask."

Then she said to me, "Use your knack to be bossy when you have to. If you're healthy, you must give orders to the sick. And it makes no difference that you're younger."

I also helped the Zacharias family. And I was the one who found them dead.

When I lifted a corner of the blanket hung over the tent door, the yellow morning light shot into the tent in the shape of a triangle and fell on the child Emma's face. She was dead. As I pushed the blanket further aside, the light revealed the mother, the father, a brother. They were all dead.

I twisted in the doorway and that movement altered the window I was making; the shaft of light reached Emma's doll. The toy lay beside the girl on the multi-colored piecework quilt, an elaborate cover which had been the parents' wedding gift, now soiled with vomit and dirt. The doll's glass eyes didn't blink. She was pink and golden and glossy. The smell in the tent didn't pucker her china nose; nothing bothered her.

I wanted to seize the lovely doll and pull it outside. But I was afraid to enter the tent. I dropped the flap to shut the dawn away from the bodies; I left the doll inside with them.

I rushed to inform the minister, *Prediger* Rahn, who lived on the neighboring farm.

"I have no time to work on the land or build our house," he said, returning with me. "Looking for bottle trees, digging graves, preparing sermons, that fills up all the hours. If at least I could find more to say. Something of comfort."

What was he telling me?

"I pray for comfort so I can give comfort . . . Blessed are the dead . . . Sometimes that seems the best, certainly the easiest to say. When it's hot, I almost wish it for myself."

"You mean you're jealous of them?" I burst out. "I don't want to die!"

"Of course not. You're young. I don't either. But sometimes one could almost envy them, don't you think? They're in a better place." He smiled at me.

I didn't answer him but I thought much about this in the following days. For myself, I decided, putting even heaven and this wilderness of bush side by side I would choose to remain alive.

Still, I wasted more than one funeral dreaming of myself dead. During the Zacharias service, as during others, I visualized myself in their place, and the mourners and the accolades in my honor. I believed I would be quite elegant in a bottle tree coffin, in my best navy dress, and the grief over me would be especially intense because I'd been so attractive, lively, intelligent. They would remember a great deal about me. I saw Gerhard in my vision, the young man in our village upon whom my interest was presently focused, looking with disbelief and regret at my corpse, wishing he had declared himself. I saw Klaus and Johann Walde and Maria — of course Maria — speaking of what I had said and done, my helpfulness during the plague — "she gave herself nursing others and then succumbed herself." Susi was disconsolate, Mama broken. Nikolaus cried, "Will Auntie Anna never come back?"

I tried to shake my daydreams away. The bench on which I sat was hard and uncomfortable. Because it wasn't standing straight, I had to push with my foot to sit level. When I got tired and let it go, my seat slanted and I felt I would slip off.

"All flesh is as grass . . ." the preacher quoted. I thought, campo grass believed it would seed and wave in the Chaco forever. I'm grubbing it out, inch by inch, from our yard. I'm burning it, destroying it.

They would say that too. "She cleared most of the yard herself. She was a tireless worker. I should have made her rest." The voices were my parents', and their words were repeated as echoes the length of the colony.

It was time for a hymn. Suddenly Wilhelm Froese stood, interrupting the service.

"God's hand is heavy upon us," he cried. "Let's repent before we're destroyed. Let's repent that some of us may live!"

Had he known what I was thinking? I thought wildly. Would he expose me in front of everyone? Impossible. But his pronouncement fell over my mental pride like a shadow. During the closing hymn I prayed earnestly that God would forgive me.

Froese himself lost two family members, first his oldest son Hans, and several weeks later, his wife.

"Hans went quietly enough," Susi confided soon after her brother's death, "but it's terrible for Kornelius."

"Why?"

"He was always second and now he's first. He had to dig the grave with the men, and he found the bottle tree for the coffin."

We used bottle trees because there was no time to prepare other wood and build caskets. There were no planks, no tools for that kind of carpentry, and with the pressure of rapid decay in the heat, burial couldn't be delayed. The bottle tree had a wide round trunk with a soft core and when hollowed out could hold even an adult.

"Kornelius found a good tree," Susi said, "but it was already morning and the service was to be in the afternoon. He told me everything later. Oh Anna, it was hardest on him."

Kornelius was awkward and shy. He seemed ill-proportioned and inept. I didn't like him. I had never given him my eye. Never.

"He cut it and loaded it on the cart, and then the ox

89

wouldn't move. He pulled at it, and pushed it and poked it. He spoke kindly. He really pleaded, and he stroked the beast. He tried everything. It wouldn't move.

"Then he swore. In Russian. He says he never spoke those words in his life. He heard the oath from our servant when he was very young and he remembered it and said it now. Then he was so scared, he began to shake and fell to his knees. He didn't mean it. 'Spare me!' he said. He wept for a long time. Then he got up and still, the ox wouldn't move. He had to light a fire under its belly to make it go.

"Once he was home," Susi continued in her even, quiet way, "he and mother hollowed the tree. It bothers him that Mother just cries and doesn't speak to him. He talks to me because he can't say anything to anyone else. 'I'm not the same as Hans,' he says. I tell him not to think of it. Poor Kornelius."

This aroused my pity, and new insight into Kornelius. "Poor Kornelius," I agreed.

Susi looked at me intently, long. She was offering him to me! I suddenly realized her story had purpose. She had a plan. She wanted me to have Kornelius. Or him to have me, whatever way it was. I felt her wish pressing against me.

"Kornelius is a good young man, Anna," she said. "But he doesn't take comfort from a sister."

There was no doubt in my mind that I had discerned her correctly. It was her look, as much as her words, that told me. But just as surely, even stubbornly, I returned a blank, unwilling gaze. I wouldn't accept him, even if she wished it. I had larger expectations of a husband than Kornelius could fulfill, and I wasn't prepared to sacrifice my wishes for Susi, or for poor Kornelius. But it gave me several weeks of worry and pain, for Susi was now my dear friend. I was sure I had failed her.

Chapter 12

Sitting down wearily at the table, Papa asked Maria, "How's Klaus?"

"Why don't you go say goodbye?" I said before she could answer.

Boldly I carried on, "He's dying. We all know it."

I wanted to effect something between the two men that would give us solace later. "Papa," I pleaded, "please say goodbye to Klaus."

He was silent.

"But what do I say? Just goodbye?" he asked suddenly. I rushed away from the table, ashamed. I belonged in the kitchen helping Mama, not counselling Papa, learning of his weaknesses.

Klaus died that night.

The following evening, after the funeral, we were alone as a family, and Papa lit a fire. We didn't want to follow the usual routine and go to sleep. Not yet. It wasn't cold but we needed the color and life of the flames, and we needed light, for there was no moon; the darkness was a bowl turned over our heads.

Baby Margarethe fell asleep in Mama's arms, and I held Nikolaus. He dozed on my lap. His face was peaceful and sweet as the dancing flames flickered their wings of light over it. I glanced at him once, though, when the fire was yellow and steady and was startled to see the dead Klaus, just as he had looked that afternoon as we posed before the coffin, gazing at him, for the photo Mr. Siemens took. Little Nikolaus was as perfect and still as his dead father had been; their features were the same. I shifted him quickly so the light and shadows would play over him, and I would know he was my dear nephew, alive.

Maria began to speak. Every phrase ended with a heaving half-sob like the tail of the whooping cough. "He spoke so wonderfully...he never complained...he was sick the whole time in Paraguay...he was so kind and so good...he loved me so much...he loved the children so much...he had his dreams and his plans, but...he was happy in Russia...we were so happy together..."

Was that how he was? I argued silently.

Maria flung herself onto Papa's chest, wailing, "I wasn't kind enough to him."

Papa seemed surprised to find her on his knees, but put his hand around her and held her, clumsily, until she quieted.

Klaus was dead, taken; he was in God's hands, and meant nothing, now, to me. But there was Maria, my thin, distraught sister, whom I had always loved. I began to cry with her, and if she thought it was because of Klaus, that was only partially true; I was mourning for her, wishing I could let her be me, for even a day or two, so she might have a brief rest from her grief. So she could anticipate marrying and having children as she had years before, instead of having just buried her husband.

Chapter 13

Every morning I awoke when it was still dark. The pre-dawn darkness was spent and thin, however, and I wasn't afraid of it. I dressed and went for a pail of water before I did any other work. Often I left before Mama and Maria were up; sometimes I said Good-morning to Mama with a full pail of water in my hand.

One morning when I set out for the walk to the well, a thick white mist covered the entire village and campo. It was warmer and gentler than the fogs we'd had at sea though, and I walked in it quite briskly and happily, thinking of the beautiful names of our villages. They were German names we brought along from Russia, many of them conveying the beauties of nature or combining words of virtue with words of place. They were lovely names. *Gnadenheim*, home of grace. *Friedensfeld*, field of peace. *Schoenwiese*, beautiful meadow. *Lichtfeld*, field of light, and *Rosenort*, place of roses. *Friedensruh*, restful peace, and *Schoenbrunn*, beautiful well.

As I walked I saw, very distinctly, how the fog lifted. It was gathered up in a single sweeping motion as if an invisible giant hand snatched away the lacy veil that covered the land. The just-risen sun pierced into the stretch of grassland where the lovely mist had just lain; the brilliant light leapt onto every drop of dew.

Lichtfeld! Yes, I thought, glorious field of light, a truly glorious and majestic field of light.

I began to sing:

> Lord, who can be with Thee compared?
> Or who Thy greatness hath declared?
> Thou Source and Life of all the living;
> Thy dazzling vestment is the light . . .

God had been gracious to us. The medical team had arrived with their expertise, needles, and precious medicine to eradicate the typhoid fever.

"And his hand is not shortened, that he cannot save," was the text our little newspaper quoted, and it tumbled jubilantly in my head, for we were safe, the danger was over. With sharp jabs of preventive injections, the epidemic could be stopped. I hadn't realized how tense and afraid I'd actually been until I knew that I was alive and no longer susceptible to catching the dread illness. I felt freed, suddenly clean, as if a hot, soapy bath had washed all my panic away. I'd wanted to live; of course, I had known I would, hadn't I? I didn't have trachoma; I didn't get typhoid fever either.

"You're so healthy, girl, it's a blessing," Mama said fondly, "All the sick people you were around . . .

"It just couldn't get me," I had laughed giddily in return.

I reached the well. We wanted to wash that day, so I had taken the yoke with two buckets. Since I was the first one at the well, it didn't take long to fill the pails. I turned slowly to retrace my steps home. The pails were heavy. Now that the mist was gone and the sun rose eagerly into the pale, hazy sky, it was hot. I began to perspire, the moisture breaking over me in droplets, on my forehead, upper back and shoulders where the yoke rested, around my waist and between my legs.

Field of light, indeed! We all got the same sun, and too much of it, in this over-lit, over-heated world; what was so remarkable about that? It was ridiculous to bring those names from Russia, as if they belonged to us, as if they could be transplanted at will, and by our naming, become, instead of drab bits of villages, the meaning of their titles. *Rosenort!* We had journeyed there just the Sunday before, to visit friends. Had I seen a rose? Of course not. I hadn't seen a single flower, let alone a rose.

Gnadenfeld. Home of grace. Oh yes, I had believed it when I walked in the cloud this morning, when it had been visible, when it covered us as grace should, a tender white blanket, when it deposited sparkling jewels on every blade of grass. But it vanished, drawing its skirts and fleeing the miserable sun, the day. It left us behind, taking with it my courage, which only returned at night with the stars, something visible and alive again, growing in the temperate evening.

Well, perhaps we knew as much, perhaps we sensed the anachronisms of our hopes. We gave our villages the ancient names, but we generally referred to them by number, in order of their founding. It was easier, more accurate.

I couldn't go on. I sank abruptly at the edge of the street, letting the buckets touch the ground so I could rest. Ten meters farther stood a tree whose shade might have helped me a little, but I didn't care enough to push myself that distance.

I saw myself, like a picture flashed before me, disembarking the *Agipe* at Puerto Casado. Instead of walking off slowly and timidly, defensively, as I should have, I pranced off, full of romantic notions and ideals that even our trauma in Russia had not diminished. I strode down, yes, as if I were a wealthy tourist in some exotic foreign resort, or an undeposed Tsarina on tour, instead of a girl, sixteen years old, and a refugee. A girl who should be ashamed for seeing only what she wanted, and too little of what really was. A penniless Mennonite refugee girl, covered with skin so fair it wouldn't turn brown in the sun like a true Paraguayan, but only redden and blister and burn. I had stepped down as if commencing a grand adventure. In the green hell yet.

And feeling so blessed! As if it were significant and very important to move to another continent, settle an unsettled place. I had worn my feelings as proudly as a Joseph's-coat.

I shut my eyes tightly, pinching tears, and turned the garment of that memory inside out. I saw the hovels to the side of the port, the half-dressed Indians, the isolation, the shabbiness of it all, how primitive it was. I was embarrassed over the girl who made those eager avowals about her new home. I decided she had been mistaken.

PART TWO

Chapter 1

Did I really expect that a suitor would arrive while I stood at the gate singing and dreaming about it? No, of course not.

Yet that's exactly what happened. Jakob came up the road to the gate where I was resting, reflecting, and wishing; we met, and three months later we married.

It was September, a Thursday, late afternoon, and I had finished clearing the weeds from the roadside between our house and the street. When I reached the gate, I was done. It was wonderful to stand after prolonged bending with the hoe. I let erectness move slowly along my spine, from bottom to top, and when straight, enjoyed the sensation as if I had missed it or forgotten how it felt. I leaned against the gatepost, rubbing one hand over the unpainted grey wood, hard wood, heavy as iron and remarkably smooth though uneven and knobby. My fingers and palm, stained from pulling weeds, were rough and calloused, yet they very clearly perceived that smooth solid texture. The post, though cut and stripped, seemed like a planted, living tree still, a sturdy friend on whom I could depend. In the other hand I held my hoe.

I leaned on the post to rest and think. At first I thought about nothing in particular, nothing more perhaps than waiting for evening, for the prongs of orange in the west which would release the lovely quiet darkness, for the time of day when with a clear conscience, we could stop working and prepare to sleep.

Then I thought about work. The unwanted plants lay in a row of clumps. It satisfied me, imagining them already losing their color, and shrinking, beginning to wilt. I often worked outdoors at such tasks, or with Papa, and I enjoyed it. I liked the wind when it puffed gently over the campo, playing with my skirt and coaxing strands of my sun-bleached hair away from the pins meant to hold them. I liked the way the earth humped up and humbly fell back as the plow cut through it, and the paratodo tree in spring with its beautiful bouquet of yellow blossoms, each long flower streaked from its center with fine wine-colored lines, and the pure white lily blossoms of the bottle tree.

I did not like the impersonal north wind drying out the soil and flinging sand into my pores and eyes, or the bush, always on the horizon, always green, but a grey green, filmed with dust, waiting stupidly for the rain to bathe it. The bush had no spaces; it was tight and unbreakable. It pressured my vision when I was weary; when I stopped to look around, it gave me no relief. I hated the heat and the perspiration that formed over my body, coalescing into drops that slid between my breasts and legs, making me hot and damp where I shouldn't touch.

But I always worked hard, and I didn't give up even when discouraged. It was difficult to quit. Every weed was a triumph. Just this one, I would say, and this one yet, and the next, and one more. Seeing those unwelcome nuisances lying with their roots in the air, removed from every possibility of spoiling something, was a pleasure. So were the seeded furrows. Just this row, and another, just to the end, and why not one more quickly, and yet another. I wouldn't stop until Papa waved or called.

"You should have been a boy," he teased me once, when the sun forced us to rest before ten in the morning. "Do you like farming?" He took a long drink from a bucket of warm water.

"I do," I said, wiping my face on my dress hem. "You have no sons here, Papa, so I help."

But I wasn't the kind of farmer a son would have been. When I put the weeds in piles, I badly wanted to do more, to gather them all and take them away, hide them completely from view. I wanted our place to look nice, tidy. I preferred the extra work of cleaning them away to waiting for the sun and wind to diminish them. Papa claimed such work was excessive and he scolded me if I did it.

"Once they're pulled," he said, "if they haven't gone to seed, they're no problem. It doesn't matter if they lie there." He only relented on one point. "Keep the earth around the house clear, if you must," he said, "but please, Anna, don't attempt to sweep the entire farm!"

I chuckled, thinking of it, and then let my attention drift contentedly to our pleasant-looking, whitewashed house. It was a small dwelling. However, the day we moved in, four months after our arrival in the Chaco, it seemed palatial, and the straight brick walls wonderfully reassuring. By then we were weary of living in tents. The epidemic had slowed the construction work, as had the seemingly endless requirements of community work.

The system of community work was traditional with us Mennonites. In Prussia, the draining of swamps and building of dikes was done together, and in Russia too it was taken for granted that every homestead must do its share in the building and maintenance of the common facilities. Here the community work system would give us wide streets, the roads to our colony center, and the village schools, and man the many trips to

101

Endstation, the end of the railway line, to transport our crops to market and bring back the products we needed to import.

When we moved into the house the grey brick structure was coated with a mixture of clay, grasses, and manure. Later we whitewashed the exterior with white quebracho ashes and flour, a process Mama and I had recently redone. The inside walls and floor were regularly smeared with cow dung and mud for a smooth hard finish.

The roof was covered with *Schilf*, a long bamboo-type grass which the Lengua Indians had shown us where to find. It was bundled, dipped in mud, and placed in neat rows over the roof frame of branches and poles. On the west side of the house we constructed a two-meter overhang, also made of these grasses over a framework of poles. This was our eating area and kitchen, the place where the table stood. The win dows and doors of our house were open; when it was windy or cold we hung sacks over them, and sometimes Papa's now decrepit-looking coat served as a door. We slept inside and stored our things there, but we lived mainly outdoors, sheltered only a little from the sun by the porch over the table and an algorrobo tree nearby.

The house had two rooms. Maria and the children and I shared a room, with the tent tarp strung up to provide a bit of privacy for me. We shared, that is, until Maria's remarriage. Then I had the room alone, and Mama and Papa had the other one.

Maria married again in January of the first year. When she announced her intention to wed the forty-year-old Ernst Hein, a widower with five children, whose wife died in the typhoid epidemic, Mama was most unhappy. It was too soon after Klaus' death, she said — what would people think? — and Ernst was too old for Maria.

"She probably spotted him in Germany," Mama said. "I

didn't think there was much between her and Klaus anymore."

"Mama, that's ridiculous," I laughed. Though Klaus and Maria's marriage was too bland for my romantic ideals, I couldn't imagine that my sister had been anything but loyal. And the way she'd fussed over her children in Germany, hardly noticing even us, when would she have seen Ernst Hein?

"His children need a mother, and Nikolaus and Margarethe need a father, so it makes sense for them to think of each other. Why should they wait?" I reasoned.

"She seems so anxious to fly from here. She barely knows the man."

"But you just said they knew each other from Germany."

Mama sighed. Sometimes it wasn't difficult to argue her into a corner. "I don't know," she said. "It wouldn't surprise me, though."

"It's impossible, Mama. You know it."

"Maria will be poor," Mama said. "And the work she'll have! A promise made one day, and she turns around with three times as many children plus one."

"She always makes crazy marriages," Papa joined in.

"We're all poor," I countered.

"She should wait, that's all," Mama said.

But neither she nor Papa spoke their protests to Maria. My sister's will seemed to have hardened since Klaus' death. No matter how trivial a detail one might contest about something she said, such as the time or day of the week something occurred, Maria wouldn't back down. Disagreeing with her only entrenched her opinion.

Lately it seemed that Maria paid me little heed, or spoke condescendingly, as if only she had grown older, and I had remained a child. But I carried the memory of my childhood when Maria, eight years older than I, had been an angel in my eyes, graceful and beautiful, someone I loved passionately. Perhaps I still hoped some miracle would make her dote on me and love me as she had then. I defended her.

"The dying came too suddenly for our liking," I said crossly to my parents, "so why not the marrying too? And remember what you said, Mama, about Reuben's Christa. Why shouldn't she be happy? Ernst is a good man. I'm glad for Maria!"

Ernst was nearly bald, but it didn't age him, for he was round-faced and possessed a cheerful smile and friendly eyes. Although he was shy at first, he seemed eager to please us and Maria; he was good-humored, too agreeable perhaps, but refreshingly cheerful.

"Oh I suppose I am too!" Mama grumbled.

I blamed the Chaco for our troubles now because I felt that its ugliness, its climate, its bleak prospects, its tenaciousness in resisting us, caused the pessimism I so often felt on our *Hof*. I remembered how desperately I had prayed for rain our first spring. It was mostly for the sake of Papa and Johann Walde; I wanted it so they could be happy. (I wished to prove them wrong too.)

Papa had been impatient to begin seeding. In spite of his lack of strength and the epidemic, he had, with my help and that of an Indian man, cleared and prepared a small portion of our land for crops. We watched the sky for rain, in order to plant.

"They told us spring comes in September. The spring rains," he said. But it didn't rain. Other than a light shower or two, hardly enough to settle the dust, it hadn't rained since April, several months before we arrived.

Occasionally the clouds piled up, massive and dark. Sometimes there would be rumblings in the distance and flashes of lightning. But no rain.

"I don't believe it rains here," Johann said. "We're simply too far west of the river. We'll never get what we need for decent farming."

"They've had a bit in the eastern villages of the other colony," Papa said. "Why they stuck us even further west, I can't figure out."

"I'll bet we could sit here for years and never get rain."

The cattle in the colony were getting thinner; some had died. There was no pasture, little water. As each week came and went without the skies releasing even a drop, the rumors hardened into fact: it wouldn't rain here, we were too far inland. The leaders of the settlement tried to encourage us by posting rain statistics of an experimental farm in the Chaco, but these didn't really stem the discouragement.

Daily, constantly it seemed, I prayed for rain. Johann said it made no difference to pray, weather was weather. But I persisted, sure that God could do something if He chose.

The drought continued, and there was much talk of leaving the Chaco. We hadn't been there for even half a year yet.

Near the end of October, the twentieth I think, the clouds rushed together and clumped up in huge stacks as they had at times before. The sky grew darker.

On our *Hof*, we kept silent as the daylight greyed. No one dared say, "It looks like rain," for fear our notice might impel the clouds on again. We kept at our tasks; I was scrubbing clothes that afternoon. But I was conscious only of the weather conditions, of the changing forms and colors in the sky. The sun was soon hidden, but it was very hot. The air was heavy, high in humidity. The atmosphere seemed charged; it seemed to roar, and yet it was terribly, intensely still. It was exactly right for the rainstorm we needed. "Oh God, let it rain," I urged in my thoughts. "Please, this time. Please, God, please."

As I felt the tension in the air, my body tensed with it. The sky became blacker, and my hands were stiff against the washboard. The heavens were poised for some fierce action. They seemed hateful. Surely they were tired of teasing us. Surely this

105

time it would rain! Lightning blitzed through the clouds. It increased, seemed nearer.

Can it rain here? I wondered. Can it?

"Oh God, please," I beseeched Him.

The wind shifted abruptly; it began to blow from the south, sweeping the *Hof* of dried leaves and sand. Quickly I wrung the wet clothes and bunched them into a basin. I hurried into the house. I was afraid, for I could feel the temperature dropping. I shivered, and my hopes dropped too; this shift in the wind would drive the full, storm-configured clouds away again.

Then raindrops clattered to the ground. Mama, Maria, the children, and Papa ran into the house. It began to thunder. The lightning came in broad white flashes. At each thunderburst, Margarethe screamed. "It's the clouds clapping their hands," I shouted to her.

The noise and light increased until they seemed directly above us; the rumbling surrounded us and shook our small shelter. It was louder and closer than anything I had ever experienced.

Raindrops bounced to the ground, raising the choking smell of damp dust. Their momentum increased and settled that dust. Suddenly the water poured down, running past the openings of our windows and doors like sheets of glass. It smelled rich and wonderful, the unmistakable smell of rain.

The rain continued. Tiny rivulets formed in the hard earth. Tiny puddles. We stood in the house, watching.

"Look at it!" Papa exclaimed at last. "Just look at it!"

"It's raining, *Opa*," Nikolaus explained.

We laughed out of relief and the child was pleased with the effect of his remark. "Whoopee! Whoopee!" he shouted. "It's raining!"

We stood and watched the rain, laughing, letting it wash away our doubts and the dogma of the naysayers.

It rained thirty-five millimeters in our village. Johann had measured it. We would need much more, but it was a splendid beginning. After the storm Nikolaus and I walked around the pools on the *Hof.* I saw with a surge of gladness the now-peaceful clouds reflected in them, the extremes of earth and heaven united in the mirror of the long-awaited, prayed-for water.

For days afterwards we spoke of the storm, and felt cleansed and pure. Spring had come. Of course, we had all known it would (hadn't each of us said it would rain eventually?) and now it was here, with its lovely after-coolness, with its moisture for our fields. Now it would come again, we were sure, every few days as we needed it. We could get on with the planting.

Regular rainfall didn't follow, however. First, three more rainless weeks, and then rain, but too little too late. We wouldn't be self-sufficient as early as we had hoped, that was clear. We needed more help from the North American relief organization which settled us.

"It's too early to call off the fat ravens from the North," Johann said, rather gleefully, I thought.

Resettlement fever swept the colony. "East Paraguay" filled the conversations of the settlers. We too discussed the possibility. East Paraguay was still Paraguay, but it sounded better: redder, richer soil, more rainfall, greater variety of fruit trees, cheaper land, closer access to markets. A two-man delegation was commissioned to explore the possibilities on the other side.

Maria's wedding, though, was happy. After the new year, rain and sunshine alternated like they should, the debilitating northwind ceased for a season, and our vegetable crops, though planted late, did well.

The first watermelons were ready shortly before the celebration. After the festivities ended, Papa sat with his new son-in-law and Johann Walde under our algorrobo tree, noisily gulping huge slices of the sweet red fruit.

"These wouldn't take second place to our watermelons in Russia," Papa declared with satisfaction, wiping his chin with two fingers and reaching for another piece. "They're delicious." He spat the seeds onto the earth.

"We'll eat our own beans and manioc this year yet," he continued. "The peanuts I planted look good. And I'm getting used to the heat, I think; though when the nights are hot and I can't sleep, then I'm not sure! How's your cotton Ernst? What do you think? Will that be our cash crop of the future?"

Was it just the taste of watermelon that could so cheer my father? The men made no effort to control their appetites. There were plenty for them and for us women, clearing away the last of the dishes. Rapidly they bit off chunk after chunk, slurping and spitting, the succulent rosy juice dripping off faces and fingers. Was my father in such good spirits because he had planted and raised them, and was now feasting on his own efforts?

A gradual change of mood came over the colony around that time. The pleasant rains, plus the relief organization's refusal to give assistance in re-settling elsewhere had tempered the widespread desire to leave. A cautious resolve to give the Chaco another chance took root. By the time the delegation returned and reported on its exploratory expedition to Paraguay's east side, only a minority still wanted to leave.

The majority forged ahead, organizing, setting up an administrative system like that of the Mennonite settlements in Russia before the Revolution. Every family head had a vote, every village was headed by a *Schulz*, or mayor, and the colony by a chief mayor, the *Oberschulz*. We celebrated the first anniversary of our release from Russia on November 25, held the first choir festival and the first preachers' conference, and started a small newspaper for encouragement and news. Eleven teachers were sent to Asuncion to learn Spanish. There would be a school for secondary students, besides the village primary schools.

A location was chosen for a colony center and ambitious plans for an industrial town developed. It began with a primitive frame saw, a mill for grinding kafir into flour, and an oil press for peanuts.

So, I reflected, still leaning on the gatepost, we had survived two years. Perhaps we had made some progress, though truthfully, I wasn't sure. We were terribly poor, living from day to day with the most basic necessities only. Did we ever take one step forward without impediments, or being pushed the same step back?

Not the least of the strange surprises which confronted us in 1932 was war. War! We were in the midst of it again.

Papa and Walde discussed the irony of having come around the world to this isolated wilderness, leaving European politics, revolutions and wars behind, seeking peace, and then finding ourselves caught between the Paraguayans and Bolivians, pitted against each other over the borders of the Chaco.

I couldn't remember the other wars of which the men spoke, but I agreed with their assessment of this one. Expending men — boys really — on this empty undeveloped place? What were they fighting over anyway?

Our loyalties were with Paraguay, of course. We belonged to Paraguay now; they had given us the *Privilegium.* Their promise that we didn't have to bear arms, so recently made, was not in question. And who knew what kind of overlords the Bolivians might be?

The war benefited us, actually, for we had a market for our milk, butter, cheese and watermelons, which provided a little cash, meat, or other staples, and we had a military doctor stationed in the town clinic. But I had no interest in the war itself. I heard the cannon thunder in the struggle over Toledo to the west of us, but shut it out of my consciousness. Columns of soldiers trekking through the village, supply trucks passing and raising dust, occasional contacts with the men of our new country: these were the fringes of life, not the center.

I was full of wishes and dreams of my own. I was a woman, and I wanted to leave home; I wanted an opportunity to use my energies, my ideas, my whole being. I chafed at still being dependent on my parents, not in a physical sense as much as the emotional one — submissive to their attitudes, their opinions, their understanding of things.

The nearly-daily evening conversations between Papa and Walde, though they were often just tones rising and falling in the night air, were burdensome to me. Sometimes they were angry, sometimes disheartened, sometimes critical, but always they knew everything. It was a powerful knowledge. Whenever my spirit wished to soar, even over small matters like Mama's fresh bread, hot from the oven, or the sudden glimmer of blue and green together when my gaze unthinkingly focussed on bush and sky simultaneously, the black pronouncements of Papa or Johann were like a rope, pulling me back.

I had two escapes, however, two places that were uniquely mine. The one was spiritual. It was a new religious experience. I expressed it in song.

I began to sing now, a hymn I knew well from choir. I sang the melody and my mind supplied the bass, tenor, and alto harmony. It was a robust song, but I made it melancholic, singing slowly and letting my voice vibrate and slide, taking many more liberties than permitted in choir.

Commit thy way, confiding,

When trials here arise,
To Him whose hand is guiding
The tumults of the skies . . .

I had grown up going to church, hearing the daily devotional readings and prayers, and of course I knew of God, His son Jesus, the Spirit; I knew of salvation, of sin, of the cross, of our hope to come. I couldn't recall a time when I hadn't known these things, when I hadn't understood the way one must conduct one's life, in faith and reverence toward God and authority. I knew that those who didn't live this way were, in a word, fools. So it wasn't as if faith had now sprung up as new as a crop did, out of something small and apparently dead. Nevertheless, a definite change had occurred within me.

Recently the phrases of the songs we sang in choir meant something. I saw what they really said. I concentrated on the words and believed them in a conscious way, and this made the choir practices a highlight of the week. They were more to me than a social outing.

"Thou art my Redeemer," we might sing. Yes, I affirmed it. "And my truest friend." Yes. "Sun of life," we continued, "that shineth to my journey's end." Yes, I cried. Yes. Oh, yes, I believed it. The words sun, life, shining, journey, were each so large and laden, so fat, that often I couldn't focus on them all as long as they deserved. Connected and attached to melody they could make me dizzy with their overwhelming weight of meaning and beauty.

I was baptized on Pentecost Sunday. There were ten of us, all young people: five girls, five young men. Each of us gave a testimony before the congregation and were examined concerning our understanding of the Bible and church.

When it was my turn I told the story of the previous Good Friday when a realization of my sin and Christ's sacrifice had

111

so moved me that tears ran down my face and I prayed for forgiveness. Wanting to communicate more precisely the meaning of my conversion, I said, without nervousness, "I thin it's something like yeast. I really feel as if I've risen, as if I've become light and . . ." I might have continued to some awful conclusion like "and ready to bake" except that I glimpsed immediately a stiffening on the part of old Mr. Hiebert, sitting in the front row, and I caught too, in the periphery of my vision a sudden, faint disapproval from other members, like a small thin cloud passing over the sun.

I should have stayed with the recitation of the texts and my Good Friday experience, I thought immediately, ashamed, dismayed. What an odd way, indeed, to speak of it. Although I didn't think God was particular about the descriptions one used, it was foolish of me to speak so in front of the adult congregation.

The slip unnerved me and I faltered, letting that sentence die, and ending quickly with a mention of my desire to join the church. I trembled. Several questions were asked, but thankfully nothing about my analogy. I stumbled and stammered, but managed to remember verses to answer them all, and I passed the examination.

> . . .There clouds and tempests raging,
> Have each their path assigned;
> Will God, for thee engaging,
> No way of safety find?

The baptism too was strange. I wanted to shiver away the uncomfortable water like a dog, but we had to stand, serious and controlled, letting it run where it would. I wasn't entirely disappointed with the day, however, for *Prediger* Rahn had gently warned the candidates earlier that Sunday morning, "You must not expect any special feelings, for this isn't something to feel, but something to do in obedience." I was actually glad my experience confirmed his statement, and I didn't regret taking the step; I had declared myself for Christ and his church.

Whatever the quality of Mama's faith — my parents rarely spoke about religious things except in church — it came out in her singing too. In spite of her age, she had a good voice. I got my clear soprano from her. She had a large repertoire of lullabies and children's rhymes which she had taught us as well as Maria's children when they lived with us. Now she sang mostly hymns. Over and over, while baking bread, stirring the beans in the pot, grubbing the manioc, or at the endless mending of thorn-torn clothing, she warbled the hopeful strains.

> Lord, Thou ne'er forsakst
> Him who waits on Thee;
> None has e'er rejected,
> Wouldst Thou then leave me?

I loved these lines. When I heard her sing them, I hummed along or joined in. "None has e'er rejected, Wouldst thou then leave me?" Of course not. He was there. He was with us. There was no cause for despair then; our Lord and Father was there. In those years my faith was very intense, and very sure.

The second world into which I often escaped was my dream of marriage. I was nearly nineteen. I felt I was ready for a husband. There was no desperation in this but rather keen anticipation, a confident expectation. These fantasies were rich with vitality and independence. They constituted a place of cheer and love and success.

At the moment, however, leaning on the gatepost, I was restless. I didn't know whom to set into my fantasy; I didn't know for whom I should hope. The earlier infatuation with Gerhard, the handsome oldest son of the Wienses in the next village, had been unreciprocated, for he had chosen someone else, and their wedding was to take place in two weeks. I didn't mourn him specifically; he seemed now to be rather too loud and insensitive, swaggering over the quiet prim Neta — but I missed having him to think about. Others for whom I once felt interest had also faded in my affections. Many of the youth were wild, unchurched characters, singing ribald and godless Russian songs, noisy and into mischief. I didn't associate with them. If only I could meet someone new.

I saw a man on horseback approaching on the village road.

There he is, I thought.

Immediately I said to myself, Anna, you're silly. He's probably a military man.

It wasn't unusual to see Paraguayan officers. In fact I knew I should vacate my post at the gate. A wise woman didn't remain in sight while an officer passed. We had heard that some children in the other colony screamed "Satan" when they first saw the soldiers. I knew, of course, they weren't devils; they were too young, small, undernourished. Still, stories spread. We believed they were immoral and hungry for women. There had been a rape, and out of that horrible news we learned to fear them and be cautious. "Never look their men in the eye," was the first rule for us women. The enticement was half done then, and it was your fault.

But my pensive mood made me careless, and I didn't withdraw into the yard as the rider approached.

I saw he was a Mennonite, but I didn't recognize him. He was a tall man without a hat, wearing a brown suit jacket that appeared, even from a distance, to be too small; it seemed to pull his arms up at the shoulders. The wind of riding had rounded his dark hair into a comical peak over his forehead.

He came nearer, and I saw he was a young man.

114

Then he reined the mare to a stop in front of me. He was thin, but pleasant-looking.

"Hello!" he said, smiling. "I'm looking for the Abram Sawatzkys."

"Oh! Oh . . . this is the place. They're my parents."

"Exactly where I wish to be then," he said. "My name is Jakob Rempel."

He dismounted. "I was a friend of your brother David," he said. "I bring you some news."

Chapter 2

When I invited this stranger, this Jakob Rempel, to come to the house, he was in no hurry to leave the street.

"So you're David's sister," he said.

"My name is Anna. I'm the youngest."

"Anna. Yes, he mentioned you." He scrutinized me thoughtfully. "There's a resemblance."

He patted the horse's neck. Why was he riding a horse? Few used horses in Paraguay.

"I knew David had family here. I wanted to come sooner, but had no opportunity."

I wished to ask more about David, but it didn't seem proper to be talking about him before Jakob met my parents.

"You're David's sister," he said again. "David was a fine person. I knew him well. We became friends when he came to Blagowersk."

He spoke in short sentences and paused briefly between them; each of them seemed important.

"David was a good man," he continued, taking two steps

and stopping. "I learned so much from him. My, he could sing! My mother would have loved him for that, though she didn't meet him, of course. She came from a musical family. I think I disappointed her in that." Jakob smiled. "But she was my stepmother. I couldn't inherit it . . . David certainly was a singer, though. With his mandolin — "

"Yes."

"Some of us would gather on winter evenings. We sang. It was a Bible study and prayer group. What wonderful fellowship we had."

But what about David? Where was he now? We'd heard rumors that he, like other Mennonites living near China's Russian border, attempted escape over the Amur River.

"Did David leave Russia?" I asked.

"You don't know?"

"Nothing for sure."

"He died, crossing."

Now there was an uncomfortable silence between us. I should have waited until he had said this to Mama and Papa.

He rubbed his forehead. "Oh, I should have tried to come sooner. I thought probably you knew. But I shouldn't have counted on it."

"It's all right," I said. "We haven't been thinking about it."

He looked at me, almost quizzically, I thought. Now, why did I say that? Even if the lives of my distant brothers rarely occupied my mind, surely my parents thought about their sons.

"I mean . . . it's okay," I said. "I mean, that you didn't come sooner."

"Well, I'm here now." When he smiled, I felt he understood. I noticed that his eyes were deep, dark, unchanging, but his smile was warm and friendly.

"I wasn't actually with him," he continued. "David was with Georg and his wife. We went over in small groups. They crossed two days after we did."

"So you weren't with David."

"I know the story from Georg — "

"My parents will want to hear it." I turned decisively and walked to the house. I heard him follow, leading the horse.

Papa greeted our guest but asked no questions until he had examined the horse, walking around it, looking at it from all sides, stroking the nose and feeling behind the ears. It wasn't a very good specimen, but it was a horse.

"To have horses again!" Papa said. "Even the smell of their manure would be welcome."

"He's homesick for horses," Mama explained to Jakob.

I heard Jakob say that the horse was borrowed, but I missed the details. He and Papa left to tend to the animal and I had to help Mama prepare our simple supper. We prepared *Prips*, a coffee-like drink made from kafir, and set out the bread and a dry crumble cake from the day before.

While we ate, Papa asked questions, not about David, but about Jakob's background. Our visitor obliged with an outline of his life, though he seemed shyer now than he had been earlier at the street. I listened attentively, for something drew me to him. I was curious. Who was he? How old was he? I judged him to be in his early twenties. And he had said nothing yet about a wife, or any other attachments.

Jakob's roots were in the Molotchna, but he was born in the Terek settlement of the Eastern Caucasus. His mother died at his birth and his father remarried. The revolution disrupted their lives; after murder, robberies and plunder in the settlement, the Mennonites fled their villages, leaving everything. They stayed in the Kuban settlement with some Mennonite farmers there, in Alexanderfeld. In 1920, when conditions stabilized somewhat, the government invited the Terek settlers to return.

"Foolishly, we went," Jakob said. "One hundred and five

families returned." Failure again, for the promises of security couldn't be kept, and hostile neighbors continued their attacks. By 1925 most of the families were gone. The settlement ceased to exist. Jakob's sister, though, married a Caucasian and stayed. The family lost contact with her.

Back in the Kuban, Jakob's parents again worked in Alexanderfeld, this time on a collective farm. When news of Mennonites who received exit visas spread through the settlements, his father begged friends for money, and took his wife and grown son to Moscow.

"We were sent back," Jakob said, "and we were separated." Unable to find his parents, he travelled to Sawropol, working at various jobs, until he heard of those straggling across the border into China.

"My father had wanted so badly to leave Russia, so I felt I must try, for his sake."

In the Barnaul-Slavgorod settlement Jakob worked and lived in various homes. Because he was alone, it wasn't difficult to plan and carry out his escape.

"And David?" Papa said.

Mama sighed. Jakob cleared his throat and told us the story he knew through his friend Georg Derksen. (Derksen and his wife emigrated to the United States.) Their preparations had taken so long that the ice was no longer safe. But so many had fled, arousing government notice. Surveillance increased; the border was tightened and people whispered that the entire zone near the Amur would be cleared. They had to attempt crossing; to wait for next winter was impossible. Even to wait for the river to thaw and cross in a boat seemed too long, too risky.

A storm blew up the night Georg and his wife, and David, crossed. In the darkness they lost each other. Then they heard David call, "Georg, Georg! Help me!" Or was it the ice that whistled and groaned? Then silence. Not of the elements, which still howled, but of human voice. Georg had shouted, long, he said. No response. Finally he and his wife, close to freezing, struggled wretchedly on.

"Georg mourned for months," Jakob said. "He felt helpless."

There was little doubt that David was dead. We could not expect a repetition of the deceased son walking with a firm gait onto our yard. Papa's look was fixed on his cup; Mama's eyes filled with tears.

I thought of my brother David, the singer, the good-looking and lucky one with a mandolin, perishing in the precarious ice and water of a river on another continent, and felt I was hearing fiction. What was real was the warmth of the evening, four people sitting at ease in the security of our yard, goodwill streaming from the sun as it sank. What was real to me was the forthrightness and gentleness of this Jakob Rempel.

"You'll stay the night, won't you?" Mama asked.

"It's too far to travel back tonight," he said.

He lived with a cousin in one of the easterly villages where the recent refugees from the Chinese city of Harbin had settled.

"You dear young man, you have no family here," Mama said sympathetically.

"But God spared me and I'll never be able to thank him enough. God brought me to the Chaco. There's a reason for it. He wants us to do something for Him here, I'm sure of it."

I marveled. It was wonderful to hear him. It would be possible to live here, I thought, with a man like that. All would be well with someone who felt called to this place.

Chapter 3

Jakob visited us again, and again, ostensibly because he had known David, but it was soon clear that he came to court me. I had no difficulty accepting his attentions; Jakob was everything I had waited for. I thought of him constantly. The brief hours we spent together, once a week at the most, often less, were the only hours that mattered. They were wonderful times. Nothing now seemed impossible or unsettled, because Jakob had chosen me; he loved me, and I loved him.

"Jakob's a good man," I overheard Papa remark to my mother. "He'll be good for our Anna."

I could have hugged my father for that. Of course, Jakob was perfect for me, and Papa saw it! I could have hugged the whole world then, I was so full of love.

When I told Jakob about Papa's statement, he was pleased. "You rode up on a horse," I teased him. "You thoroughly impressed him!"

"A borrowed horse, and not such a fine one at that!"

"Yes, but a horse!"

Even the fervent, almost innocent way in which Jakob sometimes expressed himself didn't rankle Papa as I feared it might. Jakob spoke of God's goodness or of faith in the context of daily occurrences. This was unfamiliar to us, for it seemed presumptuous, too personal, to use the words a preacher used on Sunday in ordinary conversations. When he declared his certainty that God led us here, comparing us to Israel, I sat breathless, my emotions taut. If Papa was offended, or rebutted him crossly, what would I do? But my dear father didn't contradict; he simply listened, without a nod or reply.

Only once was a visit marred. The Waldes dropped over one Sunday to sit with us after the vesper meal. When Johann asserted that we Mennonites shouldn't give up our hopes to leave the Chaco and settle elsewhere, Jakob said, "God led out his people Israel but never promised their lives would be easy. We can't expect it either." I felt an overwhelming urge to protect Jakob from Walde, for he was smiling his dreadful, wise smile, glancing at Papa as if to include him and exclude the other man. "You can't apply those stories to everything we do, Jakob," he said.

And Jakob replied, "Of course we can," just as firmly and pleasantly.

It was my turn to appeal to Papa with my eyes. Please go, I begged. And dear Papa understood. He invited Johann to walk about the *Hof*. Mama and Leni joined them and we were left alone.

Initially I felt nervous with Jakob, shivering, feeling as if my limbs were loose and would jerk away unless I hung on to them, but we soon learned to be at ease with each other. We talked about everything. He was interested in my thoughts and feelings, he said I was intelligent; he was glad, he said, that I was more than a pretty butterfly.

"I have so many, many feelings," I confessed. "I don't

know if that's thinking. You'll have to help me think."

"Of course." And we laughed.

I told him about my childhood home, about the day we left it. I described the frenzy of packing, the rush to cook and can chickens for the journey. He understood when I talked of the yellow odor of my grandmother, my mother's mother, who'd lived with us but insisted she wouldn't come along to Moscow. Her strong smell, which I hadn't noticed before, had penetrated me when I leaned to touch the lined contours of her face for the last time.

I told Jakob of Mama's concern that the old woman wouldn't live long, that she would be neglected at my aunt Martha's, her sister-in-law's. We received the news in Germany; Oma had died.

I told him how I'd gasped involuntarily along with the children when I saw the Christmas tree with its hundreds of glowing candles. The Germans had decorated it for us refugees.

He listened to my story about the small black velvet bag which Oma made for my tenth birthday, one of the few mementos I took out of Russia. It contained a photo of me as an infant, looking regal in a stiff dark dress and a bow, fat and solemn, as well as a card from my best friend Lila and a handkerchief with a lace border. But ants had chewed holes into these precious souvenirs. (During our courtship I found I was homesick for Russia.)

Jakob also confided in me, and told me stories of his life. He said that his ambition from a very young age was to please God.

"A Baptist preacher visited us when I was five or six," he said. "He talked of 'my Jesus'. That's how he referred to Christ. It sounded strange. At night I was in my little bed. It had sides like a crib. I thought I saw the Lord in the room. He was on the other side of the bars. I said, 'my Jesus' and then he was in the bed too. There were no slats between us . . ."

Jakob looked at me timidly. "Does it seem very odd?"

"No," I said. It seemed exactly right. Nothing was unusual inside the shadowless circle of love, inside that ring where anything is possible, even a man and a woman speaking out of their innermost.

"Papa told me the preacher placed his hands on my head the next day and prayed for me," Jakob added. "I've forgotten that part myself . . . I didn't tell anyone what happened in the night. Now when I say it, it seems stranger than it was. Perhaps it was a dream."

He was uncertain, uneasy, so I placed a reassuring hand on his. He accepted my gesture the way it was meant, but at that moment I felt as if my entire body had jumped into the single spot where our hands were linked.

We took a walk on the campo, and Jakob stopped at the end of the field. He suggested that we pray together. I bowed my head, but as soon as he began to speak, I opened my eyes. I didn't mean to be irreverent, but I couldn't help stealing a look at him. His one foot tapped on a stump. His eyelids, pinched together tightly, sent tiny lines like rays onto his temples. He is magnificently handsome, I thought. While he prayed that God might bless us "in whatever way He should lead" (he hadn't yet mentioned marriage specifically), I longed to kiss him, to leap into his mouth, to fly into him and be safe. But I shut my eyes quickly for his Amen, trembling like a flower when someone brushes against it.

On the Friday of the hog-butchering, Jakob arrived early, having travelled half the night. He went directly to my father, busy at the pig pen. I saw that Mama hurried to meet Papa as Jakob came to the house to greet me and join me for breakfast. "I asked your Papa's permission to marry you," he told me. "And he said Yes."

For a moment we were shy with each other, but then we giggled, fellow-conspirators.

Mama approved too, and we selected the date for the engagement and the wedding. "Anna, I hope your hands won't shake so much today that you drop the sausages and let Rolf run off with them," Mama said.

Once the work began, our neighbors Johann and Leni, and Susi and her father, Mr. Froese, came to help, so I had no further opportunity to speak with Jakob. Our relationship was not yet public knowledge, so I had to be careful not to give it away.

All day I was busy, running back and forth from the kitchen to the table set in the yard, while the sow was killed and scraped, hung and cut. Susi and I cleaned the intestines for making the sausages. We prepared the meal, a feast of fresh spare ribs. Yet I didn't cease for a moment to think of Jakob. Carrying water or knives or salt to the slaughtering table were journeys of eager longing, excuses to be near him, to tell him something in the affectedly casual, quick glances we might exchange. Throughout the day I felt feverish, as if the joy was just under my skin, thin and vulnerable as an eggshell; surely I was nearly transparent, surely the red-hot love showed.

He was so near, and yet it was still not enough. Soon, soon, I dreamt, I'll speak to him as Mama speaks to Papa. He'll be mine, and I'll butcher and plant and do everything with him. We'll work together. When he washes before dinner and calls for a towel, I'll be the one who brings it. If he has an early departure as he did this morning to come to our house, I'll have the privilege of wrapping my arms about him and wishing him Godspeed and to please hurry back. When he returns in the evening I'm the one who will meet him, and ask him questions about how it was — I'll ask him everything, for a wife has a right to know what children cannot. He'll tell me what other people do and what the men say in the meetings. And I'll tell

126

him my thoughts and what I've done that day. I'll take his coat and put food on the table, and I'll sit with him in the light of the flickering lamp while he eats and we talk. I'll put my hands into his shirt and we'll be together in the bed, my pale skin on his brown skin, and our hearts close.

All that day I rejoiced over the now-sure intimacy, over the claim I alone had on the black-haired Jakob, scraping so conscientiously on the pig ears, and cutting into the heavy swine's carcass with such measured, deliberate care. Had Susi or any of our neighbors guessed?

Soon, soon they'll know of my good fortune, I thought. Soon. Oh Susi, can you believe that Jakob is mine? Can you imagine it, Susi? He's mine!

Chapter 4

Papa reclined on the coarse grass, clasping his hands together over his eyes to shield them from the intense, white sun which penetrated even the shade under the tree.

"If only I could see a field of grain again, golden wheat ready for harvest. The bread crop! Ah, that was something to make a man proud, seeing it come up, green against that heavy, heavy soil. Then in the autumn the ripe, yellow fields. Once I had a crop, I stood in it, and only my head showed above it, or maybe my shoulders, but God in heaven, it was tall and full. The kernels fell like coins. The barns were too small that year . . ."

"What year was that?" he muttered to himself, confused. Was it . . ." He sat up abruptly and rubbed his eyes, squinting. "I never thought I'd be farming beans! Peanuts! Cotton!"

"Why don't we try wheat?" I suggested. "Could we get seed?"

Papa laughed. "It's been tried, Anna. The *Kanadier* tried. Some of our own men tried. But I won't try. I'm no fool, girl! No, no, wheat doesn't grow here. It's enough work sweating over these despicable beans and peanuts, getting them past the ants and blight and grasshoppers and pigeons and into a sack. I couldn't do it to wheat. Not here. Wheat and horses, that was Russia. Oxen and cotton, Paraguay."

"Do you really miss Russia, Papa? That much? You know where we . . .where you might be if we were still there." Letters and rumors had reached us from the Soviet Union, telling of deportations, reprisals, deaths, separation of families, one tragedy after another. "If it was so good, why did we leave?"

"You know why, Anna," Papa said, "and don't talk like that."

"Soon you'll be old, working this way," he added. "Imagine, a bride working so hard."

I wanted to protest but he lifted a hand against it. "Of course I wouldn't want to return to Russia. Not the way it is now. But," he tore off a stalk of grass, "you don't forget just like that!"

That was our last conversation. When the first good rain of spring came, filling the ditches with water and noisy croaking frogs, Papa suddenly took ill. He was dizzy, he said, and his stomach seethed with pain. The man who once exhilarated in the sharp cold of Russia shook uncontrollably beneath a pile of blankets. He was strangely quiet, though, and distant, as if he had left us; he clenched his fists and bit his lips, but he didn't cry out.

He died within a week, unexpectedly, for we didn't even know what sickness he had. There were no significant final words or farewells, nothing to mention to others; he was gone with a moan that Mama heard but hadn't particularly noted until she found him.

It was a shock, and inconvenient too, for I was occupied with Jakob and too happy to mourn the way I knew I should. Papa's death also altered our arrangements. We were married on my nineteenth birthday in October, four weeks after the funeral. It was a somber wedding, and improperly timed, some people hinted. We knew that, but Jakob must join us on the farm; he must take Papa's place.

Mama moved into the smaller room I had occupied, and Jakob and I took over the room she and Papa shared. Although I was, in a sense, mistress of the *Hof* now, I gladly let Mama keep charge of the kitchen.

In spite of the circumstances, we were happy. We adjusted quickly to Jakob's strong, gracious presence. The cycle of seed-times and harvests, and the seasons — spring, summer, fall and winter — which directed our work, continued, as did the yearly celebrations of Christmas, Easter, Pentecost, and other religious holidays, each marked by special church services and family gatherings.

For the colony, the central issue was still "Is it possible to exist here?" The years that followed our wedding contained more struggle, tension, and fighting, and culminated in the bitter departure of one-third of our fledgling colony's population to East Paraguay in 1937. They had finally decided that the answer was No.

The Chaco War, distant to me, but of utmost importance to our backward nation, also continued for several years. One day in 1935, I was in the supply depot in our town center when the siren at the industrial plant began to scream. What now? I wondered. A fire? Another death in a sandy well? What emergency this time? What further calamity? This time it sounded good news: the war's end.

Even more distant were the events in the larger world. These reached us via the news notes passed from house to house in the village, or through Jakob's conversations with men who got newspapers or listened to the voices and static crackle over a radio receiver. We heard good things from Germany: they

131

gained new confidence, and in 1933, a new leader, Adolf Hitler. Our colony sent him good wishes for the future.

While history flowed on, we concentrated on staying alive in the Paraguayan wilderness, finding some joy there, trying to live our lives before God in humility and obedience. But for me, everything was now counterpoint to a new main theme: I had become a wife. (I sincerely hoped, in due time, to become a mother as well.) Our wedding day produced, as it were, a box into which the rest of my life was placed — each successive month of our first year together, then the anniversaries in turn, and the children as they arrived in the family. Everything now connected in some way to the promise of love, faithfulness, and obedience I made to Jakob. I scarcely realized what I was saying when I pledged myself so completely; one did it, and then discovered its scope.

Weddings were the social highlight of colony life; pregnancy and births were scarcely celebrated. Maybe the precursor of birth — conjugal intimacy — made us ashamed. Sometimes the children came too often; the joy diminished with their number, perhaps. When I conceived after a year, however, I was ecstatic and it was difficult to contain my excitement within the confines of our *Hof*, to suppress it as if it were a trial to be endured. God put the flush of it on my face anyway. Jakob said I glowed with beauty in those months, and I felt the same way inside: surely nothing as significant had ever happened to anyone before.

Something went wrong near the end. I had several days of pain, followed by a week in which I felt no movement. Then the birth came too early.

"I don't think the baby is alive," Mrs. Klassen, the midwife, said. I wouldn't believe her.

"I don't think the baby is alive," she said later, as I was into the birthing process.

By then I didn't care about anything except relief from my pain. No wonder the Bible used bringing a child to birth, the hour of birth, the onslaught of the pains, to image the calamities of God's judgments! Now I understood the smug insinuations of other women — other mothers. "I don't want to frighten you, but it's something you go through because you must," Maria replied when I had asked her what to expect. All of them had acted so superior and cliquish. Smug and knowing.

And now I knew. There was nothing worse, nothing. I felt as if I was being stretched endlessly in opposite directions. I couldn't move away from the waves of agony rolling over me; my body produced the spasms against my volition, as if it hated me.

"I can't go on!" I screamed.

"Of course you can," my mother and the midwife said.

How dare they say it so easily? I couldn't bear it. The interval between the decline of a contraction and the rise of another wasn't enough for me to gather strength or breath. I began to gasp. I really couldn't bear it. I lost control. I had no will to be good, to be courageous, to bear this child. Mrs. Klassen was right: I was delivering a stone, and it wouldn't leave me!

When Mama tried to wipe my forehead with a cool, wet cloth, I pushed her away with such unexpected energy that she spilled the basin of water.

"Now control yourself!" she shouted.

I cried. But eventually, the baby was born. I was wet, exhausted, but I was finished. It was a relief to know that anything that followed would be less than it had been before; the storm had peaked.

But the birth was a horrible deceit. I would have forgotten it easily enough if I had had something for it. The child, a girl, was stillborn.

The anger I felt was an overwhelming desire to be, for a moment, the Creator. It leapt up like a flame which has caught dry wood; oh, to have control, to redden lips, to reverse events and return departed life. To bring her back!

I fell asleep and when I woke, Jakob sat on a chair beside my bed, meek and fearful. He took my hand.

"What shall we name her?" he asked.

"Name her? She's dead."

"I know, but . . ."

"Let's not talk about it!"

Later Mama mentioned that Jakob had referred to the baby as Martha.

"Martha!" I shrieked. "Where did he get that from?"

"Shush, child," she said. "You save the names you like for the next ones."

It was incomprehensible to me that Jakob would endow a baby born dead with a name, but I couldn't bring myself to ask him about it. I had already learned that a husband and wife do not share every thought that enters their heads. I only inquired: "Where were you when I was . . .giving birth?"

"I was outside, mostly. I went to the fields for awhile."

"Did you hear me?"

"Not at the far end of the field." He smiled.

"It hurt."

"I know." Jakob took me in his arms.

"I screamed because it was so unbearable. And all for nothing!"

"You're young," he said. "You have many years yet for children."

"Then, I was ready to say, never again. But I do want children, Jakob." Tears filled my eyes. "I don't know why it happened to me."

"You will have them," he answered, squeezing me tightly

and kissing the top of my head.

But it didn't happen. Then deep discouragement filled me, pressing my spirit and my stomach for months. I held it inside, knowing there were sorrows worse than mine. There had been many deaths in the Chaco already, real tragedies: a man's life snuffed out by the sliding sand of a well, as he dug for precious drinking water; a woman's life taken instantly by a bolt of lightning (which melted the chain of the Russian clock on the wall behind her into a solid metal rod); a child's life claimed by the bush (he was lost and must have been crazy with fright for the small body was found covered with cactus needles). Even Mama, after so many years of marriage, was alone. No, I told myself, you may not indulge in self-pity because of this deprivation, you must accept it and be strong.

God's comfort was real to me, like a firm bed to lie on. But as I waited to conceive, each menstruation resulted in a fresh struggle to bow before him, to rest there. The blood taunted me.

Jakob, like Elkanah, asked me, "Aren't you happy with me? Don't I mean enough to you without children?"

"Of course I'm happy with you! Of course I love you! But you're not enough!" I knew he wanted children too, but he didn't understand my desperation, the unconscious kind of inner drunkenness that motivates a barren Hannah.

My neighbor Leni Walde seemed perpetually pregnant. She had six under the age of ten, and still the children burst from her womb. So far they were all females. Maria too was as fruitful and fortunate as I wasn't. She had already added two children to the seven she and Ernest had between them when they married. She was pregnant again, and came crying to Mama about it.

I felt sorry for her, for I knew she was tired and over-worked, but I envied her too. When she complained of nausea I felt like pounding her, kneading her bulging body and saying,

135

"If I had children, I'd be happy!" She seemed to have something to lament about, always, and she scolded Ernst in front of others. "She has that man under her sandals!" Mama said.

Gossip seemed to be Maria's only reprieve. I didn't enjoy it. What was the purpose of slandering other women? Since they had children and I didn't, I was worse than them all; wasn't it clear?

Chapter 5

Mid afternoon, mid summer, the sun beaming in the west, Jakob walked with long strides from the field, his body straight, his presence reassuring: he was black and golden, blessed by the sun, and quite elegant in tattered green trousers. I watched him come nearer and take off his shirt, and saw him anew, the muscular wide chest with its black hair. My Jakob.

"I think we'll have our best crop ever," he said, joining me. "I just took a little tour."

He ran his fingers through his hair. His face was streaked with moisture and dirt, and a growth of beard shadowed his chin. "The cotton will be good this year. It's full. Really fine. In spite of the poor rains in spring. You know, perhaps we should build an addition to the house after harvest. Think about how we may want to do it."

Jakob's walk in the fields had exhilarated him. "Or maybe I should buy a horse!" he said.

It annoyed me. "Why don't we just use the crop money for living! For getting flour and sugar and tea and cloth."

"You're always the practical one, Anna," he said cheerfully-
ly.

"And you're always branding the calf before it's born."

"Mother, do you have something to drink?" Jakob called.
"My it's hot again today."

Mama brought him a cup of water.

"The cotton looks good," Jakob informed her.

"I'm glad. Mrs. Walde told me today they're hopeful too."

Jakob began to whistle. My equanimity returned as quickly as it had gone. To enlarge the house! Yes. Or wouldn't it be
nice to have a tin roof? And I'd seen some lovely material at the
store. I needed a new dress. Perhaps this year there would really be that little extra with which to make some improvements.
Occupied with my plans, I looked at the billowed sky. What
should be our priority? I saw a small dark oblong cloud, floating on the horizon. Rain? Nothing indicated rain. Smoke?

"Look at that," I said, pointing.

Jakob stood and squinted. The cloud was enlarging, growing darker.

"That's no cloud!" he burst out, stiffening. "It's grasshoppers! Get pots, wooden spoons, whatever we have. I'll sound
the alarm. In case they drop here."

Grasshoppers! Loving God, no! I hurried to the kitchen
for utensils with which to make noise.

Jakob hallooed to the next yard and the answering shouts of
our neighbors told us that others had sighted the grasshopper
cloud. Soon from every part of the village the stillness of the hot
afternoon erupted into noisy clanging, shouts, excited voices.

Jakob grabbed a piece of corrugated tin and ran into the
cotton field. Mama and I followed with pots and spoons.

"Don't overdo it, you two," he called back to us.

The campo already lay under the shadow of the cloud.
That's how quickly it moved. The advance battalions of locusts

had landed, reinforcements thick above them, a long black column, the whir of wings audible to us.

The nightmares I'll have tonight, I groaned. I had become accustomed to ants, to beetles of a dozen varieties, even to snakes, but I hadn't overcome my revulsion for grasshoppers with their grotesque box-shaped green bodies, their twig-like legs, their fearlessness. Grasshoppers didn't scuttle away, they didn't scurry for shelter. They sprang, confident, defiant and hungry. They paid no heed to people.

I planted myself in the field, waiting for that cloud with its millions of grasshoppers to rain upon us. I knew the prancing and shouting of a few people wouldn't make much difference. We wouldn't persuade a horde of locusts to change course by waving at them, by screaming, once they had decided to plunder us. But at least we were trying; we were fighting. Perhaps we could save something.

I might have stayed in the yard if it had been safe. But it provided no place of refuge, the grasshoppers would land there too. Nothing on the packed dirt surface would satisfy them, but they would drop, swarm about, pile up and whir on, searching.

The grasshoppers descended. The leaves and stalks of our crops bent beneath their weight.

Bang. Bang. Bang. Sounds of wood on metal, metal on metal. And cries, up the entire length of the village, "Away! Off with you! Away!"

I began to shout and clap my noisemakers. I tried not to look at the grasshoppers, keeping my eyes on Jakob instead as he danced in a zigzag fashion over the fields. He seemed uncertain where to expend his energies, whether in the cotton, or our patch of peanuts, or the beans. He tore wildly across the rows. I couldn't keep up.

Now the insects were all around me, and beginning to fall against me; I had no kerchief on and my hair was coming loose.

One braid slipped onto my shoulder. I was afraid to stop and wind it up again; what if I caught a grasshopper inside it? I didn't like to open my mouth to call, so I thrust out rasping noises through nearly tight lips.

I could hear them eating; yes, I was sure I heard them chomping. It crescendoed. Now Jakob was at the kafir field. I saw that the insects lifted at his coming, but many others landed in their place.

The grasshoppers were everywhere in my path, and they cracked beneath my shoes. Jakob is barefoot, I remembered. Suddenly my stomach was in my mouth; with an involuntary heave I vomited. I nearly vomited again when I saw them coming eagerly to devour the yellow slime of my lunch. I ran wildly towards Jakob, clapping the spoon against the pot mechanically.

The village cows bellowed in terror. Our faithful watchdog Rolf had run for cover, he was cowering somewhere near the house, howling piteously. The chickens squawked. Normally they liked to eat grasshoppers, but this was too much even for them.

Bang. Bang. Bang. The breaking of pitchers wouldn't raze this army, but it might scare a few away, it might save something. I became angry, determined not to scream as I felt the locusts against my legs, crashing into my back, my face. The air was grim and dusky, the sun veiled by plague, more eerie than an eclipse.

I thought of everything at once: of my blond braided hair, my anxiety for its cleanliness as if the cloud above dropped excrement; of the boyish words, "maybe I should get a horse"; of the contentment with the growing crops, growing cash. Cotton fluff good for nothing now but stuffing delusions! I had rightly chided Jakob for dreaming before it was in the sacks. But I did it too!

I was furious at the robbers writhing around me. What right did they have to spoil everything, to mar his hopes, to land on Jakob's words and eat them just after they were spoken?

God Almighty, how can you allow this? I thought with a half-sob as I sprang near the place where I had vomited and spotted them green and swarming. Perhaps I was thinking of Him most of all — my emotions were flying in all directions; my thoughts called Him, but bitterness and a moving black cloud hung between us.

I had never verbalized doubt, never rounded it into vowels and consonants, but now I doubted; at this moment I wondered if God had come with us. Had he simply delivered us across the border under the Russian Red Star to freedom, like a benevolent white-haired European gentleman, and then alighted before we reached our final destination? A silly enough fantasy to be sure, but still . . .

I don't know if anyone else in the colony doubted. One believed or one didn't; one was in the church or out of it. But as I sprang about our grasshopper-covered field I suddenly felt: God is not here. Everything happens as it will. What difference does faith make? Not everyone who prayed got out of Moscow, and some who didn't pray were released. Here too, I reasoned, it's merely circumstances, and no end of bad luck; we're alone in this inhospitable land.

What I found most terrifying was that letting these shocking thoughts sweep through my mind changed nothing. The mad activity about me continued as before. The frenzied motion of both people and creatures seemed only to confirm God's absence. If faith didn't matter, neither did doubt.

A whining sound tore the air as a branch of the paratodo in the middle of the kafir field broke under the weight of the locusts. I shouted on, danced on, beat my enamel basin drum mechanically, devoid of hope.

It seemed hours that we ran about, seeking to frighten the insects on, although I didn't know how long it actually was. We came to a kind of a finish when the bulk of the grasshopper cloud had passed over. The sun would soon set. We trudged back to the house in the half-light of day's end, exhausted, feeling the abrupt loneliness of work finished. We also felt failure, for the fields were pathetic; they were stripped and bare. Locusts still moved in the fruit trees and bushes, seeking any bit of green that might have been overlooked.

Besides eating their fill, grasshoppers deposited their eggs, and in a few weeks the fields would be hopping with their young. Then we would be busy again, trying to bury the brood before it destroyed any plant life which had survived and thrust out fresh growth, or new seedlings. (If it rained, we might replant).

Jakob skimmed the grasshoppers out of the wash basin and flung some of the tepid water over his face. It didn't seem to matter to him, but I turned away, angry. Then he went into our bedroom and drew the curtain for privacy. I suppose he prayed. I felt numb inside.

When he emerged, perhaps twenty minutes later, he said, "Let's go see how it is with the others."

There was an informal gathering that evening. Many of the villagers met at *Prediger* Rahn's *Hof*, drawn to the home of someone who might have words of comfort. But I didn't want comfort. I wanted someone to tell me it was a dream. Then in the morning the beans would be veined, the watermelon and manioc and sweet potatoes in full leaf, most of all the cotton, green, the cash crop intact.

The men formed their circle, the women theirs, and people began to relate what they felt and said as they saw the grasshoppers coming. I sat on the edge, listening first to the conversation in one circle and then the other, also distractedly watching some of the older children in the distance, still full of the eagerness and energy of witnessing a calamity, outdoing each other with adjectives of disgust, and laughing.

"I just said to the wife today that it looked pretty good this year," one man said. "I don't have much in cotton, mind you, the root plants are okay, but it was enough to get me thinking about putting in more next year. Just said it, seemed like, and there they were."

Another took up the theme. "I was thinking the same thing today. Crop looks the best I've seen it in our few years here, I said to myself."

"It looked good," chimed in a third. "I was saying to the boys today . . . "

Apparently everyone had come off the field today announcing that the crop looked good. I was grateful that I didn't hear Jakob sharing what we had talked of earlier as he met me under the tree, as if we had said the words for everyone else's ears. They had been disappointingly similar to the others', but if he kept them quiet, they would remain uniquely ours. In my despair I clutched at anything, even a conversation, to call my own.

The men compared losses. The farms at the end of the village had less locusts; the mass came over the farms in the middle. Then they discussed other grasshopper attacks, comparing them with other plagues of the Chaco, attempting to list them in order of severity. Which ranked worst: migratory locusts, leaf cutting ants, cotton leaf worms, weevils in stored seeds, aphids or birds — the pigeons and parrots and blackbirds and bobolinks, crop scavengers all of them — or plant pests and weeds? Someone mentioned the drought, another the rain if it came too heavy at the wrong times, and of course, the *Nordsturm* that could carry away half a planted field in the heated sweeping of a day.

I heard the exchanges around me as if they were spoken in a foreign language. I was unwilling to learn. In school in Russia I had sometimes tuned out like that when I was bored and thought the subject had no application for me. But this does, I remembered, trying to make myself listen. These are the difficulties of my life. I'm a wife now, a farmer's wife, and it concerns me.

No, I argued, the material isn't new, I know it all, and the order of things is irrelevant. Who cared which was worse, the ant or the grasshopper? Ants had driven an entire village off their campo. Grasshoppers could destroy our hopes for a year in one afternoon. Bird pests gobbled up our profits. The important fact was that they all existed here in one place. When one was overcome there would still be the others. In several weeks we would be combating the hatched brood of today's difficulty, waving sacks and towels and branches, trying to herd them into graves. Perhaps we would be successful and perhaps we wouldn't. But the battle wouldn't end. If we stopped to say, "Finally," or "At last" with just a bit of hope and pride, we would be crushed again.

"Come Anna," Mama said, touching my shoulder. I was startled. People were leaving. Had *Prediger* Rahn said anything encouraging? I had missed it.

I held Jakob's arm tightly as we walked home. To me the road writhed with grasshoppers, and I needed to be linked to him in case I fell.

"I've always liked those verses," Jakob said.

"Well, they're certainly appropriate," Mama sighed.

"Which verses?" I asked.

"The ones Rahn read. Didn't you hear them?"

"What were they?" I whispered.

"I know them from memory," he said. "Though the fig tree shall not blossom, neither shall fruit be in the vines; the labor of the olive shall fail, and the fields shall yield no meat; the flock shall be cut off from the fold, and there shall be no herd in the stalls . . . "

I began to cry, soundlessly. But it made me sway against Jakob and he noticed it and stopped.

"You worked too hard. Don't cry."

"It's not that. Just finish." I walked on pulling him with me. Mama, as if sensing that she should leave us alone, quickly hurried ahead.

"Finish it!" I demanded.

"Anna, you are overwrought."

"Please finish, Jakob."

"All right. After that list of calamities the prophet says, 'Yet I will rejoice in the Lord, I will rejoice in the God of my salvation.' It's a wonderful declaration of trust to help us, Anna."

He's strong tonight, I thought. The sun's rays which blessed him this afternoon have made him invincible; he's a shield for me to hide behind.

At the end of Waldes' lane we met Johann, standing on the street. He hadn't been at Rahn's place. Nor did we ever see him on our *Hof* anymore. He had wept profusely at Papa's funeral, but he didn't visit with Jakob.

"Oh good evening, neighbor!" Jakob said. "How are you keeping?"

Jakob's cheerful tone on this day of disaster would have jarred anyone who hadn't heard the Scripture he had just quoted. Even I was dismayed. I jerked my arm away from his. Johann didn't return the greeting. He rubbed his chin, then his lips as if tuning them for the words he would produce. "I don't think it looks good for any of us," he said at last.

"Wouldn't you agree, Anna?" Johann added.

He saw my unbelief! He taunted me!

"No," Jakob answered, "it doesn't look good. Yet I will rejoice in the Lord."

"Damn you, you and the preacher!" Johann snarled. "You and your verses. Damn you all!" He strode away.

I glimpsed the swollen figure of Leni Walde halfway down the lane. She was expecting their seventh child.

"Why did you say that to him?" I turned on my husband impatiently.

"Anna," Jakob said unhappily, "it's time for us all to go to bed."

Chapter 6

"The Widows and Orphans Officer talked to me this morning," Jakob said at siesta.

I tensed and twisted sideways on my cot.

"About Rosita. They want us to take her."

The image of the skinny six-year-old flew into my mind. I knew the girl's sad history. Rosita's parents were separated in Russia, her minister father arrested and sent, it was assumed, to a concentration camp, or perhaps killed. His parting instruction to his young pregnant wife was that she should leave the country if possible. She attached herself to her widowed stepmother, who travelled with her son and his family, the Heinrich Loewens.

Rosita was one of the first babies born in our colony in the Chaco. After her mother succumbed to typhoid fever, the infant was left in the care of the grandmother. The elderly woman raised her as best she could without milk of her own; she fed her tea and rice water and whatever cow's milk she could get. She loved the child dearly, so Mrs. Loewen claimed, (the baby and the old woman lived in a hut on the Loewen *Hof*) but she was terribly possessive and too elderly.

Then Rosita's step-grandmother died. The Loewens had a large family and asked the Widows and Orphans Officer to place the girl elsewhere. She had no blood ties to them, they said.

Rosita's name had already been mentioned to me several times, in casual ways, by people in the village. I always smiled politely and said "No" immediately; I wouldn't discuss it, but when I saw Rosita at church functions I watched her surreptitiously. What I saw confirmed my decision. The child didn't appeal to me at all; her large round eyes peered out of a thin face, dully, mournfully.

"She's older than the years we've been married," I said to Jakob. It was the most obvious argument.

"That doesn't matter. No one will think anything of that. They'll know — "

"But I don't know how to raise children. I need to start with a baby, that's what I mean. What do we know about — "

"Mother's here to help. She has experience."

"Mama won't be here forever."

"But by then you'll be . . . Oh, Anna, you'll do fine. Really. I don't think the age will make any difference. And others have many more mouths to feed than we do; I'm sure we'll manage that part."

"Why don't Loewens keep her? She's grown up right on their *Hof*."

"It's not that they don't want her. They have a houseful."

"I don't think they want her."

"Maybe. I don't know." Impatience edged his words. "It makes sense to me. She needs a home. We could give her one. We have no children and — " It was the wrong thing to say, but he didn't realize it.

148

"I said Yes," Jakob finished.

"You said Yes? Just like that, you said Yes? Without first asking me? I can't do it, Jakob, I just can't. I've looked at her. I don't want her!"

He didn't answer so I elaborated, "I want my own children and I'll have them! Everybody, even you, pitying me and trying to help by giving me some other woman's child! I'm young and it happened once and it'll happen again, and it'll still turn out."

Still he didn't speak. I hated the judgment of his silence.

I churned inwardly, debating it. "Is it settled then?" I asked.

"I can tell him that we've changed our minds."

"You understand, don't you Jakob?"

"No, I don't!" he snapped. "The night of the grasshoppers, when you were in such a state, I put you to bed. I sat and looked at you, and I forgot about them. I prayed that you could have a child. I can take anything, I said. Just let her have what she needs. And . . . and . . . I thought Rosita was the answer."

"Oh Jakob," I murmured, touched by his concern, but sighing the sigh I learned from Mama, which in this case meant, a man doesn't understand these things!

I said, "But it's not the same, don't you see that?"

"Couldn't you let yourself try?"

"I don't know. What if — ?"

"And think of her. Think of her."

"How can I love her and be a good mother when I don't know her and there's nothing about her that interests me? I find her . . . Oh Jakob, I want better children than she is!"

Again he responded with awful silence.

"Do *you* like her?" I asked.

"I think so . . . Actually, I haven't thought about that one way or the other. But, yes. Sure I like her. I felt it was the right thing. Why shouldn't I like her?"

"I couldn't find the love for her."

"You'd find it," he said confidently. "She's not any trouble. That's what I'm told. She's very obedient."

Obedient! The difference in our perceptions, in our understanding, gaped like a canyon between us, wide, impassable. I felt helpless before it.

"I just can't," I groaned.

"Oh Anna, why not? I want you to. I think we should. I believe it's God's will for us."

So that's what I was up against!

"I should have asked you first," he admitted, "but I didn't think you would resist so much." He got up and began to dress.

"Oh Jakob, whenever anyone even mentioned her name, I immediately said No. Surely you knew how I felt!"

"I thought you didn't really mean it that way."

"Of course I meant it. Don't you know me better than that?"

"Better than you realize I do."

He thinks he does and yet he doesn't, I thought, feeling the gap again. But there was no way to bridge it. I would have to submit. I recognized too that his motives for saying Yes to Rosita were better than mine for saying No.

"You were praying for me the night of the grasshoppers?"

"Yes." He looked down at me with a smile.

"When would she . . . Rosita come?"

"As soon as we're ready. I suggested Sunday. But Anna, I'm sorry. I'll talk to him again, if you — "

"Just leave it now," I said.

The Loewens brought Rosita and her possessions, two dresses and a blanket in a flour sack, on the following Sunday. I hoped they would deposit Rosita and leave. But no, they wanted to stay for a visit and make a ceremony out of the transfer. Heinrich Loewen and Jakob set off on the customary inspection walk around the farm.

Mrs. Loewen chattered effusively as we sat on chairs under the algorrobo tree. "I've prepared Rosita. I've been talking to her about it. I told her what lovely young parents she'll have. I told her she'll be the biggest girl in the family now. 'You'll be the only child,' I said. She seemed glad, you know. We're so many. I just can't give her what she needs. It's hard to raise a large family with so little to go around. I don't mean to complain, but it's hard, and we're so poor. She misses her Oma terribly. She doesn't say so, of course. But I guess she does. It won't be easy for her to move away, I know, and I told her that too. But I said it would be the best, I said she'd be happy someday. I think she understands. She's no trouble, you know." I nodded and smiled, nodded and smiled. (Mama got up to make coffee and left me on my own with the woman.)

"I've often said it would have been better if the old Oma hadn't raised her," Mrs. Loewen continued. "She was my mother-in-law, so I don't want to say anything bad. But I think she got too attached. She kept her a baby. Strange, you know. I think it would have been better if she'd been raised somewhere else, but what could we do? Rosita was all she had."

Taking Rosita's arm she said, "See this pretty yard? Didn't I tell you? This is where you'll live now, see? With this pretty young Mama. And there's an Oma here too, see?" She pointed her rough, red forefinger at Mama.

"What do you think? Won't it be fun here? You'll be a big girl, yes? You'll help, like you always helped Oma and me, okay? Be a brave girl and don't cry."

Rosita submitted to all that was asked of her showing no emotion. She dutifully did as she was told, and said Yes or No appropriately in answer to questions.

Though not invited to do so, Mrs. Loewen led Rosita to the house and took her inside. "Let's look where you'll live," she said.

As they emerged she ordered, "Give your new Mama a hug now." I was painfully aware of Mrs. Loewen's sharp scrutiny: in spite of her steady talking, her eyes missed nothing. Rosita and I embraced as instructed, but I knew I was falling short; I would be punished in the gossip circle for my unmaternal awkwardness. My arms felt like wood.

I noticed that Jakob, however, wasn't as nervous as I was. His eyes strayed often to Rosita (Mama finally sent her off to play with the other children and set us adults together to visit.) He seemed curious and excited, and not afraid of either Mrs. Loewen or Rosita.

It was evening before Loewens were ready to depart. Mrs. Loewen jumped from the wagon and drew me aside to brief me once more, privately. "Rosita sometimes wets her bed. Then I make her wash the sheet. She doesn't drink milk anymore. I guess she should, she's so skinny, but Oma spoiled her, you know. But she's quiet, naturally good, I guess, and it's not hard to take her, not as if she were a wild one."

Mrs. Loewen pulled on her lower lip with two work-worn fingers as if searching for something else. She found nothing and moved reluctantly to the wagon. Suddenly she walked swiftly to Rosita and bent to embrace her. As she straightened into the moonlight I saw her eyes were shining with tears, her face contorted.

With the Loewens waved out of sight, Jakob said, clearing his throat, "Well, do you women have anything to do? The dishes maybe? I'll tell Rosita a bedtime story. Come, Rosita."

She followed him to stools near the table. I heard Jakob announce his story as that of the prodigal son. I felt suddenly relieved and courageous.

"You might not know much about raising children and I know you're frightened," Mama said to me, "but she'll be a lot better off with you than with Mrs. Loewen."

"I don't know, Mama," I said, remembering the other woman's tears.

"Of course she will."

As Mama and I set the kitchen in order, I listened to Jakob's story. It was short. He tried to embellish it but he seemed unable to think of what to say besides the facts as set down in Scripture. It lasted only a minute or two. Then he prayed.

"Now it's time for you to go to bed, Rosita," he said. "Tomorrow's another day."

I showed the girl her bed in Mama's room. "Do you sleep with a doll?" I asked.

She shook her head.

"Would you like to?"

She nodded.

I fetched the cloth doll which I had hurriedly fashioned out of scraps the previous week.

"It's not that nice," I apologized. "I did my best with what I had, though."

Rosita took it without a word.

"Good night," I said.

"Good night."

Later I looked in on our new daughter, asleep, the rag doll lying against her cheek. Rosita looked startlingly different: with her eyes closed she seemed a normal child, innocent, beautiful, tangible. I bent and bravely kissed her small, narrow nose.

Chapter 7

At breakfast one morning in February, before the harvest, Jakob announced that he would go into the bush at the back of our land and seek wood for some building he might do in winter. He had arranged that the Indian Jasch would help him cut and load.

Immediately I said, "I'll come too."

Jakob glanced at Mama. "Don't work too hard, Anna," Mama said.

"Perhaps you should stay," Jakob added.

"Why? I'll gather firewood."

"It might be a good break," he agreed. "Come along. I'll enjoy the company."

I hurried to make *Prips* and wrapped some bread and cheese in a cloth to take along for a break later in the morning. I felt as excited as if we were going on a picnic.

"Where's the wagon?" I called. Since there weren't enough wagons in the settlement yet, the farmers shared them.

"At Walde's." Jakob was coaxing the oxen into their harness.

Then I felt anxious. "Did you speak with Johann about using it today?"

"I told him last week, and again yesterday."

"Did he say it would be all right?"

"He didn't say anything."

"Well, it's certainly our turn! He or Martens always have it. Sometimes I see it just standing there on his *Hof* on a day when he told you he needs it."

"Um."

"Be firm with him, Jakob. Tell him you need it."

"I told him."

"Ask his advice," I said. "He likes that. He likes to talk if you listen. Maybe it helps."

Jakob didn't respond to my suggestion, but I took it for a refusal. He thought treating Johann in such a manner amounted to little more than flattering the man, something he would not do. I watched Jakob lead the oxen to the street and to the neighboring *Hof.* I knew what would happen, and I seethed with anger.

We did what the others did, we had the same sun, the same rain, and the same pestilences, and yet we weren't doing as well as some of the others, certainly not as well as Walde. Jakob was grateful for every blessing — he always found something — while Johann complained. Yet Johann's crops seemed to thrive in comparison. What was the difference?

Jakob wasn't ruthless, he wasn't aggressive. He hesitated. He wondered whether today was the time to plant, or tomorrow. He held back, as if awaiting a sign, until I found myself urging him to do it. He usually did it then, but it bothered me. (The rhythm of farming was more naturally a part of me than of him.) We were careful, conscientious, but I knew Jakob didn't have the boldness and willingness to risk that would give us an edge.

Downhearted, I walked back to the house. In ten minutes

Jakob returned, leading the oxen without the wagon.

"Johann said he needs the wagon."

"But you told him!"

"He said something came up. More pressing than my wood."

"What?"

"That's not my business."

"Of course it's your business! You reserved the wagon today; it's plenty your turn. It always sits there, always, always, always! You told him you needed it, so insist on it!"

Mama was indignant too. "I think I'll have a little talk with that man," she said, untying her apron.

"Now Mother," Jakob said quietly, but his voice held a command, "let it be."

"Come," he said to me, "we'll walk. We'll pile some firewood. I need time to look at and mark some of the trees anyway. We can load them another day."

"But you've taken on an Indian to help, haven't you? He'll be waiting there, and we have no wagon — "

"He can cut today and we'll load another time — "

"But — "

"Come now."

The incident put me out of sorts, and we walked in silence at first, my resentment hovering around us like an odor. Each step we took on the campo carried us away from it, however. I couldn't be at odds with my husband for long.

Then Jakob said, "I don't want you to work too hard. Perhaps that's why it takes so long, with children."

"Who said that?" It sounded like an idea someone else had given him.

"Your mother. Other women. They've seen how you work. Mrs. Walde told Mother — "

"Mrs. Walde! That woman has to work like a horse and

she still has a child every year or two!"

"Well, each one is different. Maybe you're not as strongly built."

"I'm never ill. I'm strong enough! Tell me Jakob, do you really think I'm working too hard?"

"I don't know. I don't know women . . . We'll have to use Indians for the field work."

"I don't think I'm working too hard," I declared. "In the Chaco, women have to help farm. That's how it is."

"I know."

"And please don't discuss me with Mama!" I said.

"Oh Annchen," he laughed (only he could use the diminutive of my name and not be reproved for it — that is, if he did so just on occasion), "you surely know what you want and what you think."

"You and I can talk about it, if we must, Jakob. But not you and Mama behind my back."

"Okay." He added, "Your mother is wise."

"But I'm your wife."

"That you are, and I love you!" He stopped, dropped the ax, and took hold of me. "All of you, Annchen, with your energy and stubbornness too!"

I put my head against his chest; my straw hat slid onto my back.

"Don't make it sound so bad," I teased. "I always listen to you."

"I love you," he repeated.

"And I love you too."

One moment we were laughing, and then I heard those words from his mouth and mine, and we became serious. We released our embrace slowly, chastened by them — we did love each other, we had chosen to. But we heard how demanding and grave they were.

158

Jakob picked up his ax and we walked on. Above us the sky was clear, pale blue, very distant. It was early but already hot.

The old Indian Jasch waited for us and beamed to see Jakob. They conversed for quite some time in a basic Low German and then the man sauntered into the bush. Soon we heard the ax blade pinging on wood.

"Shall we have something to drink first?" Jakob asked.

We rested contentedly in the shade, unwilling to get up and work. I felt close to Jakob, as if I might safely tell him anything. Because of that, I said: "There's talk again, a lot of it, about resettlement — leaving the Chaco, isn't there?"

"Yes."

I remembered a conversation I overheard between my parents several years ago. I lay awake when Papa returned from a colony meeting in which resettlement to East Paraguay was discussed.

"What would it be like there?" Mama had asked.

"The soil is redder, richer. Lots of rainfall. Cooler too. Someone said ten degrees difference on the average. They have more fruit trees," Papa had said. "All the crops we grow here plus more. Grapes. Maybe even grain."

They had fallen asleep, but I lay wider awake than before. I visualized the setting from the information he had given. I imagined a pretty brick house on a farm with copper earth and an orchard bursting with mandarins and bananas, dates, grapes, papayas. And mulberry bushes. Plum trees. Pear trees. I skipped through flowers that bloomed along the path to the street. I strolled to the front of the *Hof* where sets of matched horses waited on the road. I leaned over the low broad fence of burnt brick to see the village homesteads on either side, peaceful, prosperous, green and safe.

It wasn't difficult now to revise the scene to include Jakob

159

and Rosita, other children as well. But before I could describe it to Jakob he said, "It's not just the weather or the hardships here that agitate those who want to leave. It's politics, people. I don't agree with their position, so — "

"But it still comes down to whether we can survive here or not — "

"It's more than that."

"I feel we're made for something better . . . And perhaps there'd be something besides farming there. More diversity. You . . . you don't enjoy farming that much, do you?"

"I don't mind it."

I bit my tongue to repress words I wanted to say, muttering instead, "Pioneering is so hard."

"We'd have to pioneer on the east side too. And we won't get any outside help like we did here."

"I don't think it's so hard there. I've heard — "

"Whatever you've heard, you make it too wonderful in your mind." He leaned forward, staring at the campo. "We have to accept this place. And we all have to work together. I don't think the people who want to leave are clear about these things."

"But is discontent wrong?" I argued. "If it makes us seek and work for something better?"

"There's a difference," he said. "We didn't know much about Paraguay when we picked — "

"When *we*?"

"When it was suggested to us. Whatever. I know your father's preference was Canada. So was mine. But if a door closes, you don't break it down. So God brought us here. I'm convinced he did it for a reason. Abraham didn't know where he was going when he was called either. But he went. All the time of our troubles in Russia, God was brooding over this place, preparing it for us. He chose us, and he chose the Chaco. I'm not leaving. Even if I'm sitting here alone, I'll stay!"

160

I sighed. Why did I push him, why did I sometimes try to change his mind? He was intractable.

"It was clear to me," Jakob went on, "crossing the Amur, that it was God who had spared me, and when I got here, I knew why."

I also knew when I arrived, I thought. But not now.

Jakob's hand swept the campo-becoming-farm land, and stopped at our *Schilf*-topped hut in the distance.

"This land will yield for us yet, Anna. It'll get better. But we can't do it in a day. If we're patient, it'll bloom. It will."

With the vision so real in his mind, I could almost believe it too. Perhaps it would be possible: perhaps we could make such utterances come true. But conquer the bush, slow the wind, ward off the sun? Could he, the dreamer, do it?

"It's not so bad, is it Anna?" Now he was tender, solicitous. "Are you unhappy with me because I won't leave?"

I shook my head, not meeting his eyes.

"I stop many times and think that it's quite beautiful here," Jakob said slowly. "I'm very happy."

"Often I am too," I admitted.

He leaned over and drew me close to him; the touch was amorous.

"Oh Jakob," I sprang back. "Not here." Not here on the broiling earth, with the clouds and sky and sun watching. In the heat. Not here! That would grant the place more honor than it deserved, and shame us. What was he thinking?

Jakob rose. "I'm off to work," he said.

Distractedly I pulled myself up to foray at the bush edges for firewood.

I contemplated my earlier dissatisfaction with Jakob. The way he loves, I thought, what he really is, his affection for Rosita, his courtliness to Mama, his way with me . . . Even letting that Johann Walde . . . Oh, how I feared that man with all

161

his knowledge. But when God, who kept the balance, weighed it all together, wouldn't Jakob come out all right, even be ahead in His harvest?

I bent for the crooked pieces of wood, and felt dizzy. I would return to the blanket and rest, just for a few minutes. I might close my eyes for a short nap. I stretched out . . .

I was perspiring profusely, and it was absolutely quiet in the bush, except for the occasional harsh cawing of a parrot that cut the thick stillness. There was no wind; not even the tiniest leaves moved. The sun puffed up, bigger and bigger, heating the air. Now I turned, and all I could see was the bush. The field was gone. The trees weren't green, but black.

I began to call. "Jakob!" There was no answer. No sounds of the ax, no voices. I dropped my wood in a pile at my feet, stumbled over it, and started to run, first one way, then another, No matter which way I turned, I met bush, broad and menacing. The woody, spiny branches barred my way. I plunged forward, stooped over. Perhaps I should crawl.

"Jakob!" I continued to shout.

A wait-a-moment plant caught my dress and flung me to the ground. I fell headlong into a cactus, and my heart pounded in terror. But I felt nothing. I extracted myself, and saw that the needles were everywhere, lodged in my body. My dress had been torn off.

"I'm lost! I'm lost!" I cried wildly. "Jakob!"

I sat up, ready to scream. I opened my eyes. There, beside me, the campo. There, Jakob, standing with a log in his hands, not far away. I had fallen asleep on our blanket; my dress and hair were wet with perspiration.

My heart slowed to a normal rhythm; I ceased trembling. I wasn't lost. I was safe; only my head throbbed. The sun had moved and I had been partially out of the shade of the urundey tree under which I rested.

This is home, I thought. I had to say it again, understanding the cost now, in the same way as "Jakob, for better or worse, until the end."

A lizard darted by me. Swift feet, long tail. Hiding? Or playing? Strange, strange creatures.

I wished for relief and for success, for something just a bit better, but the only choice I really had was to accept or not to accept. The Chaco, Jakob, Rosita.

"But God, may I please, at least, have a child of my own?" I crouched on the blanket, touching my forehead to the ground. My pounding head echoed the prayer. "Please, God, at least that?"

Chapter 8

I sat under the algorrobo, too weary to pull my chair into the open to view the wide sky, as Jakob did in the evenings. Through the branches I glimpsed a few stars, but I didn't have the strength to move my chair.

I had also been too tired for prayer meeting tonight. Jakob and Mama went; he preferred that we all attend, but when I said, "Jakob, I can't, I simply can't," he left it at that. Now the singing of hymns wafted over the village from the schoolhouse like a sweet melancholy cry. It brought tears to my eyes. I felt Jesus coming from the building to me because I didn't have the strength to go meet him there.

> Take Thou my hand, O Father, And lead Thou me,
> Until my journey endeth — Eternally!
> Alone I will not wander One single day;
> Be Thou my true Companion And with me stay.

He came to me under the tree. The beautiful algorrobo, as precious as a friend. In our early zeal to clear the *Hof* Papa nearly ordered it cut! I shuddered to recall it. What would we do without the familiar gnarled trunk and comforting spreading branches? By day, the tree gave us shade, mediating the terrible heat of the sun. Even when the rains were late or meager, the algorrobo would green in spring, bearing fresh, lettuce-colored leaves, tiny ones in graceful rows that greeted us every morning as we stepped out of our house and entered the kitchen. Its hundreds of fronds waved gently at us.

Only when the algorrobo shed its pods in the summer was I annoyed with it. I wanted to keep the *Hof* clean and repeatedly had to sweep the pods together. Jakob and Rosita liked to chew on the ripe yellow pods. "Wash them first!" I would cry, but my husband and child didn't listen. "You're worse than the Indians," I scolded.

"We as a people are becoming dirty," Mama complained. "Look at some of our young people, growing up like pigs! We're letting ourselves go."

But I wouldn't allow this to happen to my family. I hated dirt, ugliness, disorder. When I was tempted to put on a soiled dress to save laundry, I rebuked myself and took a clean one, in spite of the extra work. I swept the house every day, and the earth around the house once a week at least. I also regularly took the broom to the ceiling of the house and porch to clear the dust and spider webs.

Killing insects was a fetish with me, even if it meant chasing a cricket or grasshopper across the yard. Beetles died under my sandal with a quick cracking sound. Subduing the earth meant elimination, death.

Ah, but I didn't need to think of that now. I could sit under the algorrobo, giving in to my exhaustion, letting it run over my body, letting it drain away. I had showered and washed my hair,

166

and now there was nothing left to do but lift it periodically and shake it so it would dry quickly. The day was over, the week too, and Rosita was in bed.

Six years, I thought to myself. We've been here six years. Sometimes the days circled as endlessly as the vultures in the high Chaco sky, but when those same days were gone, it was like a swift flight.

Six years. During that time we'd lost Papa, and Mama had moved into the smaller room. I was a wife now. And we had Rosita. Susi visited soon after the girl came, bringing the gift of a dress.

"I wish they'd asked me to take her," she said. "She seems so sweet."

Rosita wasn't sweet, but she was a devoted child and Susi's comment shamed me enough to see it. In time I grew used to having her around, and even became fond of her. I especially enjoyed seeing her and Jakob together; sometimes Rosita became almost animated, and he could get her to giggle as girls that age should.

And we had made some progress on the *Hof.* We added a small kitchen. It was a separate building standing in an L-formation with the sleeping-house. The kitchen was for cooking; we still ate outside under the porch unless the weather was extremely foul.

And for six years we had been coaxing life out of this soil. I enjoyed that part. "You have growing things in your fingers," Mama said, so we divided the chores: she cooked most of the time, I did the laundry and worked the yard.

I planted a small garden between the house and street to supplement our larger fields and gardens. The winter vegetables were doing well, so far, and I delighted in everything that came up, pulling Jakob or Mama or any guests over to see what was growing. In the front of this garden I planted several citrus trees:

mandarins and grapefruit. I had plans for more.

Along the street, under the simple wooden fence which I whitewashed yearly, I planted flowers. I curved the rows up at the gate and carried them along the footpath right up to the house. Diligently I saved the seeds from season to season and collected new varieties from others whenever I could.

I had planted flowers today. Now I felt that deep ache from steady bending, but also the wonderful knowledge that the seeds were all tucked in. I could sit and not move. When Jakob and Mama returned they would walk on the path between the freshly tossed dirt which was wrapping the seeds like a womb.

Tipping my head back, I saw through the spaces in the tree that the sky was now covered with stars. It was as full as my apron had been, full of seeds. Glimmering, tiny seeds.

And Jesus came, calling in the evening. In hours like this, doubt was gone and I possessed instead a clarity and peace so perfect that it was the peak towards which every bitter struggle grasped. God was with me, Father, Son, and Spirit. His hand, ultimately, held us here. What I had grappled with in the death of our baby, my subsequent barrenness, and the calamities of our economic situation, especially the afternoon when the grasshoppers rained over us, was the bleakness of our existence, and the complexity it brought to bear upon my Christian faith. I had been struck, as by a blow, with what God's presence did *not* mean. And in this, my own suffering (during the epidemic, I had only observed), I began to understand that religion, if it was worth anything at all, must be set into human life as it really was. I couldn't shape its context as I wished.

The crux of the thing, then, was not relief, but something to be found in the whole reality of life itself. I glimpsed the way in which the puzzle might be solved. I must find God in the pain. If He was present, as I knew He was, He was inside all of my life — all the parts of it, the good and the bad of everything.

The scope of it was wide: it drew in our poverty and Rosita and our marriage and the future. It included the Chaco.

If I accepted suffering when it was mine, wouldn't I meet Him there? I couldn't expect to be spared further difficulties for they were here, and every evidence pointed to their plentiful presence in the future. But to resist them might be to miss Him altogether! These circumstances were the only ones I had in which to experience Him.

Ah, this was not new, not profound, but I felt that in this small wisdom I had received a gift. Then the quiet night air was stirred again by the harmonious and strangely mournful singing at the schoolhouse. They would be ending the meeting. Had Jakob or Mama been praying for me?

I waited eagerly for their arrival. I laughed to myself, wishing the seeds would burst up early to welcome them home. Crimsons and pinks and yellows would outline our yard. Purples and whites. Oranges. Valiant colors, all of them, the brave bright colors of the prettiest farm in the village. And Jakob would shake his head and say, "Just like my Anna!" as he did when he meant to praise me.

PART THREE

Chapter 1

It was still dark, but our rooster crowed lustily as I awoke. A cool breeze pushed the curtains aside, nudging at my eyes and washing my face with its fresh energy, and a supply of the Lord's compassion too, new every morning.

I felt strangely excited, but it took me a few moments to ascertain why. Then it was clear: a contraction wakened me. I realized that I'd been feeling the spasms in my sleep too, faintly and infrequently, but with a persistence that made me sure this would be the day of the birth. And it was November 25!

God had heard my prayer! He had indulged my desires like a father tilts his head to an infant so that little hands can pull at his hair. This time everything would be all right.

Thank-you, I whispered toward the window. Thank-you, toward Him in the dawn, in the east, heavenward. I wanted to rise, face the morning and say my thanks directly, but another contraction drew the muscles of my womb taut and restrained me. So I spoke from my bed, and waited with utter calm. Fearless, for He had answered me!

When I had conceived again, it was like spring, the gloom lifting, my belly expanding as gently as a budding tree; I was rosy-cheeked and rounded, and more energetic than ever.

"Rest!" Mama scolded. "We've got to bring you through. I'm here, let me do the work."

"I'm not tired, Mama. You should rest too." Mama's legs were thick and often swollen, and she experienced frequent discomfort.

"But you're foolish to be careless," she said. "I have no one to think of but myself."

She seemed anxious to spare me. "Don't be too certain, Anna," she cautioned. "Perhaps you'll be disappointed again. One of my sisters always had trouble — do you remember Aunt Katya?"

"No."

"No, I guess you wouldn't . . . I think the last time we saw her, you were just a baby. My older sister . . . Anyway, something was wrong with her; she always had problems with it too."

"What do you mean, problems?"

"Maybe you inherited something. Maybe it doesn't work so well for you, having children I mean."

"Oh Mama, surely this time!" I cried as if the outcome of my pregnancy rested with her.

"Aunt Katya lost seven altogether, four of them before they were half ready. Better not set your heart on it too much."

Seven! The number stung and I hurried away from further conversation. That sacred number of completion loomed above me like the stone-carved law. Oh God, I thought, I couldn't bear it. Not seven! And seventy times seven, the stretch of forgiveness; would I have to fulfill that? Failures lay before me, one upon another, as far as I could see, up to the horizon of my life, interminable.

I tried then to work less, to repress the irrepressible, to dam

174

the flow of joy washing up from its source in my womb. But it was a fountain I simply couldn't staunch. I felt it was a miracle that hope could be so large and full-grown in spite of earlier evidence against it. So what could I do but receive it? The growing fetus turned at will too, fluttering under my stomach. I lay awake many nights thinking of a baby, lacking the discipline to stop myself.

When I read Hannah's prayer of thanksgiving I noticed a seven there too. "Even the barren gives birth to seven," she laughed in victory, remembered by the Lord, given a son. Even the barren! God in heaven, be praised. I house your gift and my heart exults. I often sang:

> The Lord will hear our prayer —
> What undeserved blessing!
> To Him I may repair
> A child-like faith possessing.
> He never turns away
> All those who seek His love;
> And those who truly pray
> Receive help from above.

"It's all in His hands," Jakob said, reversing roles now to smooth the optimism, check my good cheer, prepare for the worst.

"Jakob, I want this baby more than anything else in the world," I told him one night when it was difficult to sleep because of the heat. He swung his hand from his bed to mine to touch my shoulder.

"And if you want it too much? Look at Israel, God granting their requests but then sending them leanness in their souls."

I pressed his hand to acknowledge his comment, but couldn't answer.

175

"Last week I was reading in the gospels," he said, "where a woman in the crowd called to Jesus, 'Blessed is the womb that bore you.' He answered, 'Blessed rather are the ones who follow me.' That struck me. There are things more important than . . ."

Tears rolled from the corners of my eyes into my hair. What did it mean?

"I want it too," he said. "I didn't mean that I don't. But we must keep praying, not our will but thine be done."

"I know."

I paid attention when he spoke; since I felt less tutored than he in spiritual matters, I agreed with him. But I want it and I'm afraid to say, not my will, I argued within myself. And this wanting, hadn't God put it there? I believed I had gained some submission, some acceptance of God's ways. Did this desperation to have my will this time mean that I had learned nothing after all? Was God dissatisfied with me?

It was impossible to be neutral. But I couldn't tell where the wrong or the right of my yearning lay. It was mingled: in my praise for the pregnancy I called to Him, and in my fears too. They both grasped for Him.

But leanness! Even the word was thin and unpleasant. Our lives were lean enough already. There was an insect here which resembled a twig, a sliver of a tree, with legs no wider than needles. It was lean and grotesque. No, I didn't want that!

In the last weeks of my term Mama's and Jakob's warnings caught hold within me. Certainty was gone. I hoped without foundation. Instead, foreboding: that the narrow path led on its way to heaven through valleys of unhappiness only. In this distress I asked God for a sign. Since the baby was due the end of November, I prayed that it might be born on November 25 which would be an indication that all would be well.

November 25 was a day of particular significance in the

colony. It was the day when we annually commemorated our release from Russia. On that day in 1929 in Moscow, we received permission to leave the country. Every year since then we recalled it with special services and meals together.

I fixed upon this day for the birth as a fleece which I laid before God. I didn't mention it to Jakob though, thinking he would frown on it as a foolish imposition.

Foolish or not, God was giving me the sign! It was the day of the birth, and it was November 25. I pushed off the light patchwork cover, feeling warm. My lower back ached but otherwise I had no pain. I was thankful that it wasn't as hot this week as last, and that I had slept well.

I turned to look at Jakob, still breathing deeply in the cot across from mine, his mouth opened slightly. How untroubled and boyish he looked, the dark hair askew on the pillow, his arm cradled under his head. How I loved him, my opposite, this man, my husband and lover, my teacher.

I didn't want to rouse him yet. Often I was annoyed when he slept so soundly in the morning and I had to call to waken him; it didn't seem right for a man, a farmer. I loved the edges of the day — evenings and early morning. Over the noon hour when I rested well, Jakob was alert and busy; he read or wrote in his notebook when the sun was at full strength.

This morning I was glad he slept, glad I could watch him from across the narrow passage between the beds. I could watch him fondly for a few minutes, take my leave of him, for the day of birth had come and I would pass it alone except for the midwife, and maybe Mama.

In the east the sky lightened to a pale rose, the color of our Chaco cherries, though it grew rapidly merrier. Dawn began timidly here but progressed with radiant confidence, like a woman who hurries to make the fire, sets the water to boil and even gets a start on her work before the children stir.

I turned on the straw mattress and closed my eyes. I should try to sleep again, for I would need a reserve of strength. But, November 25! Jakob and Rosita would be alone at the service, and Mama and I and the midwife would be missing. The women would put it all together soon enough. It would have them buzzing all right. I chuckled with delight.

I didn't mind missing the anniversary celebration. Not a bit. Traditionally, in the afternoon someone would give a personal account of the flight, so the children would know exactly how it had been. This year *Prediger* Rahn would do it. I would be at home having my baby but I already knew Rahn's story. We had lived in the same Moscow summerhouse, in adjoining apartments, facing the street. We had been together on the train out of the country, in Germany, on the ship, and now in the same village.

Soon I would tell that story to my own child, my flesh, my heir of those events. "My dear little one," I would say, jostling him or her on my knee, "listen to this story." The child would nestle against me. "You were born on November 25 and that's a very special day because on that day in 1929 we were still in Russia, a land far, far away, and on that day we heard we would be able to leave the country. You see, my little one, the Russians had become like wicked black bears in their huge winter coats" (the eyes of my child would be fixed on my fierce, expressive face) "and their voices were barks. They had begun to herd hundreds of our people into boxcars, taking them back, and treating them cruelly."

I was overcome with emotion as I visualized this scene with my child. My experience in Moscow wasn't only mine anymore, but it belonged to my children. I would give my memories to them as a gift. Certain details must be elaborated.

I would give them the night of the dreaded knock, when Papa's whispered "They've reached us" thundered through the room and clamped off our breath. The knock recurred twice before he could stumble to the door, but it was strange, for there was no stomping, no impatience on the other side as there should have been.

"You're free to go," the officer said. He didn't smile but he seemed relieved. Men in the government had worked on our behalf, he explained, and Germany would take those of us left in Moscow. That man, like the Egyptians who gave the Jews their jewels on exodus night, seemed glad for us.

In Riga, on the other side, we stood on the train platform and sang our thanks, tears glistening in every eye like the stars in the Chaco, with long wet lines on Mama's face and Papa standing stiff and stubborn, eyes brimming. I would tell my child everything that God had done.

But it was time to wake Jakob. My labor was beginning.

"Get up," I hissed. "Go for Mrs. Klassen. Hurry!"

I wished I could delay time now, so I would be ready. I began to shake and gathered the blankets around me for help. I was afraid.

"Hurry!" I cried.

The hour of birth had come too suddenly, and we all had to obey it. Mama bustled about me. I accepted her ministrations as my right, pleading for more. Nothing availed for the pain. I pushed the coverings aside again and begged for water for my face. Every moan was a prayer, Oh God, hasten it! Hasten the hours, and minutes.

I heard the midwife's low voice and my own unearthly groans. "I sound like a cow," I gasped.

"Never mind," Mama soothed. "You're not as wild as last time."

Mercifully, the birth progressed quickly. Within two hours the baby was delivered. At noon Jakob and Rosita tiptoed into the room to see the boy, their red-faced son and brother. We had already selected his name, David.

Chapter 2

"I have to admit I'd hoped Walde would leave," Jakob said, squatting beside me under the porch where I nursed David.

"Oh? What happened now?"

"Nothing in particular really, but . . . "

"Nothing but *their* chickens in our garden, and *their* cows loose in our fields, *their* children running here and everywhere as if the village is their *Hof*, and then it's always *our* fault!"

"Those are in the past — "

"One of these times I'll make soup from one of their hens!" I chuckled. "But then they'll want to have the supper and a living chicken in return too!"

"No, there's nothing new," Jakob said thoughtfully. "I didn't mean that. Just . . . " He sighed. "I shouldn't feel this way but I'm still disappointed he didn't leave the colony too. Even though I opposed anyone leaving."

"It would have been easier," I said. I smiled at David and his eagerness to suckle.

"Just look at your boy, Jakob! Such an appetite! He drinks

181

as if there won't be enough." I put my face to the baby's, touched his nose and cooed, "There's enough, child, there's enough. Plenty!"

I lifted my head and laughed. "He, at least, has everything he needs. Enough of everything." David had bounty, for my breasts were full of milk.

But Jakob's thoughts weren't with me or David. He sat down on the ground, rested his arms on a pail, and stared into it.

"It's easier, I suppose, having that group gone. Even if Walde didn't go, the overall tension is reduced," he mused.

From the side of the house I could hear the subdued conversation of Mama and Rosita as they picked grapefruit. A cow bawled in the corral. Flies buzzed about us in the heat, but still the village seemed quiet and at peace. And I was comfortable, my bare feet on the packed earth, David resting on my knees, his head crooked in my arm. But Jakob was troubled. He still mulled over the events of the past months, when the arguments over whether to leave the Chaco and re-settle elsewhere had finally resulted in a separation. One third of the colony's settlers, one hundred and forty families, moved to establish another colony on Paraguay's eastern side. Two hundred and eighty-four families stayed in the Chaco.

The break was painful for both groups, and particularly discouraging for us who remained. Would their leaving prove us fools?

Nevertheless, it had also had advantages. The decision made in Germany, to put twenty-five farms in each village, thirteen on each side with the twenty-sixth as the school property, was motivated by the wish to provide strong community life in each village with a school, church choir, and youth group. But economically, this plan was disastrous. The campos in the Chaco were too small to support twenty-five farms.

The fronts of the farms were narrow and often there were

no more than four to eight hectares of land available for cultivating and planting. It was too little to provide for a family's needs.

With one third of the settlers gone, however, the rest of us could stretch out; the farms could be enlarged, the numbers per village reduced. It provided a new beginning.

But Jakob often sat alone, absorbed in thought.

"I don't know," he sighed again. "He was your father's friend, but I find him a hard man. Hard . . . "

"Well, they stayed, and we can't change it," I said pragmatically. But the tension with our neighbors bothered me too. I had noticed Johann's abrupt absence on our *Hof* after our marriage, although he was unfailingly friendly to me when we met at church or village functions. I had not been able to establish a relationship with Leni. I'd expected that our new baby might give us something in common, for she and Johann had their first boy soon after David's birth, but still she kept to herself, as if I would always be young and never able to catch up.

Sure, it bothered me. I raged and talked and stormed about it; that helped. Jakob was a peaceable man by nature, and the dissensions, touching his own reactions to others as they did, perturbed him more. But I too wanted peace. I wanted beauty and order, but people were not like the flowers in my seasonal arrangements. If we women could erase the tensions in the colony the way we cleaned the children's faces with a bit of spittle on two fingers just before going to church, we would. If I could make Jakob and Johann good neighbors, I would already have done it!

"The cotton crop was good. They'll regret that they left," Jakob said, his mind jumping back to the recent split.

"We might be sorry we didn't."

"It was a foolish move. Oh well, never mind that. More will be accomplished now, with unity and — "

I stopped him with an impatient cluck. "*Tsk*. Unity? Us here, them there, waiting for the others to fail? That will be unity!"

"That's not — "

"You men will find other things to fight about," I said. "You always do."

I wiped the perspiration from David's forehead and shaped his damp fair hair into a tiny curl on top of his head.

"Oh Anna."

He rose. "I'll go do the chores." With long strides he went to the corral.

I caught some of his emotion from seeing his firm brisk gait. I had said too much. But wasn't it true? Men were like that, unable to meet each other in the middle. Women didn't conduct long meetings and argue. How could we?

I turned my attention back to David. His hunger stilled, he drew more slowly; his eyes were closed. I contemplated him tenderly. He was a pudgy, well-formed baby. When others told me he resembled me, I said, "The forehead is narrower, that's Jakob's. And his eyes are deep. He'll be a thinker."

The infant's mouth fell open and I loosed the relaxed gums gently from my breast.

Rosita came to me with her apron full of fruit. I nodded approvingly and she rolled them out into a woven reed basket beside the door. Rolf nuzzled her.

Rosita pressed the dog against her leg and returned to me, looking at David and touching him lightly on the cheek. "He's asleep," she murmured. "Shall I put him in his bed?"

I relinquished David into Rosita's thin, careful hands and went to the corral. Perhaps I could say something to Jakob to undo my glum prediction.

I had no idea then how it would all come true, how much reason we Mennonites would still have to quarrel with one another.

Chapter 3

The sun glimmered suddenly through the parting clouds, the misting rain stopped, and the clothes I had draped over the line fluttered. Instead of hanging straight and heavy, the wet wash began to ripple, each piece alternately, as if wind chased wind between them.

"It's clearing," I said aloud. The fronds of the palm in the garden waved the same minute graceful tempo as the wash on the line. My spirits danced along.

For five weeks it had been cloudy, drizzling, and cold, making the streets and roads a quagmire. It was a miserable task, trying to keep warm, for we had no extra clothes. In the evenings and frequently during the day we huddled around the stove to drive away the chill and cold that kept settling deep into our bodies.

My biggest worry was that the clothes wouldn't dry properly. Every day I mentioned this to Mama and Jakob, as if they didn't know it. I hung the clothes outside when I could, to air them, but they often drizzled wet, and then at night the tiny

187

kitchen was cluttered with damp garments hung on every available hook or chair. We had so few clothes that when it rained long and was cold I couldn't keep up with the laundry either; we wore soiled garments.

The year before we had suffered another drought. How we longed then for rain! Now we waited over a month for it to dry. When the sun shone it was never long enough to dry everything thoroughly. A musty smell puffed out of the boxes and wooden trunk in which we kept our things, the salt wouldn't sprinkle, the sugar became wet and lumpy, the flour moldy. Our one leather case grew green fungus on the edges.

I also worried about the children. David was four, and we had added a daughter to our family: Tina, born in 1939, the year the war began in Europe. I took her into my bed at night, and David, who usually slept on a mattress on the ground, crowded in with Jakob so he would be off the damp earth. During the day I tried to keep them playing actively, or sitting close to the stove. They mustn't get sick.

Now, the sun came out with all its wonderful promise. This time it might grow warm, even hot. I scrutinized the sky. It had changed and I felt certain it signalled more than a temporary break in the weather. In the south the cloud covering was thin and in the north and east it had parted like a curtain to reveal the lovely mild blue it had hidden before. I smiled and watched the clothes skip gracefully; they were drying!

I returned to the house with light steps. Mama was bent over the wood box, feeding the fire.

"The sun is out," I announced to her broad back. "The clothes will dry properly this time, I think."

She raised herself ponderously. "Oh that's good," she said. But she didn't turn. She lifted a kettle lid and then replaced it, slowly.

"Anna," she said, speaking to the wall by the stove, "you

know . . . you know that Maria feels it's not fair if I live only with you. She says she needs the help too. You have fewer children. I think I should move over there now."

And that's how fast the happiness could disappear, how fickle it was, out the door faster than a bit of fat sliding off the knife at slaughtering, whizzing through the air to the dog.

"What did you say?" I set the empty enamel basin on the small work table and looked at her in astonishment. I had heard the words, but they were too unexpected for me to absorb. Move to Maria's?

Mama remained at the stove but turned to face me, holding one corner of her apron in each white hand. "Maria says she needs help too, and you have fewer children. It's only right if I go there now." She spoke quickly, as if she had memorized the sentences.

"You mean move there, to live?"

The idea, of course, wasn't entirely new. Maria had complained; she had dropped remarks. But Mama usually responded, "This is my place. This is where I belong."

Now Mama said, "You know Anna, Maria really has her hands full. Is it fair if I live only with you?"

"But, Mama, they don't have room!"

"Maria says they'll find room."

Mama leaving? It was not to be believed. Sometimes I had wished I could be alone. I had wondered, why doesn't she live with Maria a while? But these were moments of pique or disagreement, and they were rare. Mama and I understood each other. Our personalities meshed better than Maria's and Mama's. I always felt that Mama genuinely enjoyed us, that she loved us, that we gave her happiness and solace. So how could she say she would be leaving us?

But I knew she wouldn't say it unless she meant it.

Maria is selfish, I wished to say, and she's thinking only

of herself and her problems. Yes, she has ten children, but her oldest is sixteen and well able to help. I have three and one coming soon and they're all young; even Rosita is small for her age.

I had more angry sentences waiting on my tongue which I wished I could spit at her: does Maria look over here and suppose I don't work hard? Does she think my life is easy because you're here? She overestimates what you do. She imagines she's more tired than I am. She sees my flowers. Ah, she says, you have time for flowers. She sees my swept *Hof*. Ah, you have time to keep the *Hof* clean. She sees Rosita and David and Tina with their neat, clean clothes. Ah, she says, you have time for that. You have Mama here. Over and over: you have Mama, you have Mama.

Even if you go, Mama, I reminded her in my racing thoughts, Maria still won't find time for flowers. What does she know about it, as scatter-brained as she is? Her garden will still be in weeds, the *Hof* won't change. She'll learn that she won't get to the bottom of her mending either. And I'll manage everything! If she thinks that you make the difference, then you'll both see!

My lips trembled but I forced myself to be calm. I said almost carelessly, "It seems sudden, Mama. I'll talk with Jakob."

Mama was also controlled. She held the apron edge, but didn't twist or move it. She refused to look at me directly, however, and thus revealed her uncertainty.

A rush of compassion, unbidden and as swift as a memory, came over me. I saw Mama, her lined face and that sighing, creaking, heavy and unwieldy body. Her face was red from the fire, but she was as tidy as always, every hair tucked into the braided bun under the grey kerchief. She seemed no older than when she arrived in Paraguay, no older even than the days of my childhood in Russia. But of course she was older; she had aged, and now I saw it. The old woman opposite me was

190

more than seventy. And Maria and I would fight about whom she would help?

"I talked with Jakob already," Mama said. "He said I was free to do what I think best."

"But this is your farm. Papa's."

"My farm? No. It's yours. Jakob and I have discussed it."

"But I mean it's your home!"

"That doesn't matter." She sighed in her characteristic way.

Then I knew! Suddenly I was sure of the reason she was moving. Mama felt more at home with Ernst and Maria now because they agreed about Germany! They agreed about the Chaco and our future.

"It's because of the German business, isn't it Mama? Because of Germany?" I accused.

Mama's bewildered eyes met mine.

"Now what does your old mother have to say about that?"

"We all have our opinions, Mama. You have yours. You've expressed them. It's because you don't agree with Jakob, right?"

Mama reached for a bowl of chunked sweet potatoes, and lifting the kettle lid, dropped them into the soup.

I blinked. I saw my mother, pathetically aged. I saw the house, a hut with a mud floor, uneven walls, cracks in the whitewash. Small rectangular windows without screens, bare, open. Not even a curtain over the window in the kitchen. A few utensils on the rough work table, and two basins. Several dishes, just enough for each of us and a few extra. It was winter but I comprehended it as if it were summer, with flies attracted to the milk and swarming into the room, black flies and silt settling on everything.

"That's the reason, isn't it?"

"Maria needs help. Doesn't a mother want to be fair?"

"So it's all decided and this is the announcement?"

She nodded.

Oh, who could speak freely here and who would listen? When Jakob said "She has to do what she thinks is best," he didn't realize how his ideas drove wedges into families, how his rigidity exasperated powerless women. Mama moving to be fair, she said, and I knew better: she and Ernst and Maria looked at things the same way.

I visualized them sitting in that mess of a house, not any better than ours, dirty babies crawling over the manure-and-mud hardened floor, Mama unhappy with their running noses and untidiness, but agreeing with them! Mama would pronounce that we were all sliding downward here, isolated in the Chaco, losing our culture and manners. She and Ernst and Maria would sit in the boiling night swatting mosquitoes and bask in their membership in the German *Bund*, the association formed here which would bring them back to that wonderful land when the war was over. Mama would fill their ears with stories of the Ukraine, all the way back to her girlhood, how she came from good family, about the near-gods in her line: her father, her grandfather, great-grandfather; she'd even found some relationship, some distant connection, it seemed, with Cornies. She could say, "We're German," in her wise, sure way and her children and grandchildren would nod. Dreaming of going back.

But I didn't have that luxury. Not with Jakob. We would sit, the two of us, under the same moon on the same hot night, and he would share, in his measured sentences, his concern about the direction the leaders of the colony were taking us, about Christians mixing in political matters that belonged only to the state, about the battle songs and love songs and sports being taught to our youth.

How had it all started? We had people in our colony who

had recently studied in Germany and knew the temper of the times. They were here with us, trying to help us, trying to show us the identity we had lost or neglected. We were Germans, something we might justly be proud of; we knew our race! These teachers and leaders energetically began to promote nationalism, "the German people's movement," in our colony. We here in the Chaco must understand ourselves as part of the unity of all German people, they said. We must work together to maintain our high cultural legacy and also prepare ourselves to return someday to the *Reich*, to the land of Germany herself!

To me, this philosophy was attractive. It contained hope and seemed quite simple and obvious. Nevertheless, the nationalistic movement had brought, not unity or progress, but conflicts and disagreements and tensions worse than any we had known so far. The issues were debated intensely and soon became more than philosophical differences. They spawned bitter enmity. The sides formed: "German" vs. "anti-German."

I remembered a conversation Jakob and Mama had several months ago as we sat or stood around a heap of uprooted peanut plants, our brave harvest, beating the peanuts off their stems and gathering them into sacks. Even little Tina helped. I had her at my side and showed her that she must be very careful to get every nut off the root system. This was work I enjoyed most, work we did together as a family.

"It's because you came through China, Jakob," Mama said that afternoon. "You haven't experienced how good Germany was to us, what they did for us. Only the Germans responded to our call for help. We were about to perish, there in Moscow. Many of our people had been sent back or exiled already, and we were next. Who came to our aid? Germany. Barely able to manage for themselves, still trying to recover after the Great War, the Germans didn't abandon their brothers in their plight. The need of a German concerns every German, they said, and

— "

"I'm not against gratitude," Jakob broke in politely. "But I'm afraid that this nationalism discourages us here. To talk of returning makes us unfit for the battle at hand. He who puts his hand to the plow and looks back is not fit for the kingdom of God."

"You weren't in Germany. You weren't there when they rescued us," I flashed, in defense of Mama.

There was surprise and displeasure in Jakob's face. He was quiet a while, then he addressed Mama again.

"We appealed to Germany in Harbin too," he said. "Yes, we're German. I don't mean that. But I'm uneasy. This emphasis on returning there after the war and building a German world unity, even giving up our long practice of non-resistance to do it . . . And making us think of comfortable lives and material well-being instead of God . . . Of earthly kingdoms, of Germany instead of Christ . . . It's wrong." He didn't raise his voice but he was absolutely unbending in every statement.

Mama continued the argument, her voice rising. "Look at the Indians! Is that what we want to become?" She waved a peanut plant in the air. "They're contented here, living as they do, filthy, pagan. And contented to be so! No," Mama shook her head vigorously, "We mustn't forget who we are."

"We're in Paraguay now."

"We're not Paraguayan! We had better make sure we don't become Paraguayan either. It would be a sin!"

Fear seeped into me like the sure movement of water finding its level.

"Don't discuss it with Mama," I begged Jakob that night.

"As you like," he said. "But let me clarify it for you at least. Do you know what we Mennonites are lacking here? *Gelassenheit.* Resignation. Tranquility. We must learn to leave ourselves quite purposely in the safe hands of God."

He talked to me a long time about why he opposed the nationalistic movement among our people in the colony. It made sense to me too, but I couldn't help but pity him for he had hoped that the peace snatched from us in Russia would be reestablished here in the distant lonely Chaco. He dreamt of a humble, separated, settled community, working aggressively, occupied with God's Word, peaceful towards men. Instead, the conflicts boiled inside our settlement. And they affected him too; he also struggled to maintain the attitude of *Gelassenheit* he wished for us all.

It affected all of us. And it had entered our family. Mama liked the teacher who led the "German people's movement" because she believed posture and order and discipline were important. Her grandchildren must speak German, sing, grow plum trees. They mustn't lose their culture or religion or language. For her they belonged together, were one.

I understood these concerns, for I felt them deep within myself. But I was married to Jakob, and what he believed was my belief too.

Mama stood at the stove stirring the soup and asserted that though she would move, it had nothing to do with the German business. "Maria's my daughter too," she said, insisting she had thought long about it and wanted to be fair.

But I didn't believe her.

I stepped to the porch. "Look!" I nearly shrieked. "It's clouded over and drizzling again!"

Chapter 4

It was dark and late, yet as warm as day. Moonlight glimmered weakly upon the earth, touching it with mystery and a measure of sadness. I lay half-asleep on my cot.

I woke, hearing the faint clomping of oxen, the creak of a wagon, and voices. That would be the village men returning from their meeting in town. I was wide awake then, waiting as I always did for Jakob.

"Fine widow you'd make," Mama remarked when I'd confessed once that I missed Jakob if he left even for an hour or two.

"It just seems easier when he's near," I explained.

I heard David snoring lightly in the other room, and from small beds at the end of mine the even breathing of our young daughters puffed towards me, as pleasant as wisps of smoke, like the fragrant smell of a palosanto fire. All the children were asleep, all was well.

Because the quiet night carried the noises of the travelling men a considerable distance, they seemed an especially long time arriving. I wondered how many other women were awake; I imagined that in each one of the silent houses, perched like doves along the village street, a woman waited, unable to sleep, all senses attending the open window, thinking of her man coming home.

The men's thoughts were probably not with us women; they would talk of other things, but still they would be weary and their tiredness would urge the oxen forward on the long narrow road that gleamed silvery in the moonlight.

I got up, lit a lamp in the kitchen, and set bread and cold beans on the table in case Jakob was hungry when he arrived. Then I returned to the bedroom and crept under the sheet again.

The wagon reached the village and eventually stopped in front of our *Hof.* I heard Jakob and our neighbor across the street, Wilhelm Froese, call "Good night" as they sprang down from the cart.

No voice answered them. Only a strange silence and a nervous cough. Anxiously I pulled myself up to the window and peered out. Jakob had been unusually curt with the children and me before he left for the meeting. Tensions in our village, as in the entire colony, were mounting.

I saw his tall form moving to the house. He'd gone perhaps ten paces when Johann Walde's clear brittle voice jumped after him. "You're a hypocrite, Jakob, you know!"

Jakob stopped.

"When you needed help you were ready to be German like the rest! Even now you benefit from their help. You sang their anthem, didn't you, and were willing enough to congratulate *der Führer* Hitler in '33? You're a hypocrite!"

Jakob turned immediately and retraced his steps. "I shouldn't have. I realized it and changed my mind!"

Walde burst out again. "Who are you anyway? Who are you? Will you give your daughters to the Paraguayans then?

Have your children speaking Spanish?"

"That's not what — "

A voice which I couldn't identify called, "So you'll glad-ly sit by and let the communists take the world? The Germans fight Russia, Jakob! Think of it!"

Walde again, "You hide behind your piety, but you're a hypocrite. And you're a lazy farmer. Crawl into a hut with the Lenguas!"

I recoiled from the window as if struck.

Jakob answered in a low voice. I caught the single word, "Non-resistance."

When it began, Jakob supported the German association in the Chaco because he was interested in the colony's education-al progress. But he soon withdrew from the *Bund* and all it represented. When we were given the opportunity to register for German citizenship in anticipation of a future return to the Uk-raine, assuming Germany's victory over the Soviet Union, he refused to do so. He and a small minority. Johann Walde, on the other hand, was a keen supporter of the German people's move-ment.

The issue, as Jakob spoke of it, had shifted a little, and now revolved around the matter of non-resistance. Those who promoted close ties with Germany were willing to give up the old principle of the Anabaptists. In the settlement of Mennonites in Eastern Paraguay a group of youths had even gone to Ger-many to enlist in the army. For Jakob such sacrifice of Jesus' teaching was incomprehensible.

A leather whip whistled over the backs of the oxen and with a creak the wagon began to roll. As it labored noisily on, Walde flung a last mockery into the air. "Stay in the Chaco, you stupid fool! I'll be back in the Ukraine when the war is over!" The words hung in the windless night.

Then the roadway in front of our gate was empty and the

199

sounds of the wagon diminished like an echo. I lay still in bed, waiting.

The lift of the latch, his tread: Jakob was inside. Then outside again, and gone a long time, it seemed. Finally he returned to the bedroom.

"Hello," I whispered.

"It's late. Aren't you sleeping?"

"No. Did you see the food?"

"Yes."

Jakob undressed and eased his body into the narrow bed. Lying on his back, face to the ceiling he asked, "Did you hear them, Anna?"

"Yes."

"They're angry at me. I spoke up at the meeting . . . I couldn't help myself."

"What — "

"Some of them are such rabble," he said bitterly. "They talk like irreligious men. Of war! Of actually fighting! It's nothing to them anymore."

"But not all of them. Surely not all of them."

"No. But preachers too. So I was angry. I spoke what I felt, and others spoke, and we were all rather sharp with each other."

"Who else?"

"Walde, of course. He's eloquent. Ernst."

"Ernst Hein? Our brother-in-law?"

"Oh he blustered about, all excited. And I couldn't help speaking up to oppose him."

"What did you say?"

He turned on his side to face me, though his gaze went past me to the window. His nose caught a bit of moonlight along the bone and looked like an ivory-colored horn between his deep-set eyes.

"We all said the usual. They talk of loyalty to Germany.

How they helped us. How they're fighting communism. How we belong to them. How we can't live here. I said we should glorify God instead of a nation. They sit around the radio set, evening after evening, following the war like boys."

But I too had rejoiced at every piece of news from the German *Reich* that reached our village, passed from house to house like a wind bringing rain! I too hoped that Germany would save the world from the Bolsheviks, that they would somehow be able to undo what had happened in Russia.

"How far should the church mix with the state? Not this much. Not at all. We're to be separate from the kingdoms of the world. Peaceful. And we must stay on the firm platform of biblical teaching."

In Jakob's words I heard the sentiments of *Prediger* Rahn, the most rigid and uncompromising of them all. From the very beginning he had wanted us to forge our own path, stay where we were. He venerated the Chaco, people said in derision.

"It was like a testimony meeting," Jakob continued. "All those stories about wonderful Germany and the horrors of communism — "

"But they're true! Communism is — "

"Yes, Anna, I know all that. But is it our place to take revenge? To wield the sword against evil?"

"Oh . . . " he moaned. "I wish I'd never joined the *Bund* in the first place. Now I speak up and am hated more than those who stayed out of it right from the beginning."

"I pushed you to do it."

"No, it's not your fault. Most of us have thought of leaving at one point or another . . . "

"Even you, Jakob?"

He smiled ruefully. "Even me."

"I'm hated, Anna," he said after a pause. My husband was bereft. And I couldn't say, oh, surely they don't hate you, surely you exaggerate. I had just witnessed it.

"Why did I open my mouth? Why did I speak? Oh . . . "

What had actually happened at that meeting, I wondered? Since when did Jakob regret speaking his truth? Since when did he care what others thought? Care that he was hated?

"I wanted to grab Walde and shake him good. But I saw the light in the kitchen. I knew perhaps you were awake. So I held my tongue and fists, but otherwise . . . "

This was even less like Jakob. "I love you," I said anxiously and slipped out of bed to lie beside him, comforting him in the only way I knew.

Several weeks later, on a morning when I was rushing with many urgent things, I saw Jakob and Johann together at the fence, each on his own side. They rarely stood and talked in a neighborly way, and I could read through the corner of my eye, that this conversation was not about the weather either. Carrying slops to the pig, I noticed that Walde's hands waved in the air. Snatches of his speech blew by me with the hot wind. Feeding the chickens, I observed he had stopped talking (but was impatient to begin again) and Jakob's hands gestured agitatedly.

I nursed our newborn Gretchen and put her down to nap. I ran to the piled dishes, and then to the garden to dig sweet potatoes, and then to the kitchen to watch the cottage cheese on the back of the stove. The men talked on.

Wisdom counselled minding my own affairs. I had work enough for two, three, four days . . . The cottage cheese curded nicely. There! Into the cloth bag it went, to drip.

But those arguing men outside began to annoy me. They stood hatless in the strong mid-morning sun. They were wasting time, time that was precious. There was enough work for them too, on both farms. I washed my hands and dried them on a clean towel. I patted my hair to check if the pins were in place and dropped my apron on a chair. Then I marched out of the kitchen toward the opponents.

Neither of them noticed my coming. The exchange seemed to be reaching a climax: both gestured, both talked at once, and the words fell like blows: "Germany . . . non-resistance . . . Bolsheviks . . . the *Bund* . . . culture . . . Paraguay . . . fools . . . progress . . . " They began to shout.

I meant to separate them. I meant to say, "Now shush both of you and go to work." But I was too late.

Jakob's fist shot over the fence and caught Walde on the chin. I gasped as the smaller man fell. He floundered on the ground like a beetle on its back. He shook as he rolled sideways and pushed to his feet. A faint reddish circle marked the place where Jakob had hit him.

When Walde saw me a startling vulnerability flickered across his face, but by the time he was standing, his rigid dignity was restored.

And Jakob! His right arm now dangled limply at his side and the other, partly forward, fingers clenched, also ready to strike if required, relaxed and fell awkwardly away, shoulders hunched in defeat. He didn't acknowledge me in any way.

I didn't leave with Jakob. I stayed, staring at Johann, and he at me. His eyes moved over me as if to measure me. I saw that he was scarcely taller than I. In the steady look I gave him in return I intended to tell him that the years' difference between us had fallen away, that I didn't think of him as Papa's friend anymore, that I didn't consider him worthy of respect just because he knew a lot, that I didn't care that he was the mayor of our village. He was my enemy and I wasn't afraid of him. I would tell him that I despised him. I hated him.

"Johann Walde," I said coldly, "I beseech you to leave Jakob in peace. You — "

"And I, my dear Mrs. Rempel," he interrupted with sarcastic gallantry, "beg you to refrain from commanding me to do anything. Do save your rebukes for your husband." He acted as if he would leave, then added, "But let me say just one thing before I go. Remind Jakob of it too. I didn't have time to tell him. We hear reports that thousands of innocent German civilians, German women and children and old men, that is, are being killed through the bombings on Germany. And Mennonite boys from the United States have also participated in that. Think of that when your husband and Rahn visit with the American missionaries who come here wanting to instruct us on neutrality."

"Once! For one hour, perhaps, they talked. Rahn — "

"Oh, and this yet," he continued, interrupting me again as if I had nothing of consequence to say, "Jakob isn't beyond fighting either. As you yourself have just observed."

And then he walked away. The back of his shirt was covered with dirt and bits of dry grass, but he strode away in a posture of victory. I was left sputtering, my resolves in disarray, watching his mussed back until he disappeared behind a hedge. Oh, if I could see him squirming on the earth again! If I could rip him apart!

My shoulders twitched in frustration and helplessness. I went to the chicken house to check for eggs, and then hurried to the house. The potatoes wouldn't be cooked in time for dinner unless I peeled them right away.

Jakob waited for me inside the kitchen. For the first time in our marriage, he raised his voice at me. "You had no business doing that, Anna. You humiliate me."

"What do you mean?" I flared back. "You hit him because I walked up?"

"You don't need to get involved!"

"I'm on your side, Jakob."

"Your side in this matter is silence. Learn your place,

woman! Learn silence!"

He brushed past me and went to the sleeping quarters. My hands shook as I tied my apron. I checked the baby, then looked for Tina. She was happily playing house in the garden. Leadenly, I joined her for a minute in the fantasy that I was a guest for supper and then rushed back to the kitchen to prepare our noon meal.

When Rosita and David ran in from school I greeted them as cheerfully as I always did. I performed all my duties. And Jakob stayed in the bedroom until noon.

I had to carry on as if nothing was wrong. Inside I was crying, a poor, miserable, trapped mouse; I wanted to escape, to run out of the village and never come back. But I was trapped. I wanted to die. I had marched to judge like a Deborah and was debased, on every side. Now I just wanted to die rather then return from battle!

But I called Jakob and the children to eat, and we had our dinner as usual. No one would have guessed that anything was wrong. Only when I took up the crying Gretchen after the meal and pressed her soft infant cheek against mine did the tears flow. I cried in self-pity and deep despair, and I cried for her too, born female.

Chapter 5

The division in the colony over the nationalistic German movement became even more complicated when sharp disagreements and opposing parties developed within the pro-German group. Tensions came to a head on March 11, 1944. A group of men stormed into the town center and began to attack their opponents. The American Mennonites working in the colony called in the Paraguayan military to prevent further trouble in the colony.

Every year afterwards when we tore the devotional reading off the calendar on March 11 we remembered, each one silently of course, how tempers boiled over and erupted into violence, how blows became public and required the policing of the state. These developments tainted us all, whether we had participated or not, like a scarlet burning embarrassment.

That May the colony mayor and the high school principal, head of the nationalistic movement, were expelled from our settlement.

"Like goats to carry the sins of the people out of the

camp," scoffed a supporter.

"Those who sow wind, reap the storm," said an opponent.

And Jakob explained to me, "Kneaded dough merely rises again. We must be thorough and remove the leaven completely."

The foreign element of political activity was formally, publicly removed. "We say with Daniel 9:5, we confessed we have sinned, and have committed iniquity, and have done wickedly, and have rebelled, even by departing from thy precepts and from thy judgments . . . " Non-resistance was now deliberately reaffirmed. Eventually the church which had been divided over the issue was reunited.

Jakob visited Johann to ask his forgiveness.

"I should go too," I worried. "Or could you tell him for me?"

"I'll speak for you," he said.

Germany lost the war. That ended hopes that her triumph would free us from our struggle in the Chaco. We had all been chasing a snake through the grass and now it lay dead on a blood-stained patch of sand. It was particularly disappointing for those who had neglected their farms, expecting to be "home" in the *Reich* soon.

I suppose I might have felt satisfied, in the end, for Jakob had been on the "winning" side. But I didn't feel anyone had won. Perhaps he had been right, but we both were chastened; the entire colony carried the scars of those bitter years. I often wondered, too, whether even in the restorations, in the reconciliations, justice was done. Perhaps it was simply impossible.

In the future, we would be reluctant to speak of those experienes. It was because we were ashamed. We wanted to forget they had happened. Just because peace was restored, repentance declared, didn't mean we were wiling to talk. Though God allowed Scripture to reveal David's adultery and murder, did the king then describe it in his songs? In telling the story he might stir the lust and the covetousness that drove him to arrange the death of a good man. So too, we kept quiet.

The shame I felt was unlike anything I had known before, for it wasn't a recollection of adolescent naivete, nor the realization that innocence was altered by enlarging experience, but rather an intimate knowledge of violence and hatred within me. For months I battered the images of Maria and Mama and Walde in my mind, carrying on angry conversations with them, lashing them with my words. I was torn between the views of my mother and sister and those of my husband. I was unhappy with them all. These emotions and attitudes only washed away gradually; they wore away with time rather than through any holiness or even graciousness on my part.

I was stripped of my boldness. For many years following I was more subdued in my spirit, unable to trust myself. No longer did I see what I had been; I looked fully at what I was.

Chapter 6

The years when the children were small (and Mama suddenly gone in the middle of them) didn't stay in my memory in ordered chronology. The dates of the births were vivid enough, and each child proceeded to grow up through all the proper stages, but the events themselves flowed together into one long line which seemed in retrospect, marked mainly by weariness.

It had made a difference, of course, that Mama was no longer on the *Hof* to help me. Perhaps I appreciated for the first time how much work she had done. At the same time, however, I discovered that I could manage fairly well alone. I even kept up my flower beds, though now their beauty was wrung out of the edges of my strength.

Gretel, named after my mother, (though we usually called her Gretchen) as Tina had been after Jakob's, was born a scant year following her sister. I who had struggled to have even one child, now had three in rather short order. (Nothing was predictable with me, it seemed.) Gretchen's birth was followed in ten months by a miscarriage. I didn't regain my strength sufficiently between these pregnancies.

Then Jakob and I both suffered attacks of malaria. When I recovered I was still not well, but I forced myself up in spite of my weakness. Daily necessities and the dependency of my family pulled me up; I couldn't easily shake the nagging compulsion of my duties: there was always a child to nurse or feed, or a meal to prepare. Cooking, washing, gardening couldn't wait. I helped Jakob on the fields too, with planting or harvesting.

The concerns of the day pressed upon me before I was fully awake and there were times when I prayed earnestly that I wouldn't renege on the dawn but have the willingness to rise and run my course as the sun did. Run until the children were in bed in the evening. Then I sewed and mended until my eyes were too heavy to keep open. Insects whirred about me and the lamp. I had to move my hand through them between every stitch, to clear them away. When it was impossible to remain awake, when I was no longer angry at the winged nuisances but let them gather, I snuffed out the dim light and stumbled to bed.

One evening after just such a busy, full day I dropped onto my cot and began to sob.

"What's the matter?" Jakob asked, immediately beside me, his hand on my arm.

"I'm just so exhausted. That's all."

"But what's the matter?"

"That. I'm exhausted."

"Are you sick again?"

"No. Tired."

He let me cry.

"I wish I was a little girl like Tina or Gretchen," I sniffled. "Then I would climb on Mama's lap and be safe. I wouldn't realize I was consuming her time, keeping her from her work. I would take her love and her lap for granted, like they do mine, and be safe . . . "

"I'll hold you," Jakob said.

"I know."

Yes, he wrapped his arms around me and comforted me, but he would feel my body against his and his passion rose. He was a man, I didn't hold it against him, but that's why I didn't want his consolation. I was unwilling to face another pregnancy.

I want to be a child again, I thought, a young girl without responsibility. Without the obligation to nurture or care for anyone else. Neither the children nor him.

"What's the matter, Anna?" Jakob asked, puzzled as I began to cry anew.

It was nothing but tiredness. But if he wanted other reasons, well!

"We're so poor!" And "you're no farmer" (but I didn't say that aloud.)

And "I get nowhere! Today I cleaned the garden. I felt I was bent in two when I finally finished and tried to stand. But never mind, it was clean. But maybe the bugs take the plants. Or it won't rain and they'll shrivel. And for sure, in a few days the weeds are there again. And then I make noodles for the soup. How many minutes did it take to eat? Hours of work, for that. I made pickles. How long do they last? A few days at most."

"But we enjoyed eating them," Jakob said. "It's not without importance, Anna, that we enjoyed that meal. The noodles nourished us. We all had enough."

"Don't you get a little joy out of it?" he probed. "Seeing the garden clean, and all of us eating heartily at the table?"

"Not when I'm tired."

"But otherwise?"

His voice was so gentle, it softened my frustration. Still, I viewed my life compacted by fatigue into a thick woven rope of

213

unending, always repetitious tasks.

But I had to admit, "I suppose there's a bit. Before I start. The determination to have it done and finished. I get something from that, I guess. Because I can't bear to leave it. Because I care."

"Yes."

Jakob got into his bed.

"It would be easier if I didn't care," I said.

Jakob laughed. "Oh Anna, you're a good woman. That's why you care. You're a good mother."

I was silent, thinking: and that's another thing! I'm not a good mother. I'm impatient with them. I push them away with my hurry. I'm never finished with them either. And I want riches. I'm proud. I don't pray enough. I'm not submissive. My temper is too quick.

"I love you, Anna," he said.

"I know. I love you too."

"Will you be all right now?" There was longing in his voice. But I pushed it aside. I had to.

"Yes. Good night."

He knelt to pray aloud, but I didn't hear the end. I fell asleep. I awoke abruptly some time later and saw that Jakob was gone.

Then I heard the latch and his steps. He came into the bedroom with a snow-white queen of the night, the elusive cactus flower that opened only to the soft light of the moon or at dusk or dawn.

"Where've —"

"Just walking," he said.

"It's beautiful. It's simply beautiful!" Even in the nearly dark room, lit only by the moon, the flower was radiant, the slender delicate petals a luminous white.

"Suddenly in the shadows along the fence I found what I

wanted, a shining white head," Jakob said happily. "I wasn't very careful taking it off. I scratched my hand on the cactus spikes that guard it. It even bled."

I reached out my arms to thank him with a kiss, and what was the use of holding back after that? I knew what would happen and didn't care. He smelled fresh, of earth and air, his cheeks were cool, and the bristles on his chin tickled my ears.

My intuition about the consequences were correct. But I lost this baby too, the third one, this time in the sixth month. It would have been our second son.

Another memory . . . It was a Sunday evening, but had Gretchen been the baby, or was it later, with Liese? I don't remember the time, nor why the trip was so late and long. had we been to the Harbiner Corner, visiting Jakob's cousin? I think so.

Jakob and I sat on the grey seat in the front of the wagon and the children sprawled on the floor in the back, covered with blankets. It was hot and humid, however, and they wouldn't stay under the covers. It wasn't cold, David exclaimed.

"Stay under the blankets!" I ordered. "It's because of the mosquitoes. Look how they bite you!"

The insects hovered around us in eager clouds, whining in our ears and landing wherever they could.

"Children, stay covered!" I exhorted them repeatedly, waving my free arm frantically over the baby on my breast to keep them off her. Rosita tried to help the younger ones, but they didn't understand and began to cry.

Jakob stopped the wagon and went to the road edge and broke two branches from a tree. I climbed into the back with the children. With one hand I held the baby, with the other I moved the cluster of leaves vigorously over them to hold the mosquitoes at bay. Rosita did the same for the baby in my lap.

I began to sing. (I felt the mosquitoes biting my back and

legs.)

> When I see the evening shadow
> Softly falling o'er the meadow
> All my trials seem forgot
> All my trials seem forgot.

I loved the simple, lilting melody, with its octave leap of
hope in the middle.

> And the hours have swiftly vanished,
> Sorrow, tears and grief are banished,
> There's a day that endeth not.
> There's a day that endeth not.

"I don't know," I said to Jakob, "I'll miss the evenings and
night. Endless day?"

"Not then, you won't."

After the children were asleep I crawled with stiff limbs
back to the seat beside him. A cool breeze fanned us now and
the mosquitoes disappeared. A gleaming full moon rose majestically on our left. It was so huge and close that I felt I could
reach up and pluck it out of the sky, yet I wouldn't have dared
touch it. It shone as if holy.

Then I glanced down and saw that the baby's eyes were
wide open. And there I saw the moon again, there, small and
luminous, reflected in the dark pupils of the little one's eyes.

"Oh Jakob!" I whispered, "She's staring at the moon. Her
eyes are so big. I guess it's the first time she's really seen it, and
she's thinking, 'Now what in the world is that?'"

I chuckled. "That's the moon, my little one. That's the
moon." I crooned and rocked her until she fell asleep again.

I recall that we talked together until we reached our village, and that the moon stayed with us during our journey. What

did we discuss? Nothing profound, probably; probably our hopes and plans for the crops and the cows and the children. Simple conversation, the talk of poor pioneers gathering courage in the night.

And I also remember the Sunday in spring, walking to church, when I realized I wasn't tired anymore.

That evening I offered to let the children play and go for the cows myself. It had rained. The sweet fragrance of the 'yellow kitten' blossoms wafted into my nostrils. I found some of those bushes and touched clusters of the tiny furry flowers to my lips and eagerly inhaled the lovely sensuous odor. The 'widow-wood' bushes were also blooming, and the rosy brown hues in their various stages provided a striking panorama.

Gretchen was two, it was half a year since I lost the boy, and I was alive again. My body survived winter, it was full of strength, green! I stretched and began to run, gulping the air and its perfume; I ran like a child, calling the cows to come home.

Chapter 7

We had lived in the Chaco for twenty-five years and paused as a colony to celebrate the anniversary of our founding. On that cold, overcast day I sat in the crowded church, squeezed between our youngest daughter Liese, seven, and my mother, eighty-five. (Though she rarely attended public services anymore, Mama must, as an original pioneer, be present on this special day.) I was worried. I tried to listen and remember and reflect, and I did it too, but I was tensed for betrayal.

It happened this way. Next to the restless, always wiggling Liese, sat my friend Susi. Since the Paraguayan dignitaries hadn't arrived yet, we leaned our heads together and visited in whispers. She said, "Kornelius is talking of going to Canada."

She didn't need to fill in the details. Susi and her elderly father Wilhelm Froese lived on the original farmstead; the youngest son, Abram, still single, did the work. But it was Kornelius, married and with seven children of his own, living on the *Hof* next to theirs who was the acting head of both units. If he talked of going, that meant they were all talking of going. If he

219

went, they would too.

"Are you serious?" I breathed, shocked.

"No matter how much it improves here, there'll always be the northwind. And the heat. You can't correct that."

For the briefest of moments I thought, what if I had married Kornelius? But it wasn't a wish and I dismissed it immediately.

"Do you know what's going around?" Susi continued confidentially. "That only the poor and the stupid stay here."

She spoke within the privilege of friendship, probably thinking I would appreciate this information, but she didn't know that this comment wounded me deeply. I felt she had already forsaken us, and rejected me; I trembled inwardly as if I had been left alone.

I couldn't answer either because the service started, even though the guests of honor still hadn't come. With great shuffling and clearing of throats we stood to sing the magnificent opening hymn:

> Holy God, we praise Thy Name;
> Lord of all, we bow before Thee;
> All on earth Thy scepter claim,
> All in heav'n above adore Thee.
> Infinite Thy vast domain,
> Everlasting is Thy reign.

I gave myself wholeheartedly to this song. But when I sat down on the hard wooden pew I felt as if my energy was consumed. I was tired, for I had worked with other women the whole previous day preparing food for the festivities, and I hadn't slept well. And the northwind and sun could never be altered, and only the stupid and the poor hadn't yet grasped this irrefutable fact!

I told myself to concentrate, for today was an important occasion. I placed a restraining hand against Liese and gave her a warning look. She had better be a good girl or else! it said. I placed my firm hand on her leg. The speaker was mentioning changes. I thought, this blond baby of ours, already seven, tells me of the changes. We have made progress indeed.

Liese wasn't born at home like my other children, nor in the colony's first hospital, a simple adobe clay shelter with a thatched roof, paneless windows, dirt floors, and primitive equipment, without a sterilizer, without a doctor to call if something went wrong.

No, she was born in the colony's new brick hospital which boasted five cisterns, electric light, a sterilizer, a dentist's room, a pharmacy, and a laboratory.

She was born at the end of the drought. That was followed immediately by a second winter of eight months without rain. Those years, and also in 1950, we had terrible grasshoppers, but now there were poisons for them and the insect plagues. And an experimental station had been established and new grasses and crops were being developed. An agricultural worker from North America introduced a buffalo grass that was perfectly suited for the Chaco soil. How this would enhance cattle farming! Although our struggle was far from over, I could wish a farmer as a husband for my Liese. It would certainly be easier for her.

And what would Liese know of oxen? There was hardly a team of them to be seen on the farms or streets anymore. Horses were used now; a better strain had been developed. And already the colony had purchased several trucks for transporting our produce to market. Roads were being improved; the proposed Trans-Chaco highway would link us to the capital, Asuncion. We had a new modern cotton gin; our colony head had travelled to North America, seeking credit for the colony; yes, we had made progress!

But still, the stupid and the poor and the wind and the sun . . . Susi's words beat against me. The crisis had continued in the form of one family leaving, and then another and another. The return of one of them to the Chaco after trying life in Canada was a small triumph for the "Chaco patriots," as those like Jakob, who would see nothing bad in the Chaco, were called. But it hadn't stopped the demoralizing outflow, some going to Canada, some to Brazil, others to places like Germany, Argentina or the east side of Paraguay. It was a slow, troubling migration, for we feared, "Who will be next? Can we trust our neighbors' words or will they leave tomorrow?"

Obviously we couldn't trust anyone if Susi, the faithful and uncomplaining Susi, also entertained such notions.

Now the preacher was reminding us of our arrival in this unfamiliar peculiar place. Some women, he said, sat down and cried. Not me, I thought ruefully. Not me. I was a silly and courageous girl; the women might have cried, but not the girls!

I let him talk on and looked at my bare, tanned legs with their pale hair. My heavy black shoes, worn only on Sundays or special occasions, pinched my toes and pushed the thick leather of my feet into narrow forms to which they weren't accustomed. My toes and soles were soft when I arrived here, and I had been proud of my shapely ankles and feet.

How many kilometers had they walked in twenty-five years? Too many of them barefoot too, all on the soil of this wilderness (I included our house with its mud and manure floors). Before sixteen I travelled days from one continent to another, and then for twenty-five years I didn't step anywhere but the limited earth of this one small sequestered settlement.

Mama's weighty body shifted suddenly against my shoulder. I saw that she had slumped without realizing it; her eyes were closed. I decided to let her nap.

"What helped us through the early years?" the speaker

asked. "Trust in God," he continued, "and the Mennonite relief organization's help; our feeling of personal freedom; the friendly reception of Paraguay; and the realization of the sorrier fate of so many Mennonites in Russia who hadn't been able to leave."

Add "no alternatives" to your list, I thought, and also "love." I was the age when I started dreaming about boys; one hoped, and that helped, even if they died of typhus or turned rebellious with it all, going off to Puerto Casado or Asuncion to work, not coming back. With Jakob, I had stopped wishing and basked in his steady, faithful acceptance. That kept me here. Add "my humor and energy" too, though it might not be much beside Jakob's piety or the calm submission of a Susi.

What the speakers said in their reports (of our release from Moscow, the various groups that came here, our early struggles with plagues and death) was also true: God had been with us. In the fiery heat, or as by cloud, He was here.

A song sang itself in my head as I listened to the stories I knew.

> We'll tarry by the Living Waters,
> Tarry by the Living Waters,
> Tarry by the Living Waters,
> Tarry by the Fount of Life.

God's grace was water for sunbaked and parched soil; it was rain for the separations and cracks and tears, for the tensions and divisions and loss of people we'd experienced in the colony. These, of course, wouldn't be mentioned at a public festival, with delegates from other places listening in. And even if Susi left, He wouldn't leave. God was everywhere.

I felt better, having worked my way to this point. I had to put my hand on Liese's leg to hold her still again; she kicked at

223

the bench in front of us as if it were a ball.

Near noon the official Paraguayan visitors finally arrived at the church. In the stir, Mama woke. I pushed against her to assist her in sitting straight.

The men's choir sang in Russian, "We Praise You." And what was this? Tears oozing from Mama's eyes and sliding down the rivulets on her wrinkled cheeks. Immediately my lips began to quiver and my eyes filled with moisture. I dabbed at them with my white handkerchief. I suppose I cried because Mama did and also because I recognized most of the words of the Russian hymn.

Exiting after the service, Susi walked close to me and said, as if the lengthy service was merely a moment's interruption in our conversation, "Kornelius is only talking of it though. We're not sure at all if we will."

"Well, I'm staying," I replied cheerfully, "so it's not only the poor and the stupid left behind."

Susi seemed puzzled by this. "Oh but I never meant you," she said.

Then something funny happened. I saw a woman who looked vaguely familiar, though she must be a visitor. She was middle-aged, somewhat red-faced, but pleasant-looking too; her blond hair was greying, yet she was smiling and youthful and happy.

It was me, reflected in the tiny mirror in the vestibule. For an instant I hadn't recognized that woman and thought those things about her.

My hair was tidy and I was relatively young, yes, forty-one, especially compared to my mother whom Susi and I had to support walking down the aisle. I would celebrate a silver anniversary of my own in two years — mine and Jakob's — and I was still the same Anna as ever. I had gained weight but Jakob never mentioned it.

"Jakob!" I announced later. "We've survived!" I told him that I hadn't recognized myself in the mirror. He found it amusing too; he believed that such a thing could actually happen. I laughed and laughed, thinking about it, but I could see by the expressions on the children's faces that they found their mother's error odd.

Chapter 8

I wasn't surprised that David became a teacher, and a good one too. Even as a boy he was interested in everything. He caught armadillos and turtles, killed snakes and lizards, and then turned them over and studied them. He climbed trees and held cicadas between his fingers, and captured spiders to examine. He loved to read, though we had very few books. He was also a serious boy, and absolutely honest like Jakob was. So it was no wonder that he became a minister as well.

I forgot the details of his childhood — the crawling and first steps and illnesses and school experiences — but clearly remembered the sweet-water clarity of his spirit, and that intense curiosity.

One evening at dusk, with reddish traces of the sun's departure on the earth's western edge, and the half-moon and her companion, the Evening Star, shining brightly, Jakob and twelve-year-old David and I searched our fields and bush for the cow about to give birth. We found her; she had managed. She was in the field with her calf so we could return home satisfied with our mission; but first we sat awhile to rest.

We listened to the breezes stirring the leaves of the paratodo and yellow quebracho trees near them, and the urundey at our heads. The wind whispered. It sighed and seemed to speak the same mysterious and melancholic sounds as certain other voices of the earth, voices Jakob and I had heard, but David never: the ceaseless lap, lap, lap of waves in a bay, or a mountain top towering into the sky, or a river rushing swiftly to sea with the clouds in its face. David had never seen a train or a mountain or a river or a pine forest or a ship. But he didn't seem to mind; and he still dreamt of worlds beyond ours, and had questions about how things could be.

Now he asked, "Papa, I sometimes wonder and I just can't figure it out, how can life go on and on and on, and never end; I mean even after we die. I just don't understand, do you?"

"Not everything."

"How could God always have existed? I want to know how He got there."

"It's hard to understand," Jakob said. "We can't."

"I try to go back and back and back to reach a beginning."

"You just have to believe it."

Typical childhood questions, yet David sat long after they had been answered and puzzled at them some more.

"But it's wonderful, isn't it, David?" Jakob said.

"Yes."

From that unattainable realm of the supernatural, David usually turned to our stories, Jakob's or mine.

"Papa, could you tell me about Russia again?"

Then Jakob would bring out all the stories and the names, as unfamiliar to David as things he hadn't seen: Molotschna and Chortiza, the mother colonies, and Moscow and the Amur, Harbin, Riga. All the names which were the Edens and Egypts and Red Seas of our history, gardens whose gates were closed, stations of salvation. And I was silent, listening to David's questions, and pondering. What did he imagine when he heard them? Did he see them at all as they really had been?

An owl shrieked near us and we jerked, and then laughed together at our fright. The bird hooted again, an eerie call, vibrating as if it had a stone it its mouth.

As we walked home, David marvelled, "It's so wonderful and quiet here in the Chaco."

He and Jakob always found the landscape beautiful.

David's best friend was Theo, the only son of Johann and Leni Walde. The boys kept the narrow path between our adjoining yards smooth and bare of weeds by all their running back and forth.

"There's always one thing or another between us," I commented to Jakob once when Johann had reported finding our cow in his kafir field, "yet our boys are inseparable."

"It rebukes us when the next generation won't perpetuate our sins," he replied.

Theo was garrulous, witty and confident, speaking about matters with the same air of authority as his father, his back straight and his head tilted to increase his height. When the boys were in a group I noticed that David supplied statements from which his partner's quick humor could spring and then he roared with the rest at Theo's comical Low-German one-liners.

One day, it was in 1957, the year he started to teach, David said to me, "Theo's going to Canada, Mama." Books were scattered around him on the table but he took a break from his studies at my urging. I brought him a glass of freshly-squeezed grapefruit juice.

"Oh?"

"His father has a rich cousin over there, who's going to pay his way. Theo will work for him until he can repay it. He tells people it's a visit, but he told me that it would be a one-way

trip. He'll work on his immigration papers once he's there . . .
He says I should come too."

"And?"

"I told him we don't have the money, for one thing. But
you have a brother there, don't you?"

"He's not that well off. He's invited Oma to come. He did
say once he would try to help if we wanted to move, but . . . "

"Theo offered to pay for me once he's established."

"Oh?" Theo, I thought, is as free with his offers as a
rooster with his crowing.

"He says we're like froggies in a dry well here, staring up
at the sky. He says there's no future in the Chaco."

"Froggies!" I was irritated by the silly, diminutive word,
but I tried not to show it. David didn't readily confide his
thoughts and I wanted him to continue.

"He says there's a world of opportunity up there. He
figures all the smart ones will leave Paraguay."

I had heard that line before. I sighed. "Do you want to go
to Canada?"

David took some time to answer, drawing carefully to the
bottom of his tumbler for the last of his drink. "No, I don't think
so. I feel this is my place. I'm nearly ready to begin teaching. I
don't want to think of leaving, not now at least."

Three months later I stood beside David at the airport. I
came for Theo's sake, because he had often been in our home,
and for David's. Theo had a new hat and shirt and he waved
jauntily to his old friends, embraced his parents rather casually,
and was lost into the belly of the plump DC-3. David waved,
and as the plane lifted noisily into the air, he and I walked silently home (we had moved into town by then.)

David didn't reveal his feelings, but I believed I knew
them. Theo hadn't kept faith with David and the dreams they
had together. I had heard them boasting about their future cot-

ton fields and cattle herds, but Theo hadn't taken even the core truth of the big, overblown boyish plans seriously.

I decided that David was also envious. Theo would travel, see other places, earn much money, and my son would stay in a limited world with only the stars for any sense of life beyond the Paraguayan hinterland. Theo flew away with a light heart while David with his responsibility and dedication and loyalty must stay. He had absorbed — lapped it up like a kitten its milk — Jakob's commitment to this place. David wouldn't be able to leave because Jakob's zeal would always ring in his ears. There was nothing I could do to change that.

"Will you miss him?" I asked cautiously.

"I don't know."

"You think he'll write?"

"He said he would. I don't care, really."

It might have been true. It might have been that I was more hurt over Theo's departure than David was.

David fell in love with Katie Walde. Would we never be rid of the Waldes? I wondered. Our relationship was politely cordial following the stressful break and reconciliation of the 40s, but it would probably never lose the strain all the past events introduced. It was easiest simply to move in different circles; why struggle unnecessarily? But how could I keep that family, that man especially, at the fringes of my life when even our children unwittingly brought us together?

That aside, I also asked myself what David saw in Johann's youngest. Her hair was dull brown like the soil, and pulled back into a loose bun at the back of her neck. She could have worn it shorter, even curled, as some girls did, but apparently she didn't want the bother of the work. Katie's face was plain, quite unexceptional in every way.

She was, I knew, intelligent enough. She was a year younger than David and a fellow-student of his at the teacher

231

training school. When we learned of David's interest in her, I remembered earlier comments he had made: "Katie's shy at first, but when she gives a presentation she seems to lose that. She'll make an excellent teacher." Another time, as if marvelling, "Katie knows nearly as much as I do about the animals and plants of the Chaco."

Yes. As a child Katie was the one in pursuit of the chickens or running with her dog far through the field to the bush, out of sight, or perched in a tree, and one might even walk under it and be startled by her solemn face, for she didn't laugh if you discovered her there. She had seemed wild to me then, and her fine hair didn't stay in braids. She played alone rather than with our Tina or other girls in the village.

I followed Jakob's admonition not to seek to dissuade David, however, and when Katie visited us, I tried to like her. On the first visit we two women had a few minutes alone in the kitchen. I was nervous. Then Katie confessed, "I really don't know much about cooking or baking."

No, I thought, your mother had all those older girls to help and left you to your own devices, and now you're helpless in the kitchen.

But I said, smiling, "If I notice that David's getting thin, may I send something over for him to eat?"

She giggled and said, "Of course."

I was pleased that I had replied so light-heartedly, for it provided a moment of understanding between us.

Apart from that one exchange, however, Katie made no effort to gain my goodwill; she stayed shyly at David's side as if glued to him, directing her entire interest his way. His family mattered not one whit to her, I felt.

After the visit when I knew David was waiting for my opinion, all I could say was, "Katie will be a wife with whom you'll be able to talk, with her being a teacher too."

David and Katie were engaged. They saw each other frequently during the courtship and engagement, and also wrote each other daily letters. I felt this was excessive, but Jakob, so strict in some things, was surprisingly tolerant about it. "Let it be," he said.

Three weeks before the wedding: David was sitting in his room at his table, writing that day's missive. I wanted to bake and urgently needed sugar. He would go, he said. After he left the house I was overcome by a terrible desire to read the letter. I was alone and gave in to the temptation. I fixed the exact position of the sheet of notepaper, pushed under a book, in my mind, and lifted it out to read. The handwriting was uneven, rushed-looking.

> My dear dear Katie. Again I sit down and express my longing to see you, to talk with you as we did on Saturday. The days are so long and empty when I have nothing to look forward to in the evening. I dread next week because I'll be in the village alone, and I won't see you once. But I'll be preparing the house and everything there with you in mind. Now it's only three weeks, and then you'll be there with me. We'll always and always be together. I think of your beauty and your very soft skin and I long for you. I can't bear to have only my thoughts of you and not the real person. But I must wait. Soon I'll be able to hold you and know that you are completely mine, by all rights.
>
> We'll work together in everything, won't we, even after we have children. I don't see why we can't do it that way: I'll help you with them and with things on the yard and house, and you'll help me in my work. You will be able to advise me and suggest things. It is wonderful to share with someone else my

233

dream of advancing the educational work in
our colony, of serving our people and truly advancing the lives of others through our service.
Perhaps I'd dreamed such a thing might be
possible — to have a partner who understands
this, but I guess I was still surprised when it
truly happened, when I got to know you and
love you. You were so quick in the classes. I
noticed that about you right away.   You
mustn't be so shy about yourself though.

I knew I should put it down, but no, I kept on. I couldn't
stop.

Isn't it strange how we went to school in
the village all those years together and didn't
regard the other as anything more than another
child, even a nuisance? Do you know my first
memory of you? I was at your place, with Theo
probably, and I saw you sitting with a turtle in
your lap. You were stroking and talking to it.
Theo said, "She's crazy. Talks to animals as if
they're people." Oh Katie, I smile to think of
that now. You with your gentle, little-child-
like way still. You with your ideas of caring for
animals on our yard. You have so many
thoughts and so many moods. I love you,
Katie!
But I was troubled about what you said
Saturday, that your father doesn't like me. That
he's not happy with us. I'm troubled, Katie, not
because I think it's such a concern but because
it so affected your spirits. Please don't worry
about it. (Don't you think it's the same as when
you mentioned that you felt Mama didn't like
you? You're taking her boy away, that's all,

and it's hard for her. But she'll get used to it. She works at things.) And just remind yourself of this: soon it'll be just the two of us, and what will it matter what anyone thinks then? I wait for our wedding day, for then we'll be together and we'll be able to talk about everything. Then we'll have time to know each other, and nothing he or anyone says will affect us.

When I leave you these days, I feel I've not even begun. You're still a mystery and a wonder to me. But soon you'll be mine and you'll not need to pull away from me when I have my arm around your waist and jump into the tree in the lane. Have you really climbed it two hundred times? Oh yes, I believe you, you've counted. It's something you'd do! Katie, you're so silly and you make me laugh, but the longing to climb after you in the tree and never let you down until I've possessed you and . . . .

When I came to the place where David stopped I was covered with perspiration, though I'd scarcely breathed during my hurried perusal of the closely-written lines. I felt as if I'd memorized them and wouldn't be able to forget them, for even as I replaced the sheet of paper, which I now despised, the flame of my curiosity reduced by its satisfaction to powdered ashes, and left the room, they followed me. I shivered in spite of the heat, afraid. (He had judged me in the letter, but I didn't dwell on that. Fair or unfair, I deserved it and more for what I had done.)

I was afraid for David, uttering those innocent repetitions and not knowing yet what he would suffer in that marriage, and afraid because I had intruded into the place where a mother should allow much, much distance. To read the longing flowing from his pen, seeming to him a pure and easy passion, was no shock, but rather pain that I had taken on myself needlessly and wouldn't be quickly rid of now. Yes, I read it and knew from experience the complexity of that longing — with its restlessness, power, joy and shame, its humor, even the grossness if one wished to be really truthful and comprehensive, and then her already leaping from him into a tree. Better to pretend that nothing existed than to see so clearly his entry into the mysterious intimacies I already knew. Did I feel he wasn't ready? That marriage was safe for me, but not to be entrusted to a son whom I had first known totally helpless? Perhaps my motives were as pure and over-simplified as his; I was a mother, I wished to spare him.

Still, I would have allowed him everything, had I had power to avert the tragic ending of his love affair with Katie. She drowned ten days before their wedding.

I was preparing for bed, unwinding my hair, when I thought I heard David's voice outside on the *Hof*. The frogs in the ditches and dugouts, full of water from the very heavy rains of that week, croaked loudly. They seemed to be animals a hundred times larger when they began to croak and honk from every waterhole, so I didn't think further about David's voice. He had set out on foot to visit Katie in the village several hours earlier, but wouldn't be home until later, again walking. Then Jakob came in saying Katie was dead, she had drowned. *Prediger* Rahn had driven David back in the wagon.

I wanted to rush immediately to my boy.

"Leave him, Anna. I talked with him already."

But I didn't heed him. "Don't worry, Jakob," I said. "Do you think I'll chatter all over him?"

I leaned against the closed door of David's room. There was no line of light under it.

"David, are you in bed?"

"Yes."

"David?"

"I'm okay. I'll talk in the morning."

"Good night, David."

I returned to Jakob. "I had to let him know I knew, at least."

"She was in the dugout — the one at the back of their land — behind that strip of bush Walde has. Perhaps she went in after some animal. After one of their ducks perhaps. Once earlier, she'd said, there was a heron there, more than once even. She's not a swimmer. Not a good swimmer. She was in with her clothes."

"Who said all this? Who discovered it?"

"Johann."

I turned quickly. I stepped in front of Jakob at the window. I had uncovered something important; something missing a long time and given up as lost had been found.

"Jakob," I whispered. "Johann did it, don't you think?"

"Anna, what are you saying?" But my husband didn't move a muscle of his neck; his head was motionless and his eyes studied the path of moonlight crossing the garden. Then:

"Rumors will be scattered like duck's down. We won't add to them . . . Anna?"

"Yes?"

"You must not suggest it to anyone."

"I won't," I said.

"Poor, poor David," I moaned, thinking of him lying awake in his dark room.

"It's a terrible thing for him," Jakob said.

"So, instead of baking honey cookies for the wedding tomorrow, there is a funeral?"

"Tomorrow at ten."

* * * * * * * * * * * * * * * * * * *

David taught in one of the outlying villages and didn't come home often, but every visit reminded us that he was still mourning; he was pale, quiet, unhappy.

"Why did it have to happen to him?" I agonized to Jakob.

Then Jakob showed me some verses he found in Lamentations: "It is good for a man that he bear the yoke in his youth. He sitteth alone and keepeth silence, because he hath borne it upon him . . . But though the Lord cause grief, yet will he have compassion according to the multitude of his mercies."

"Should I show him?" he asked

"Yes, they're good," I said.

For myself, I decided to ask Susi's advice about David. (Her family ended up staying in the Chaco.) She spent a day helping me apply a fresh coat of whitewash to the inside walls of the house. She earned a little money for herself doing this for people.

After we had worked and talked about everything else all morning, I swallowed and said,

"Susi, I've often wondered how you got over what happened to you . . . the rape . . . in Russia."

My friend placed her coarse brush in a nearly-empty pail of caulking material carefully so as not to splash it, and looked at me in alarm.

"Do you mean . . . do you mean?"

"I heard your father tell that story."

"He did?"

So she thought that no one knew? "I'm sorry. I shouldn't have mentioned it."

"Oh, I don't know. It doesn't really matter. I never . . . I hardly ever think about it. It's a long time ago." She wiped a rough hand over her forehead. "I had no idea that you knew."

"Oh Susi, I'm sorry." I hurried to mix another bucket of whitewash. But she followed me.

"It doesn't matter, really. I don't think of it. I guess I was just surprised that you knew."

"I think of it often when I see you."

"Why?"

"It seems so terrible I guess. And you've suffered so well. That's what I've wondered about, that you're serene and . . . so gentle." I was eager to praise her. "How did you forgive?"

"Oh my," Susi said, her voice hollow.

"I did it for my mother," she said. "That's how I saw it."

"Your mother?"

"They took anyone. What did it matter to them whether the woman was old or young? I think it would have killed my mother. I was glad to be there, to spare her."

"But for you . . . I mean, wasn't it terrible?"

"Of course. I was young though. I had time to recover. It's been a long time ago. I was still flexible." Susi glanced sharply at me as if to make sure this wouldn't be misunderstood. "She was old, at least it seemed old to me then. I felt I spared her. It was bad enough for her, having to hear it behind the door. God made me able to endure, to sacrifice. That's how He made me . . ."

After a pause, she said, "Mother cried a lot. About everything it seemed."

We returned to our painting.

"How can I help David?" I asked.

Susi sighed. "I don't know." She brushed steadily with short even strokes, the whitewash sinking into the wall as if only water. When it dried, however, it would be a sharp clean white.

"Do you remember that Mr. Kroker who was here, studying us — the Chaco and the Mennonites. Writing a book or something?"

Susi murmured affirmation.

"He was in the school, and somehow he and David became friends. Being curious, David probably asked him questions, and of course anybody likes to talk about what they know. Once he even came to our place. Do you remember that? I was *so* nervous. Then he just walked around the land with Jakob and David, looking at plants, and couldn't stay to eat, after all the preparations I had made!

"I guess David told him he'd never seen a stone," I went on. "Then Mr. Kroker went away, to East Paraguay, I think, but he returned for one visit. We went to church in town one Sunday and suddenly David spotted the jeep. He got all excited and when we asked why, it came out. 'Mr.Kroker said he'd bring me some stones,' he said. 'He told me it's not right for a boy to grow up without stones. He says a stone seems dead, but there's life in it if you sit and look at it.' David said this while we were riding on the wagon. Sure enough, we got to church and there was Mr. Kroker, standing outside talking to someone.

"David went right up to him before I could stop him and shook hands. I heard him ask, 'Do you have the stones for me?' I was feeling ill at ease already. Did he think the man would carry stones in his pocket?

"Well, of course Mr. Kroker had completely forgotten. Remember his voice, how hearty and loud it was? He boomed out to the men near him, 'This boy has no stones and I said I'd bring him some. I forgot all about it, my boy.' He slapped David on the shoulder and said, 'As if I don't have enough to think about!' They all laughed. I don't think he meant it unkindly, but David is so sensitive, you know. I could see the disappointment even from the back because his ears got all red. He blushes worse than any girl I know. Then Kroker said to David, 'Well, boy, you'll have to grow up without stones after all.'

"It wasn't unkind, but really, it was too cheerful. Couldn't he realize what he was doing? David acted as if he didn't mind, but I saw his face and knew better."

"I heard that Mr. Kroker said good things about us Mennonites in his book," Susi said.

"Yes, I heard that too . . . . But you know, Susi, that's the look I see on David's face now. If I could do something! If I could just help!"

"I don't think you can," she offered. "Of course you can pray."

"I do."

"That's all then. The rest is his."

"It's so hard on him," I protested.

"Yes. We all pity him. But time will help."

"I can hardly bear it!" I cried. "I see him suffering and so unhappy, and it nearly makes me sick. If I could just do something!"

Susi sat down, took her glasses off, and pressed her palms against her eyeballs. "Maybe my mother didn't have it any easier than I did," she said, as if to herself. "Maybe I didn't spare her at all."

She reflected. "But you're strong, Anna. And so is David. He's an adult."

I prepared refreshments for us. We drank our cold coffee, and then, having confided so much already, I said, "I have such a struggle, too, trying to sort everything out. I never thought she was the one for David. I was sure he'd be unhappy with her later . . . Now she's gone and I'm glad it didn't work out, but he's so broken-hearted. Either way, he's unhappy. I wish I understood why things happen, even in the beginning. It torments me . . . Really Susi, I wish something would happen to me instead; it's easier than watching someone you love with such a burden."

"Who knows?" Susi said gently. "Each of us has a load to

carry and who can say whose is the hardest?"

"I don't know . . . . "

"Don't worry about him Anna. Both of you are strong and will get over it."

"Oh Susi, you say that because you're an angel," I said.

Then she went on to tell me she had refused a good offer of marriage once (she wouldn't divulge the name) because she felt she must stay with her widowed father and care for him. I happened to know — at least local rumor had it — that Wilhelm Froese would have remarried if only his children had encouraged it. I recognized with a shock that even an angel might sacrifice more than is necessary. Thereby, she unknowingly helped me the most: I must let David own his sorrow.

Chapter 9

Jakob plugged the cord into the wall outlet while the girls and I watched. As the fridge began to hum, Liese clapped her hands.

"Now we'll live like kings!" I declared.

We certainly felt we were: we could make ice, keep milk and soup and meat fresh, and the leftover breakfast coffee was cold for supper. It was a wonderful, almost unbelievable convenience, still a luxury in the colony, and at first we all opened the door much too often, just to see the gleaming shelves and our cold food.

We bought the fridge after my brother Peter in Canada died suddenly of a heart attack and left some money to Mama in his will. She immediately insisted on dividing it between Maria and me ("I don't need anything," she said). It wasn't a large sum in dollars, but in our circumstances it was a rare gift and made possible the purchase of our first modern appliance.

The small white fridge, set on a table in one corner, symbolized a new and easier phase in our lives.

In 1956 Jakob was offered a job at the new butter and

cheese factory in town, and decided at once that he should accept it. We sold our farm to Isaak Pauls, whom Tina later married, and bought the K. Hiebert place in town (they emigrated to Brazil). The move meant that David and the girls could live at home instead of boarding out during their high school studies.

We were also able, in this exchange, to purchase some pasture land on which we kept a small herd of cattle to supplement our income. On our *Hof* in town we had a cow and chickens, and planted a garden. Occasionally I did laundry or cleaning for North Americans living in the colony. So, although our means were still modest, we lived more comfortably than we had before. Our house was larger than the one in the village; it was built under one roof instead of having the kitchen and sleeping quarters separate.

Our years in town were good ones. The children were no longer small, we had a regular income, Jakob enjoyed his work and we were in good health. Of course, I always had enough to do — the work never ran away — and there was David's sorrow and my worries over Liese. But still, they were good years. I didn't miss the village as much as I had feared initially; it seemed that we had entered a new world with all the excitement of new beginnings, even though it was only a few kilometers distance and the essentials of our life remained quite familiar. I missed the algorrobo most of all, though I now had a beautiful lapacho tree with purple blossoms in spring, providing a wide, round shade for our chairs.

Our life in town had a pleasant and regular pattern. Every morning at six the siren at the industrial plant blew. I was already up, ready to milk. (I reluctantly gave up milking in 1970, because of the rheumatism in my hands. Then Jakob brought milk from the creamery.) At quarter to seven, the siren sounded to warn him and the school children to be on their way. At seven

244

it whistled again and then I thought, now he's at work, or they're at school, and I would pray for each of them. The whistle announced noon, when they came home for the noon meal, the big meal of the day. It whistled to signal the end of siesta and again at two, when the afternoon work hours began. And again at six. Jakob came home, drank cold coffee, and we worked in the yard or at tasks around the house, and ate supper at 7:30. My work fit into this rhythm: I didn't mind being alone and I welcomed them home. It was the right amount, I thought, of both.

Mama came to live with us again, in town. This time it wasn't her decision, but ours, the children's, made for her. She acquiesced; now she felt that whatever we decided she must obey. She decided she was old, too old; she wished, she said, that she could die; she lost her confidence.

"You'll have it better in town," Maria told her. "Nearer doctors and so on."

"Mama's been with me fourteen years," Maria said to us. We understood her suggestion, and offered Mama a room in our new home.

Fourteen years ago I had said to Jakob, "Mama's moved and now we're alone, Jakob, just as we were when my parents disappeared so you could court me." We had fourteen years of evenings under the algorrobo, we and our children, not shy and eager as lovers, but as a family with ordinary conversation like comfortable, everyday clothes.

Now I took my mother back as one who needed care; I took her back as a child.

As Maria and I settled her into her room in our house, Mama rubbed her eyes, looking earnestly at us. "I see you're doing everything I once did. And you're already a grandmother, Maria!"

Maria was a grandmother; Nikolaus was a father. The boy I nurtured with deliberately spilled milk, the small companion I

245

once favored in particular, was a father and remembered nothing much of me. He was no longer winsome, like a newborn puppy curled in my hand; he never spoke to me anymore, he didn't seem interested when I sat beside him at a family gathering and tried to tell him the story of how puzzled he was when we first stood on the bare staked-out *Hof* in our village, looking about for our home.

"I can't believe either that my boy is a father," Maria laughed.

That's what has happened to the years, I thought. He's a father and I take my mother back to be mothered: to be old and dependent and weak in my house.

But I was patient with her, more patient than I had expected to be, tender with her numerous ailments and lack of will (no easier, I felt, than the irrational stubbornness of some older people I knew), and gladly sat with her for an hour or so many afternoons, doing handwork, visiting with her. When I resented the demands of her care (she could walk, but otherwise did little for herself), I hid it. I guarded our relationship fiercely. Who listened like a mother does? Now I had her with me, and I could talk and talk of every bit of news, everything the children brought home, all my worries and concerns, sharing even my tears, and she heard it all, though she said little; she was a mother and she took it and stored it up, as in a bottle.

And, with her increasing dependence and frailty, I could also listen to her. Now I asked questions about Papa; I asked about their years in Russia; I received her stories and probed them, unafraid to be interested in my parents' lives as I was when I was younger, thinking then it implied submission or a style of relationship which I was hoping to reverse.

At ninety, Mama fell on her way to the latrine and broke her hip. It became infected, and too weak to resist the malfunction of her body, Mama's overall health deteriorated rapidly.

"She's approaching her end," the doctor warned us.

I undertook long vigils at her bedside. I clung to her. Although I was exhausted from staying awake, each time I left or slept at home I feared that Mama would die while I was gone.

I wished that my aged parent might be released from her pain, and yet, to be motherless! I wasn't ready for that. I had been the last child, the baby born to Mama at the end of her childbearing years, and I hadn't had her long enough. I was relatively young.

Then the doctor, quoting Scripture said, "What man is he that liveth, and shall not see death?" Yes. but what a thing to say! That was part of the terror too. I wasn't so young after all. Mama would die, and then I moved into position. I was next.

Now Mama seemed not to hear my news about the children and Jakob. She scarcely noticed the roses I brought.

Once, however, she whispered, her voice dry as the wind, "I didn't know if it was right to send you off to help others in the epidemic."

"Mama, that was fine."

"I sent you out into the middle of it. I prayed for you constantly . . . . I couldn't have forgiven myself if you'd caught it . . . ."

"Nothing happened, Mama. Klaus died on our very yard, so it was there too, had it been my destiny."

"I prayed constantly . . . God spare her!"

At night when she woke, Mama commanded with a puff of breath, "Sing!"

I sang her favorite hymn, the one she taught me.

> Lord, Thou ne'er forsakest
> Him who waits on Thee;
> None has e'er rejected
> Wouldst Thou then leave me?

I knew the verses from memory and sang each one slowly, savoring the simple, beautiful melody.

> All my pain and anguish
> All my grief and care;
> All my greatest burdens
> Thou wilt surely bear.

My voice was steady. It hovered in the still, moonlit room
as sure and miraculous as a hummingbird at flowers. On the last
lines, however, unwanted tears began to run down my cheeks.
The timing was confused, the notes not true, but I sang on, the
haunting doubtful strains of faith . . .

> When the shadows lengthen,
> And the night is come;
> Safely through death's valley
> Thou wilt lead me home.

. . . Thin as a thread, as tenuous as a spider-line strung between branches over a trail in the bush. But holding.

At dawn Mama murmured names, of her sons David and
Gerhard and Reuben, my brothers. She didn't mention Peter or
Abram in Russia (still alive, as far as we knew), nor Papa, nearly thirty years dead. And nothing of us, her daughters. She died
peacefully in the early evening, during hospital visiting hours,
with both of us and our husbands around her bed.

Our children came home that evening to mourn with us.

"She was so old and tired," daughter Tina tried to comfort
me, "isn't it good she's gone to a place of rest at last?"

"And what do you know of it?" I wailed. "To have no
father or mother left alive on earth?"

The tone was too angry. I saw that my grown children crept timidly outside to sit in the warm darkness. Only David lingered a moment before leaving me at the kitchen table with my head in my hands. Jakob sat beside me, his arm over my quivering bowed back.

* * * * * * * * * * * * * * * * * *

When I sewed quilts I rarely had time to plan the pattern properly in advance. I used up the scraps, trying to make the design as pretty as possible. Generally I was surprised how pleasing the results were. My eye played with the pieces later, selecting the blue triangles or the green squares, perhaps the yellow or brown pieces, fascinated with the way they zigzagged over the bed.

In the same way my life ran alongside my children's lives; I followed them. My life was no straight road, not as a mother. Instead of travelling one path it ran in all the directions they took, as if instead of going to our colony center, as one had intended, one turned to one village and another and then another.

I loved to watch my children. Loking at them was like gazing through the window in the morning, facing the blended demands and wonder of a new day. When the sun was rising, the world was mysterious, for everything was hopeful and possible. My life had so much of that awesome beauty: our five, our children . . .

True, Rosita was no student; she couldn't seem to grasp sums or push her pencil into proper, neat forms. Day after day I had to help her with her homework, while she tried and failed. It was a mercy for her and me when she was allowed to quit, for though I had come to love her, her academic inability tested my patience daily. But she was gentle, and a hard worker.

When she was sixteen she went to work in the hospital,

249

preparing meals for the staff and patients. She was a capable cook and liked this job. She gave most of the money she earned home, though I discovered when she married at twenty-eight that Jakob had kept careful count of it. He paid her back in cattle.

Rosita married Isaak Giesbrecht. I suspected the marriage was unhappy, less because of Isaak than his widowed mother, Mrs. Giesbrecht, who lived with them. Of course, there was no other place for the woman to go, but she was domineering and not about to respect Rosita. People hinted how shamelessly she ordered her daughter-in-law about. Rosita tried to comfort herself with her children, but they were as helpless as little rabbits too, as if expecting to be struck at any time.

Rosita was the most faithful of the children in visiting us. I told my other girls this: Rosita comes over every time she's in town, and she doesn't rush off right away either. Isaak was of the sort who didn't complete any business in a hurry, so when Rosita came along she had the freedom of a half day or even longer to do her shopping and spend with us.

She burst in one August day holding a letter from Russia. Her father was alive, and had traced her. She asked Jakob to read it aloud. The letter informed the newly-found daughter that the imprisonment was finished, he still had his faith, and would she please reply with information about herself. Never had I seen Rosita so overcome with emotion: the tears streamed down her cheeks and didn't want to end. She cried nearly silently, but it was a flood of happiness. Jakob spontaneously kissed her wet cheek.

Rosita kept the letter and three subsequent ones — the last one from a distant relative informing her of her father's passing — in our dresser with our papers, and sometimes when she visited she re-read them to herself, her lips soundlessly shaping the familiar words, her face flushed with contentment.

Tina married the same year as Rosita, at nineteen. She also married an Isaak, the Isaak Pauls who bought our place in the village. I thought it fitting that the one most like me (people said) lived there, working and sleeping and raising her children in my former place. She even ran over the street to Susi, to borrow things and talk a bit.

Then Susi would tell me, "She's so much like you! A younger Anna!"

Was I so quick, so efficient, so meticulous? Always in a hurry?

"Didn't we sit and talk though, Susi? Talk for hours? Tina never stays. I get tired watching her."

Susi said, "Most of the time we snatched our conversations here and there. You were always on the run." I shook my head, not remembering it.

Tina, my blond, wiry baby, born running, it seemed, and bossy. Even at an early age she commanded Rosita and David about. They stood in awe of her. Perhaps we all did. We marvelled at her energy and determination.

She was a good girl, and never rebellious. She learned easily in school, though after two years in high school her interest flagged when Jakob told her she didn't need to continue longer than she wished. Then she spent four weeks with Mrs. Niebuhr, learning to sew. She learned to sew everything, and to make nice patterns. Because of that course, she became acquainted with Isaak, a nephew of the seamstress, a quiet and unassuming young man, but sly as a fox with his farming.

Once on the farm, Tina sewed for others, and also sold tomatoes, cabbages, eggs, cream, whatever she had. Isaak disliked delivering the products to customers or taking them around to the shops in town; he thought it a bother for the few guaranies, but he did it, admiring the thrift of his wife. He was in charge of the crops and animals, but he did her marketing as

251

ordered.

Isaak and Tina fared well, and I never worried about them. I even prayed less for her than my others. Tina was healthy, could afford what she needed, and raised seven children; she was a good wife and mother.

Gretchen, though, started like a little brown bush-chicken hiding in the compost floor of a thicket, slight and shy, a waif with her tiny face and large blue eyes. She seemed less equipped for life than Tina, on the edge of the village social groups, tagging after the other children, and never reaching them before they had run to another place. She often sat alone, daydreaming. She was disorganized and untidy with her things, although not with herself, for she combed her hair too often and made a proud fuss about second-hand clothes.

I guarded and shielded her. The older children weren't allowed to tease her. I'd say, "Tina, please help Gretchen" when Gretchen had chores or studies. I knew it wasn't quite fair to demand more of Tina and Rosita than of Gretchen. But the deficiencies had to be compensated, I felt, and somehow I wasn't able to teach her to take charge of the washing or to cook properly or clean. She was an intelligent child but learned only what she chose.

She was barely thirteen, and already alluring to the boys! I watched the young people and could tell. The girl's pretty helplessness portended no Chaco male any good, with her lack of domestic skill, but it attracted them one after another.

Fortunately she picked the best of them.

Ewald Janzen became an important man, second only to the colony head eventually. Gretchen, the wife of a colony administrator! And she managed it! It seemed almost a miracle, though she always had household help. (They had the money for it.) They had four precocious, beautiful children.

My daughter Liese, who sometimes lectured me later, told

me why I was so fond of Gretchen's children (she told me I was always praising them to others). "You think it's all because of Ewald," she said. "But just watch Gretchen, she doesn't know how to organize, least of all people's lives, and that's the best thing for them. Letting them be, you know. She's tolerant and patient, and she lets them jabber and jabber, and she listens. She really listens to them, and nothing they say shocks her."

Liese had no experience of her own, so I didn't know whether to believe her or not, but it was true, Gretchen had out-witted me. My worries were a waste. People knew and noticed her, still quiet and aloof, but sure of herself. And Ewald's attraction to the slender adolescent he fell in love with continued twenty-five years and beyond.

"She was irresistible," I told Jakob. "I know I babied her too long, but with that smile flashing like sunshine for extra attention . . ."

He agreed. So she wasn't helpless. She knew her way just like the rest of them.

Chapter 10

Seen from the air, the Chaco looked as I had expected: immense stretches of bush rolling like green waves, hazy, dense as fog, the roads cutting straight through it, the villages tiny and neat.

I was flying to Asuncion.

Now that we had an airport, the capital could be reached in a matter of hours instead of weeks now.

"I've always wondered what a bird must see," I had said before leaving.

David's children (he married Irene Peters two years after Katie's death; they had four sons and a daughter), waiting with their parents to see me off, stared.

"Didn't you think Omas have thoughts like that?" I asked them.

"Aren't you scared, Oma?" ten-year-old Jakob asked solemnly.

"No."

We older people were allowed wisdom, I mused on the trip, but the younger ones didn't believe that we knew pleasure, desire, adventure. They supposed we had no imagination left. They didn't realize that wisdom came out of those things, out of the range of emotions and experiences, the joys and sufferings we had experienced. And still did.

Would Liese accept what I wanted to say to her? Or would she also think, what does Mama know?

Annaliese, whom we called Liese, was our prodigal. She was always a stubborn one, never a girl who would grow warm on the lap or under a mother's words. She had her own mind.

For example, she was musically gifted, so we bought her an accordion. She learned quickly, and played well. She could figure out songs by ear in several attempts. One night when the sky was filled with brilliant stars she began to play the children's song,

> Can you count the stars that brightly
> Twinkle in the midnight sky?

The lilting folk melody drew me into the yard. I sang along,

> God the Lord, doth make their number
> With his eyes that never slumber:
> He hath made them everyone . . .

She stopped. She refused to play if I sang.

"Why?" I wanted to know. "Why can't I sing?"

"I just don't want you singing when I play," she said.

Even if I hummed, and she noticed, she would cease immediately, no matter if she was finished the song or not. She was sixteen, so I couldn't force her.

She took lessons for several months, then decided she didn't enjoy playing. Finally after a year in which she hadn't taken the instrument out of its case once, we sold it.

Jakob listened to Liese when she talked and pushed her comments and questions upon him. But he wasn't strict enough with her. He demurred, saying, "The girls are your job."

"She's too smart," I complained. "Girls don't need it. It will only be hard for her later."

Jakob was amused. "Now Anna. Where do you think she gets it from?"

"Not from me," I retorted. But he chuckled.

Liese was a beautiful girl, with my features refined to perfection, her body tall and slender like Jakob's. But her hair was red. Reddish blond. It was not a good color to have in our colony.

"I hate it! I hate it!" she complained.

"Well keep your hat on then, so it doesn't get so red," I'd say. "So you don't burn and peel and have so many freckles."

She had ideas on every subject. "I was born on the Day of Heroes. That's special for a Paraguayan. Better than David's birthday on November 25. I'm Paraguayan!"

She asked, "Why in the world do you have that verse in the living room about looking to the hills for help? Of all the thousands of verses in the Bible! There aren't any hills in the Chaco!"

Was I so tired of mothering, I wondered, that I allowed her to speak like that? I didn't even try to answer her much of the time. I let her talk back to me.

Liese saw and heard things and then carried them home to us with the rage of an uncontrolled grass fire. "I heard Mrs. Friesen yelling at an Indian beggar woman. She even grabbed a broom! My Sunday school teacher! And Mennonite dogs hate the smell of Indians. They're bred prejudiced. Why do we call them 'the brown ones' as if they have no names! The children laugh at them, spit at them. They throw stones at them! They say they stink! And you know what else? Our teacher says the Paraguayan people are shiftless and immoral and their blood is stained with the worst of European and Indian society. It's not fair! And I don't believe it either!" Then she would finally be out of breath.

She learned that some Mennonite men whored with Indian women.

"They buy them with a watermelon! Or a kilo of rice!"

"It *is* wrong. Yes." Jakob said.

"Why doesn't someone preach about it? How we treat them like pigs?"

"You don't know what's already being done about it," Jakob said patiently. "I'm sure the men will be dealt with. We don't know all the prayers and tears shed by our people in secret. There are many —"

"Secret! Silent! That's for sure. Why doesn't someone do something?"

"You don't know everything about it. It seems so simple to you. It's complex, more complex than you — "

"If anyone's said there are simple ways, it's you, Papa!" she interrupted. "Trust God, think about his greatness, thank for his mercy, trust and pray and obey. Simple solutions! You have them! God will provide. That's where I get it from!"

And that's how Liese talked, always exclaiming, defending the Indians, defending the Paraguayans. Sometimes I ended the discussion, but not quietly as Jakob might. "Liese, you talk about how much sin you see. You want peace and goodness but you're a whirlwind yourself, raising dust and rebellion everywhere you go!"

"Nobody understands me!" she flared.

She was right: we didn't understand her, and she didn't make sense. We loved
her but were helpless before her contrariness.

And now I had to fly to the city because of it. When Liese completed high school she didn't want to study as a teacher or nurse, the two career possibilities for women in the colony. She wanted to work in Asuncion. She found a job in a German pension, cleaning rooms and helping in the kitchen.

That was bad enough, but then we learned she had a Paraguayan boyfriend.

She was in danger, we felt immediately, and we had to do something. Jakob and I stood together on this. We couldn't keep her in the colony, that was clear. So if she wanted to go away, she would go to Canada. By nightfall I had written the letter to the single daughters of my late brother Peter's wife, and explained everything. If they could help us out now, get her settled, we would repay it when we could.

"At least there she'd be with our people," I reasoned.

My mission was to travel to Asuncion and persuade Liese that she must go.

When I got there and told her, our Liese said, "Sure, why not. I'll go. Might be fun. Something new."

"Really? You think it's a good idea?" I said, surprised.

"Sure. Why not?"

I had her unexpected consent, so we began to work on gettingher passport and papers to leave. Then I wanted to get home. I had enjoyed the taxi ride from the airport to the hotel in which Liese was employed, seeing the continent's oldest city, marvelling at the red hues everywhere — in the soil, trees, and flowers — but Asuncion was too noisy; I couldn't sleep properly. Dogs barked throughout the night. It seemed as if packs of wild hounds roamed the streets. As they ran by, free, the dogs inside every house on the street howled with envy. Then, long before the sun was up, the streets clattered with the creak of cart wheels and the calls of the farmers and vendors going into the center.

I was annoyed at the constant, unorderly traffic, the stifling humidity, the garbage on the sidewalks, the untidiness, and the hills to climb while walking to shop or do business. I was vexed that I needed Liese for every transaction, for I knew no Spanish. And I hated to pay for everything — my lodging, meals, taxi trips, each tiny sweet or fruit. The Latin culture, the bright colors, the clutter of yellow blossoms under trees, the heavy sensuous smells of food and warmth and trees and flowers and people overwhelmed me; if I were young, yes, but it was all too much. I wanted to be safe, home. In our romantic capital I realized what had happened. I might have disliked the Chaco, but I had carved my home there, and now I missed it.

I returned on a dry miserable winter day, with the wind blasting and driving dust before it as if it were a cauldron of boiling dirty sand. The huge bottle tree at the end of the garden, so graceful and interesting when green, stood in its winter nakedness, an ugly and gnarled skeleton. A few half-puffed pods hung alone on the strangely twisted, leafless branches.

But the algorrobo on the neighbor's *Hof*, following some cycle of its own, able to anticipate spring without a single sign of it or even a decent rain, wore a fresh coat of delicate green leaves. And the lapacho, though buffeted by the wind, bloomed mauve.

The following week the weather turned unpredictably to a deep cold which worked its way through shivering skin to the core of our legs, arms and bodies. We sat in church on Sunday wearing several layers of clothes, trying to look our best and still keep warm. After the service we returned home for bread and sausage and cups of hot coffee. We stayed close to the stove, Jakob pushing in wood periodically to keep it blazing.

I sighed and yawned, tired but reluctant to leave the warmth of the kitchen. Our homes in the Chaco were now built with a view to keeping out the sun (we too had added a porch for shade around the entire house) but when it was cold, the buildings were as hard to heat as tombs.

Suddenly Jakob was on his knees, praying for Liese. I slipped down beside him. With a fervent voice, he pleaded with God, begging him as a child begs.

In her first letter from Winnipeg, Liese reported that it was unbearably hot; they were having an unusual autumn hot spell there. She described the colors: bright reds and oranges and yellows. Her cousins took her for a drive to the Ontario border; they had taken pictures which she would send later.

"My dear Liese," I wrote, "it's so strange for me to think of the seasons being the opposite in Canada. Here in the Chaco the paratodo has put on its yellow lacy dress, its bells as you used to say, so we know it's spring. And soon you will see winter. What will you think of the snow, I wonder, which I haven't seen for thirty-nine years . . . "

For the first year, I wrote her every week. She reciprocated with lively, engrossing letters, full of descriptions and humor. She would not admit to any homesickness. Another half year, and she sent us a picture of herself and a certain John Friesen she was dating. This was very interesting, she said, for his grandparents had been part of the *Kanadier* group that came to Paraguay several years before we had, though they'd turned back at Puerto Casado without even seeing their land.

* * * * * * * * * * * * * * * * *

Ten years later Liese and John and their children, Robert, Amelia and Miranda visited us. We liked our son-in-law John; he was friendly and enthused about all he saw. He also spoke enough German (a mixture of the High German and dialect) to communicate. The children, in spite of their strange-sounding English names, were lovely children; they looked at me with such awe and respect that I was immediately fond of them. We

261

developed special relationships, largely through hugs and kisses and funny gestures, since they hadn't learned any German.

When I chided Liese for not speaking German in the home, she said,"You don't know what it's like up there."

And she said, "I speak a very good English, people tell me. I don't even have much of an accent, they say."

"Everything's changed here," she said happily, dozens of times. "Huge semi-trailers humming along the paved Trans-Chaco. Produce going in and out. New buildings. In the Co-op, you have everything you could want now!"

John and Liese toured the colony buildings and Ewald's air-conditioned office. They stayed for a week at Ewald and Gretchen's air-conditioned house. They visited the meat plant, the hog farm, the peanut industry, and the milk plant where Jakob worked. They saw the colony ranch and experimental farm.

"Now there are hills here at last," Liese said mischievously, pointing to the plaque, still in the same place on the wall. "Little hills, perhaps, but still hills. Hills of cotton, hills of peanuts, little hills of soil beside all the ponds dug out for the cattle ranches. Hills everywhere!"

"Now we struggle with materialism as much as I've heard that the churches in North America do," I said.

She laughed and laughed, until I was upset, wondering what I had said that was so hilarious.

"Oh Mama, I'm sorry," she said at last. "It just struck me funny because you made that statement with such pride."

Our Liese, as direct as ever.

One afternoon after siesta she came out of the bedroom she and John used during their visit with a triumphant smile on her face. She went to the porch and gazed at the grey sky, think with dust as if a dirty pane of glass had been placed in front of it. For several weeks it hadn't rained, and the last week had been particularly hot, the *Nordsturm* especially wearing.

"I just love it!" she called to me.

I was puzzled.

"John's been giving me a hard time. 'It's not that bad,' he was always saying about everything. He figured I'd really exaggerated the Chaco. Now . . . " Here Liese laughed merrily and threw her hands into the air to emphasize her delight.

"Now he's lying in there stark naked. Absolutely naked and flopping from side to side on the hot sheet like a fish, moaning about the heat! So I try to comfort him in his misery. 'This kind of weather,' I say, 'makes for a real nice bloody sun.' Since he thinks the sunsets are so incredible here. And then he tells me to beat it!"

Liese stood on the porch and giggled about her husband's discomfort, grateful that the sky and high temperatures proved her point.

"Mama," she said, "it's wonderful to be home." And she drank tereré, the Paraguayan herbal tea drunk as a cold infusion, like a man and leaned forward in the earlier intensity, asking questions.

Again, she couldn't let the matter of the Indians rest. It was all I heard some days, for it was David's theme too; he had left teaching to work on the Indian Settlement Board. He took John and Liese to see the Indian settlements.

"I remember their savage, wild dancing cries in the night," I interjected when the Indian business was brought up again at a family gathering, "and their orange fires. It was something that made me shiver. It sounded inhuman. They were like animals when we came."

The children looked at me quickly, but disregarded my comments. They went on with the conversation, the projects and programs, Liese probing with her observations, David, patient and confident.

When I heard the mission reports now, I was amazed at what had been done with our native compatriots, but I was worried, for they outnumbered us now. How could we few help so many? They seemed to stream into the colony for bread and for work.

Our son-in-law John let Liese sit under the tree and argue while he and Jakob went to the museum, or to farms. I had to listen to them as I worked in the kitchen, the window open to their words.

"As a Christian I believe I should pray for the Paraguayan government," I heard David say. "I should support it as far as I can without actually compromising my faith. When the Jewish captives were in Babylon, they were told to pray for the peace of the captor country, they were to wish it well and work for its good, and that would result in things going better for them. We are to be supportive; I won't fight against it. Or get involved either."

"But David," Liese said, "that's exactly the part that puzzles me. Okay, you accept it, work along, pray for, like you say. I'll accept that. But you only pay lip service to it. Really, you turn around and say, but we can't advance with such a system. And you set up your own government! You run your own affairs!"

"We don't have our own government."

"Sure you do. You're a little state of your own up here. You have plenty of government. Maybe not a president, but a mayor, and you run your own schools, hospitals, roads, cooperatives, everything!"

"We decide internal things. It's a cooperative."

"Call it what you will. It's government. I just don't think you can argue that you're under the Paraguayan state. Sure, somewhat. But you're a state within a state. And the church is mixed right in with it. You're into government up to your ears!

264

You can talk piously about praying for the regime because it let's you do what you want so far. But if that changes, how will you pray then?"

I joined them at intervals with drinks, peanuts, chocolate candy and then fresh buns, hoping to effect calm and a change of subject by my interruptions and the food, but they talked around it.

My precious Liese, I thought sadly, a beautiful, efficient woman but still whirling the sand in our faces.

She talked of colony pressure on citizens, blackmail, cooperative monopoly. (Where had she heard so much again, in so few weeks?) Of the colony and the church as an unwieldy and unholy union? Of racial prejudice?

"And you value silence about these wrongs, more than justice?" she accused David.

"You haven't changed a bit," David replied. "It's more complicated than it looks, you know."

"Yes, but try," she pleaded. Her voice grew shrill. "Try at least! Separate things, unravel them, pull them apart. Lose your peoplehood if you have to, but strive for righteousness."

David was exasperated. "It's easy for you to talk! You left the Chaco! You people from abroad with all your answers. Stay here and see what you can do. Otherwise, mind your own business and don't judge."

Liese leaned back in her chair. "Don't jump on me as if I've touched a nerve," she said sarcastically. "It's not as if I'm asking you about your sex life with Irene, you know."

I was unhappy with that, and David was startled too. "Is that the way you people from Canada talk?" He stood and left, without farewell, on his motorcycle.

Liese entered the kitchen, disgruntled. "Boy, he's patronizing."

"He and Irene are coming for supper. It will be fine then

265

again. If you don't start an argument."

She was silent a moment. "Mama, I really do care about these things. It's not just . . . " She stopped, staring at the floor.

"Liese," I ventured, "how is it with you. Inside, I mean. Your faith?"

"I think about it a lot," she admitted. Tears filled her eyes. "All those other things . . . what I think and ask about them . . . it's part of searching." She walked to the bedroom.

My children, my children, I sighed. What could I do but pray for them and make supper? We would have a house full for the meal again, and I must try again to keep the conversation small and light and full of laughter, to arrange it as nicely as an arrangement of flowers. During the whole visit I must try to keep peace.

Chapter 11

On the last day of November, when Jakob (seventy-six years and four months to the day) lifted his faded straw hat off the hook beside the screen door in the kitchen, pressed it firmly over his white hair, and pulled the latch away from the door for the third time in one morning, I couldn't help but express my impatience with him.

"Well, Jakob," I said, "where are you going now? Again?"

I was cutting noodles and pushing them into a shallow black pan, spreading them to dry. The skin of my hands was loose, as old skin is, but every motion I made was deft and swift and skillful. How many thousands of times had I made noodles? After more than forty years at it, I certainly knew what I was about. They sagged away from my knife consistently thin and even, the dough perfectly smooth, and nearly white.

In a pot on the blue gas burner to my right, yellowish water with bits of parsley, onion halves, an anise star, and peppercorns churned against a small plump chicken, dispensing steam and a delicious aroma into the room.

I knew what Jakob was doing, even though I faced the

middle room and couldn't seem him. For the third time in one morning he was putting on his hat and leaving the house.

"It's too hot to go out, Jakob," I said, my back tensing against the grey chair. "You should rest. The doctor—"

"I have my hat," he said, his hand still on the door. "It's no cure to sit still."

"But Jakob, you know what he said." I stopped my work, the long knife stationary in the air. "You must take it easy now."

After a short pause, I asked, "Oh, did you read the mail? Was there something today? David brought a letter, didn't he?"

Jakob dropped his hand, but didn't answer. I turned. He stared at the devotional calendar on the wall above the table where I worked.

"Is it December the first?" he asked.

"It's the last of November."

"It says December 1."

"But we read the page this morning. We tore it off, that's why December 1 shows already." I pinched salt out of a chipped saucer and dashed it into the boiling broth.

"Oh, yes."

"Jakob," I said, pleading, "why don't you stay in? Do you need something to do? Perhaps you . . . "

But then Jakob opened the door, shoving my words aside. What would I do with him, so recalcitrant now? I sighed and resumed my cutting.

Spurred by misgivings that I hadn't been firm enough with him, however, I rose after a minute or two to open the door and call after him.

"Jakob? Jakob! Please don't go walking now! It's too hot!"

Hearing no answer I stepped onto the porch, letting the screen door close with a sucking sound behind me. The brilliant white light of near-noonday burned into my eyes and the heat pushed its hot fingers against me. Immediately, reflexively, I braced myself against it the way I always had — by thinking, it'll be a bit better this evening when the sun has set. It'll be easier to bear after the summer. We'll have respite then.

(I hadn't, though, "gotten used to it" as visitors from other lands sometimes suggested; if anything, it was more difficult now; yes, it seemed worse now, after fifty years of such summers. But the ability to wait for the darkness or for the shy shift in the wind direction or for the pleasant autumn had stretched, perhaps, become elastic. And now at least, we had decent shelter, better houses, fans, something to aid us against it.)

I couldn't see Jakob, nor hear the sound of his worn black thongs slapping against his soles after every careful step. Although the cicadas were shrilling, filling the upper octaves of sound with their high-pitched, insistent chirping, the overall effect of nature at this time of day, the peaking of the sun, was a pervasive stillness. Silence.

I walked the length of the verandah and looked up the driveway to the palms that guarded the posts of our gate. He wasn't in sight.

Why must he leave his chair and notebook so restlessly, so often?

Shielding my eyes, I looked into the magnificent and flawless sky, that clean pure blue sky upon which flat-bottomed clouds of immaculate white hung in clusters. That deceptive sky. More than once I had marvelled at it. How did the burning rays of the sun get through and leave the sky so unscarred, so un-rent? The color itself reminded me of middle-latitude Russia; it seemed to belong to my distant childhood, with time to idle in the garden or edge of the field, gently pulling tender bits of grass to chew, and then sitting and imagining what shapes the clouds formed. But the same wonderful blue existed here and

269

mediated this oppressive, tropical heat.

I felt perspiration gathering on my chin and forehead. The thermometer mounted beside the green shutters of the bedroom window registered over forty degrees.

I must go inside. It was cooler there, the shutters were closed and a portable fan manufactured wind. I had plenty to do before dinner.

I called Jakob a last time. Once again he had foolishly gone walking. Well, there was nothing I could do. I wouldn't chase after him on the streets. He would find his way back without me.

I retreated into the kitchen and sampled the chicken broth. It was perfect. The first noodles were dry so I set water on the gas burner for cooking them. I cleared the table, wiped the red-flowered oilcloth, and set out the bowls and spoons. I squeezed some grapefruit juice, which Jakob enjoyed so much. When the town siren announced noon time, he would turn back and come home to eat.

He still knew what the siren meant, and would walk laboriously back from wherever he had gone, the old thongs clicking behind him. Erectly, for he refused to stoop, he would return for our meal together. Jakob, the pioneer, now an old man, would proceed patiently and pathetically up the street, one foot after another on the hard, hot, dirt walkway, while the younger men on their motorcycles or in cars sped past him. They did not notice him in particular, or if they did, they saw a man whose head they might want to pat briefly on their hurried way, to reassure him that it was very useful and fine, indeed, to be so ancient.

In the past two years the eight years difference in our ages had asserted itself for the first time in our marriage. I was heavier and not as hasty on my feet as I had been but I felt competent and energetic, my mind still quick, eager, young. I was

68.

But Jakob was 76 and weakened. Inside the baggy olive-colored trousers and blue cotton shirts he always wore he appeared shrunken; often, too, he seemed unaware of what happened around him. He might tell David or a friend a long story, and every part of it was in the right place, nothing missing. Then I spoke to him about something and a moment later he had forgotten what it was. He mixed up the days of the week and the hours of the day. It was increasingly difficult to converse logically with him.

The town siren blew. Now he would come. I changed into a fresh apron, and took a loaf of bread out of the pantry to cut. I heard the whine of motorcycles on the street, people going home for dinner and siesta, the happy voices of children finished with school for the day.

A motorbike turned onto our *Hof*. It was David. What did he want. He had come earlier to drop off the mail.

David stepped off the bike, strode to the door and said, "Papa's had a heart attack. I'll take you to the hospital."

I comprehended his message immediately and a tremor of fear washed over me. I purposefully checked it. I switched off the ring of flame under the simmering soup, removed my apron and placed it over the back of the chair with the one I had worn all morning, and smoothed my hair. As I closed the door behind me, I saw the two glass bowls and plates waiting in their usual positions. I thought: it happened while I was setting them out.

"Alfred Kroeker found him at the monument," David said.

"The monument! He walked that far?"

"Alfred saw him leaning against it and then slump, so he ran over."

Then David said, "He's already dead."

"I told him not to go!"

"Come, Mama."

I perched awkwardly behind David on the small Honda. He slowly drove me to the hospital where Jakob's body lay.

Chapter 12

Jakob was dead, and I was a widow, an alarming new thing to learn. I would move my head at a sound, expecting his step. I woke, forgetful, happy, thinking of something to tell him until I glimpsed the cot opposite mine in perfect order, unused, the colors of the patchwork quilt smooth and cheerful in the first rays of day. The bed was already made up, always made up. Then I remembered he was dead. He died the last day of November and on December 1 we buried him.

I recalled little of the funeral. Every few hours my daughters gave me a pill. This made me angry later and I told them so, but they blamed the doctor who ordered the prescription and told them it was best for me. They presented me with a cassette tape of the service. I listened to less than half of it before I turned the machine off, not in grief, but in disgust. I wouldn't repeat something that was finished.

The only part of the funeral that was quite clear in my memory was the burial. It was nearly noon when we reached the cemetery; it was as hot as the day before, and we huddled under the few shade trees of the graveyard or umbrellas. My grandson

Ewald stood behind me to hold a large black umbrella over my head.

The wind blew in sporadic gusts. It carried swirls of dust about the forlorn cemetery as if they were tufts of dry grass. It brushed over the mound of dirt beside Jakob's grave, played with the leaves of *Prediger* Klassen's Bible so he had to hold them secure. The wind wants those pages, I thought, to carry them along out of town, over the colony, to where it disappears into some part of the huge, unbroken, green Chaco bush. It also tugged on the flowers and the ribbon banner, "Our beloved husband and father," that garnished the casket.

The wind danced over Jakob, thin and empty-looking, the gaunt, handsome features exposed for the last time to his family and friends and the burning sky. Play, wind, play, I thought, staring at the body, you won't carry him off; he's gone. Far past the Chaco by now. Home.

> In the midst of the street of it, and on either side of the river, (read the preacher in a sorrowful, sonorous voice) was there the tree of life, which bare twelve manner of fruits . . . . And there shall be no more curse: but the throne of God and of the Lamb shall be in it; and his servants shall serve him . . . And there shall be no night there; and they need no candle, neither light of the sun . . .

Who would miss it, I asked myself, wiping my handkerchief over my brow.

> for the Lord God giveth them light; and they shall reign for ever and ever.

During the first weeks of December I sorted through

274

Jakob's clothes and possessions. I sat down eagerly with his notebooks, two of them full and the last nearly so. The latter lay with his tattered Bible on the table, the other two were in the bottom of his drawer. I knew approximately what they contained and hadn't been curious to see them before, but now I hoped to meet him again in the close lines and letters. Page after page of yellowing paper was written with dates and Scripture references beside them, outlines or several sentences for the occasional sermons he gave in the village services. Dates, Scriptures, often parts of verses written out, outlines. No wonder biblical phrases fell into his conversation like seeds spilling through a hole in a sack, steadily dropping out.

My heart quickened when I spotted my name. My name with my maiden surname: Anna Sawatzky. It was dated October 5, 1932, the time of our courtship. Ah, what had he said then? He had written, "The sun stands still. The moon does not move." The reference was Joshua 10:13.

I turned quickly to Joshua 10:13 and read, ". . . the sun stood still, and the moon stayed until the people had avenged themselves upon their enemies. . . "

I read it again and tears rose in my eyes. Now what, oh what, did that have to do with me? With Anna, his bride, Anna Sawatzky, his lovely bride, not quite nineteen!

Impractical Jakob with his visions and ideas! Dates and one neatly-written Scripture reference after another: his diary! But how did they connect with life as we had lived it? Life was a naked window, with nothing to shut us away from the groaning of creation, very little better than nothing at all, an unadorned and hewn-out opening in clay or brick walls, allowing in a bit of light. Years and years we had lived as one with the struggle and cruelty of the earth, feeling and tasting it all in its relentless bitterness, not able to escape. Meanwhile, he sat and wrote, inexplicably linking the sun and moon and the battles of

Israel with my name. When I was Anna Sawatzky and he courted me; I was full of loving sentiments and dreams of the future, and his idea of romance was the miraculous halt of the sun upon Gibeon!

I searched for meaning here but couldn't find it. Sometimes it had been hard to live with this mild yet rigid opposite. He made me feel I must reach the position he held. He indulged me as if I were a child, needing life explained, and smiled on my incomprehension of his views with the epitaph, "such, after all, are the strange ways of women."

But . . . oh, God, how I missed him! How I had loved him! I wanted him again, even here in these notebooks, speaking to me. He must not disappoint me.

I continued to flip the pages. Beside the date July 16, 1959, I found the title, "My Life Story," and remembered his wish to write his story for our children. Two lines below the heading he had penned, "I was born on March 4, 1905, in a village in the Terek settlement, the Caucasus. My mother, Elizabeth (Neufeld) died when I was young, so I didn't know her at all. My father was a kind man."

The rest of the page was blank.

In the last notebook he had attempted it again, this time with the title, "Our life in the Chaco of Paraguay."

"Those of us from China came to the Chaco in 1931," he wrote, "and settled in the Harbiner Corner. But I didn't stay there long, as the father of my bride, Abram Sawatzky, had died, and I moved to his place to take over the farm."

That story, too, was left unfinished.

I packed up Jakob's clothes and had them delivered to the mission for Indians, and I gave the notebooks and Bible to David.

After that, there was Christmas to think about: the cleaning and annual re-whitewashing of the walls, baking, selecting and making gifts. I did everything as accustomed, and finished embroidering the pillowcases I had started for my granddaughters, but I felt as if I watched myself perform, clumsily, like a play the youth group might present, ineptly prepared and amateurishly acted so that the air between stage and audience was filled with embarrassment and hope that the curtain would soon close in the middle to hide it from view. Christmas was long and hot.

Then, January. I was still alone. With the sudden loss of the deep, familiar pattern of the two of us, Jakob and Anna, that imaging of life in male and female with which I had lived so naturally so long, I didn't know myself or where I belonged. I recalled dead, buried Jakob in minute detail, but was distant and confused about myself. Who was I? I felt tired and ill, and wondered if I had ever experienced a summer so hot, with so little rain.

When my children came to visit and comfort me, I complained, "I feel alone. I'm afraid here." If they suggested I go home with them for a few days, however, I refused to leave the *Hof*.

They annoyed me, laughing and talking about everyday things as if their father wasn't dead. When I brought some memory of him to their attention, they abandoned it after one comment. And the grandchildren were restive, noisy, banging doors, shrieking, whooping on the porch near the window. I didn't know how to calm them. It was Jakob who had kept them attentive and expectant with caramels and other treats hiding in his pockets.

I regretted, oh how I regretted, that I had sometimes been irritated by my husband. I thought especially of my impatience over his failing faculties during the last months of his life and my specific failure to keep him in the house the morning of his death. Why hadn't I anticipated what the consequences would be? Now his nobility and strength of character loomed above me; his virtues cast no shadows.

He had been right; it was fitting that he died slumped against the monument erected for the fifty-year jubilee celebration of the colony. It was an imposing structure, heavy and grey, three tall vertical pillars representing the three facets of our success here: faith, work, unity. Towering over the silver pine and lapacho trees which alternated down the middle of the wide roadway leading to it, it proved Jakob right, for it was the same color as the Chaco earth. Above the trees it looked as if the brown clay and sand had been thrown to heaven and remained suspended, the soil of this impossible land lifted as an oblation to the one who fashioned all places, and this one too. Jakob had said, "He had his eye on it. For us." And the boughed green of the trees, like leaves under flowers, said what he had said, "the campo is rich and fruitful. It will reward our labors." What I didn't like though, was that they had planted cactus at the monument base.

"Mama," Tina scolded me when she visited, "you're letting the roses go. They need — "

"Roses," I said glumly. "How can I think of them?"

Earlier, I had developed a keen interest in roses. No activity had given me as much pleasure in the last ten years as the planting, grafting, watering, spraying, pruning, and then harvesting of the magnificent blooms. I gradually acquired and tended over fifty bushes, with as many varieties and colors — reds, corals, pinks, whites, yellows. My reputation grew and I was frequently asked to supply bouquets for weddings and other special occasions. When one of the nurses at the hospital informed me of a patient without flowers in the room, I made him or her an arrangement. It gave me much satisfaction.

Now my daughters took turns tending the roses. And Tina kept after me. "Mama, I'm warning you, we'll stop coming. We

278

don't have time to do this. You have to do it."

"Let them die," I said crossly.

I waited for the visits of my children, but after they came and went, I spent hours struggling with bitter mental recriminations. They were busy, uncaring, too quick with their words of comfort.

David dropped in one evening after the Wednesday prayer meeting. I was in bed, but awake, watching the white curtains fluttering in the breeze.

"Are you sleeping well these days, Mother?" David asked, having let himself into the house and coming directly to my room.

"Yes, quite well," I replied.

The silence that followed was long and inconclusive. I hated the years that brought me to this: lying under white sheets, my hair uncoiled, the braid loosened, and my son standing at my bedside, seeing me like that, tucking me into bed as it were. If only I could be a young mother again, putting him to sleep, and having him beg me, "But can't you stay here a little bit longer, Mama?" Now I wished I could keep him in the room until I had fallen asleep.

"You must rest much, Mother," he said gently. "Papa's death has shocked you. You're simply overcome with sorrow."

It was true. Perhaps he understood. God bless him! The brush of his hand on mine remained a warm indentation which comforted me until morning.

But another time when he came, he rebuked me. I had pouted, "What am I good for now? Who needs me? I lived for Papa, and now he's gone, so why should I still be here?"

"There's much you can do, Mother," he replied. "This is the time in life to pray. You can have a ministry of prayer. Pray for your children. Pray for me. Pray for the church. Missions. Make lists."

My time to pray? Lists! Well, it sounded wonderful enough, but how could I pray if I was lonely, and my life was out of balance? When my thoughts were illusions and memories tempted me with their sweet familiarity? When my feelings dipped repeatedly into despair? Someday David might know how impossible prayer was now. Easy advice, I thought, for a young preacher to give.

All my life I had resisted dirt and insects; now I saw a cockroach in the kitchen and fussed until the cupboards were lined with jar lids of poison. Then I dreamt of cockroaches with feelers longer than a man's arm waving before me, scratching my face, searching for something, feeding on my drool while I slept with my mouth open. I cried out, woke, and discovered I was soaked with perspiration.

Another time I dreamt I climbed trees, shouting, ecstatic, calling to the hawks of the Chaco; I held their beaks and they carried me where I willed (I felt the sensation of flight), down into the lair of foxes, stroking their long lovely tails, and stalking cattle with a gigantic jaguar, killing the cows, the calves, the bulls and their owners, their wives and their children. I was surrounded by snakes and ordered them to sting; one by one I went through the colony; I knew everyone, and the beasts obeyed me.

Again I woke exhausted and wet.

Sometimes even during the day my eyes closed on a darkness that I couldn't blink away. To the right a pinhole of light shifted whenever I moved my head; it insisted on staying at the periphery of my vision. It seemed as if the black space before me enclosed tangles of lizards and eels of immense proportions, but I couldn't see them, for they were chameleon-like and couldn't be distinguished from the night around them or the dark oozing oils in which they writhed.

At the beginning of February I suddenly thought of the picture which hung in the children's room for years. "Where did the picture of the angel guarding the children go? I want it back."

The next day Gretchen's son Peter appeared with the picture in this hand. It had been freshly framed.

"Where shall I hang it, Oma?" he asked, looking at me in a strange way.

I was ashamed of myself. "Take it back, Peter, my boy. Take it back. I gave it to you children."

"Mama said I should hang it up here," he said, "and I'm not to bring it back home."

I told him to put it on the nail beside the calendar in the kitchen. The scene of the angel who hovered protectively over the children, clinging fearfully to one another as they picked their way over the broken bridge across a chasm, would help me while I ate.

"I'll give it back to you," I promised. Peter nodded and darted out the door.

When he was gone, I knelt at my bed. "Lord Jesus," I cried, "please have mercy on me. I have been strong, and now I must be strong again."

Since Jakob's death I looked forward to sleeping (and I slept much) because, as well as bad dreams, I also had good ones, of him. He stood at a distance, and I ran to him. I didn't reach him, but the joy and the residue of that excitement even after I woke made me wish for night, in case I experienced it again.

Now, after praying, I was filled with a desire to sleep. At the same time I knew my motivation was wrong. I decided that I wouldn't sleep in the middle of the afternoon, long after siesta, and that the next time I dreamed of Jakob I wouldn't move. "I'm coming later, Jakob!" I'd call, but I wouldn't take a single step. God had given me Jakob, He had taken him away; at any rate, I was still alive, still His, now I would bless Him.

I put on a clean dress and walked to the nursing home where my sister Maria lay bedridden. She was glad to see me.

"Look Anna," she said. "Look what Nikolaus brought." She pointed to a handful of wheat stalks stuck in a jar.

"I heard they're trying wheat in the Chaco again," I said, "but I hadn't seen any. It's a type better suited for here, I guess."

"Nikolaus has a good crop."

"How many hectares?"

"I don't know. He's experimenting, I think. His Edith doesn't want him to plant wheat. Stick to peanuts and cotton, she says. She's afraid to try anything new. She worries and worries."

"She forgets that in farming it may turn out good as well as bad," I said.

"It's not the kind of wheat we had in Russia."

"But it's wheat," I countered. "I wish Papa could have seen it."

"He died without seeing anything turn out well here."

When I returned home, I remembered that Maria had wheat on her bedside table but no flowers. I put on my gardening gloves, took the flower scissors, and went to the garden to cut her a bouquet of roses.

AFTERWORD

Two days ago I fell on the plank I had lugged to the low spot between our yard and the street, badly twisting my ankle. Now I'm in the hospital for a few days to keep me off my feet.

This afternoon Gretchen brought me six coral rosebuds from my garden. But she couldn't stay to talk.

As soon as she was gone, Johann Walde stepped into my room.

He entered it without hesitation, rather jauntily, as if his presence was the most natural thing in the world, looked directly at me with his wide smile and said,

"Hello Anna! How are you doing?"

"Johann Walde!"

I had heard he was in the colony, visiting his oldest daughter Agnes. (She's the only Walde left here; Johann took his family to Canada in the middle sixties. His wife Leni died several years ago.) But I certainly never expected him to call on me.

"Yes, it's me!" he announced. And it was Johann Walde indeed, somewhat thinner than I had remembered, his hair grey. His face was red — too much sun too quickly, a common error of visitors to the Chaco — but under the white brows his eyes were still a clear pale blue, still tireless and quick. He held a new straw-colored hat in his hand.

"I'm sorry to hear about your foot," he said. "Good it's just a sprain and not broken. Soon you'll be up and walking again."

"I hope so."

He set the hat on the end of my bed and moved nearer to me. I had recovered from the shock of seeing him, but I was baffled and wary. What did he want?

"Well, Anna, it's cooler today than yesterday," he said, "but still hot enough, isn't it? I was just talking to the folks at the radio station — now that's a comfortable place to be, air conditioning! I was wondering about the weather statistics, how

285

they compare to earlier years. But it's pleasant enough in here too, isn't it?" He looked around the room. "One can do a lot with proper curtains, wide porches, and so on. If you had waited with your accident until later, you could have been in the new hospital though! That's going to be a splendid place when it's finished, isn't it? I walked through it this morning too. I don't think any hospital in Canada will be cleaner and nicer. Of course, you don't have the equipment that some of the big city places have, but still, it's quite something. There have been so many changes in the twenty years I've been gone. Changes, changes, changes! Progress! You people really live well down here now."

He rambled on, looking at me steadily. "Maybe you're not so aware of how everything has changed, but when one is away, as I was, you really notice it. It's possible, I see now, to live here. It's not that bad, after all, is it?

"We who live here have also noticed the changes," I said.

"Well, I came to see daughter Agnes again. And my grandchildren. The winters aren't that pleasant in Ontario and I have money to travel . . . You know, in Canada people often put signs on the back of their cars, on the bumpers. There's one I saw recently I liked. 'We're spending our children's inheritance.'" He laughed pleasantly, but I didn't respond.

Apparently thinking I didn't understand, he explained, "You see, instead of staying home and letting the money sit in the bank until they die and giving it all to the children they travel, and use it up! Well, I have enough money. Maybe I can travel and leave enough for them to divide too. Not for a while, though, I hope!"

Johann laughed again, but this time I detected nervousness.

"I'm thinking of living here again, " he said.
"You are?"

"Sure. Why not? I find it quite pleasant here now. I could build a house with air conditioning."

I wanted to say, Won't you be ready for an old folks home soon, like me? But instead I commented "I see that the former residents of the Chaco are coming back, one by one. The *Chaqueñas* just don't get the place out of their blood."

"But how are *you* keeping, Anna?" Johann asked, changing the subject and stepping a bit closer.

"Fine."

"I read of Jakob's passing," he said. "Has it been hard?"

"Of course."

Walde gestured toward a chair in the room. "May I sit down?" I nodded, and he carried the chair into the narrow aisle between the beds the (other was unoccupied) and seated himself.

"So how are you doing, Anna?"

How many times would he ask it? "I'm in bed," I said, "and I don't like it."

Then he asked me to marry him!

That was the purpose of his visit, he said. After Leni's death he had been lonesome and when he read of Jakob's passing in our small colony newspaper, to which he still subscribed, he had begun to often think of me. He remembered me sell, he said, how fine-looking and solid and neat I had been, always in a clean dress, a clean apron, and my hair in place. He had always considered me attractive and energetic; more than once he had said to himself, she's a fine-looking woman.

You're saying more than you should, Walde, I thought.

I said coldly, "You should have been looking at Leni, not me."

"Now Anna," he smiled indulgently, "of course I did that. But one sees others and makes some general observations."

General observations! He could still make me feel foolish.

"I'm old and leathered like the rest of us now," I said.

Johann made a long speech of proposing, not giving me an opportunity to respond. When the spouse is gone, he said, one starts fresh; older people needn't desist from matters of the heart; we were both healthy. He had seen me in the store last week, and then he had known that he must go through with what he had contemplated and wished for so long. He would ask me, for he knew that he loved me. I also needed to know that he was well off and had a nice house in Ontario, though if I wished we could travel and live in both places.

His words unwound like yarn from a ball of wool. I couldn't retain the details. He talked about his last twenty years in Canada, the joint business with son Theo, and how well they had done together. He described his house, Leni's death, Ontario, Canadian democracy, and the Mennonite churches in St. Catharines. I heard him talk about the climate of southern Ontario and praise its fruits. Yes, I watched his mouth and eyes, but I heard only the themes, for I was floundering over the incredible statement that he loved me.

Finally he stopped for my consent. Then I looked down at my hands on the yellow hospital blanket, and said, "No. No. It hasn't occurred to me to marry again."

"I've given you no preparation," he demurred cheerfully. "I might have sent a letter or had someone else mention it to you first. But I was determined to see you myself. I've been thinking about it longer than you have, so it seems a very good thing to me. But I'll gladly give you the time you need to consider."

"No," I said.

"Are you worried about my age? Think of it this way, I'm no older than Jakob would be."

To mention Jakob and his age! Weak, forgetful Jakob at the end, compared to this dapper man. But I wouldn't compare. One was chosen, had chosen, and one grew loyal.

I felt very calm, though I didn't trust myself to look at Walde. "I've no inclination for it," I said firmly. I saw his hand, the flecked slender fingers, reach for his hat. He set the fancy thing on his lap.

"I'll leave you to think about it," he said. "You need time to consider it. I'll return tomorrow."

"No," I repeated.

Walde stood. "Anna. . . "

I raised my eyes to meet his. They searched me, they tried to reach me, they were warm and appealing. "Please consider it. Pray over it," he said, quite gently. "I'll come back tomorrow."

He replaced the chair, waved, and left me. His shoes clicked briskly on the tile floor. He was seemingly unworried that I had said No, not needing a final look, confident that tomorrow he would have the response he wanted. He had asserted his superiority over me again.

I sat on the bed, the high white bed with its very firm mattress, as if paralyzed, rehearsing the strange event. Oh, I was thinking about it all right!

His words were preposterous, amazing: I love you! We didn't say them easily, even as husband and wife, not our generation. What could he mean by them? I recalled that I had been aware of his approval of me, thinking as a young woman that he liked me, as an adult likes a child, is charmed by, is fond of, thinks well of.

But our subsequent hot words, neighbor to neighbor, and the long thick silence across the short space to the Walde *Hof*, the loathing, the disputes over chickens, fences, the polite barbed remarks, our terrible fight over our stance to Germany. The villagers were together at weddings, funerals, prayer meetings, worship services, always together. And one struggled to love during the whole time the preacher talked about it, seeing the difficult person on the bench opposite.

He had thought of me in the womanly way; he said I was fine-looking. A beauty! Well, Johann always knew what he was talking about. He was an expert on matters, great and small.

I had always tried to carry myself with dignity. I learned from Mama lessons about impeccable attire, even if patched, and firm carriage. If I could, I wore shoes, instead of going barefoot. But if shoes weren't available, one thought of one's feet and remembered, at least, that they shouldn't be cracked, wide, brown, flat. One tried to walk as if they were enclosed in stockings and soft leather.

But, had the enmity been nothing to him? I had hated and he admired? Had he outdone us by not letting it touch him? I detested this possibility, for it diminished both my anger and my small victories (for I had forgiven, I believed, though not without struggle). His smoothness flattened my emotions, reduced my memories.

I composed an answer for tomorrow. First, I decided, I would outline his faults as I observed them over the years in the village: his domination of village politics and many of the men, his way of excluding those who didn't agree with him, his confidence which was probably pride, his ruling word in his house which was more likely cruelty to a worn wife and many children. He had a temper. He was tight with his money. He had acquired it at the expense of his Indians and other Mennonites.

Second, I would speak quietly of Jakob, of our years together, his good qualities and mine, how we prayed and worked and talked under the algorrobo, of his notebooks with their evidence of meditation on Scripture, how he loved me. Everything I would tell Johann about Jakob would have the same meaning: this is what I'm used to from marriage. This is what I had. Are you a man like he was?

Then I would tell him I would never be party to his snubbing of my husband. And I would inform him that I'm well

290

enough set for money myself; I don't require his. He should know how it is in the Chaco now. Jakob started in cattle, modestly, just a small herd, but it was a good investment. Now Tina's Isaak looks after them for me. I pay the pasture fees, but I'm well provided for. David went over everything with me after Jakob died and I was surprised at how much I have. If I want to visit Canada, I can do it on my own. I would stay with Liese in Winnipeg. I don't need Johann to show me about.

Planning these rebuttals made me weary. I would call a nurse to lower my bed. Perhaps I could sleep and forget that Walde had come.

I realized in that moment that I didn't want to share the story of my marriage or Jakob's qualities with Johann. Wouldn't it betray our intimacy to pit that union against what Walde offered?

Nor did I wish to expose Johann's sins or argue with him. Besides, what had I been dreaming? That I would be fluent and persuasive, and that he would listen to me?

I didn't know what I would stay instead, but I knew for sure that I would not marry him.

I wouldn't re-write my history.

When the nurse came to assist me, I was laughing to myself.

"Are you all right, Mrs. Rempel?" she asked anxiously.

"Oh yes," I replied. "I'm just thinking of something funny."

The nurse helped me find a comfortable resting position.

"It must be funny," she said, giving me a puzzled look as she left. I was still chuckling.

What would she say if I told her that I had just received a surprising marriage proposal, and that my answer was No, which meant I might sum up my life as a victory? I was filled with delight because I remembered that Jakob had seen this: me,

Anna succeeding in the hot wilderness, surviving and more, under the unmoving sun over our heads.

I saw myself leaving the boat in Puerto Casado, sleeping lightly that first night on Chaco soil because of my excitement, sitting with Papa and Johann in the dawn. Then already, though fascinated by him, I feared him. He had mocked and stumbled me. When he exerted his will no one opposed him. On the trip and in our village we let him be our authority; we let him tell us how the Chaco had been opened to us Mennonites, and what a mistake it had been, how it was before and how it would be in the future, making predictions and pronouncements on the rain, the epidemic, the schisms and rifts, places where it was better — Germany, Canada. He was the son to Papa that Klaus was not. And he refused to believe God led us here.

He robbed my hope, my perceptions of the place.

But Anna, I reminded myself, pulling the blanket higher over my shoulders and closing my eyes, now you must be careful. Don't blame Johann anymore. You mustn't forget what you've learned, and how Jakob's words sprang to life.

The Chaco also had its power, slow and irresistible, to change my mind. Oh yes, at sixteen I acted the fool on the shores of the river. With the determined will of a romantic adolescent I hid from my sight the primitive huts of the Indians beside the port, the many signs of uncivilized, unchecked nature, the poverty. Heedless of the warnings, I called the Chaco Home. I intended to love it.

I discovered what it was like and realized that was impossible. But I had to stay.

Now it was — now it had become — what it had been earlier. The Chaco remains as it was! I had found it again. Pale golden wheat and roses of all the shades of the sunset; and me, old and widowed as my dear mother was, but the same Anna; and my sister Maria, also alone, bed-ridden, but the two of us sisters with one blood, and close again.

Life moves us in circles, I thought, but they're the circles of a coil; returning to where we've been, we find we have moved ahead, upward.

The Chaco is home; it comforts me. It has my memories and my children. Nature here is beautiful. To my grandchildren this is obvious; they can't understand how anyone could be unhappy in this wonderful land. They're right, of course, as I once was, and have learned to be again.

I don't want to live anywhere else, or travel now. This place is all that I wish until heaven.